DARREL OF THE BLESSED ISLES

IRVING BACHELLER

1st WORLD
LIBRARY
Literary Society

Darrel of the Blessed Isles

Irving Bacheller

© 1st World Library, 2008
PO Box 2211
Fairfield, IA 52556
www.1stworldlibrary.com
First Edition

LCCN: 2007935388

Softcover ISBN: 978-1-4218-9342-6
Hardcover ISBN: 978-1-4218-9442-3
eBook ISBN: 978-1-4218-9242-9

Purchase *"Darrel of the Blessed Isles"*
as a traditional bound book at:
www.1stWorldLibrary.com/purchase.asp?ISBN=978-1-4218-9342-6

1st World Library is a literary, educational organization
dedicated to:

- Creating a free internet library of downloadable ebooks

- Hosting writing competitions and offering book publishing
scholarships.

Interested in more 1st World Library books? contact:
literacy@1stworldlibrary.com
Check us out at: www.1stworldlibrary.com

1ˢᵗ World Library Literary Society

Giving Back to the World

"If you want to work on the core problem, it's early school literacy."

- James Barksdale, former CEO of Netscape

"No skill is more crucial to the future of a child, or to a democratic and prosperous society, than literacy."

- Los Angeles Times

"Literacy... means far more than learning how to read and write... The aim is to transmit... knowledge and promote social participation."

- UNESCO

"Literacy is not a luxury, it is a right and a responsibility. If our world is to meet the challenges of the twenty-first century we must harness the energy and creativity of all our citizens."

- President Bill Clinton

"Parents should be encouraged to read to their children, and teachers should be equipped with all available techniques for teaching literacy, so the varying needs and capacities of individual kids can be taken into account."

- Hugh Mackay

To the Memory of my Father

PREFACE

The author has tried to give some history of that uphill road, traversing the rough back country, through which men of power came once into the main highways, dusty, timid, foot-sore, and curiously old-fashioned. Now is the up grade eased by scholarships; young men labour with the football instead of the buck-saw, and wear high collars, and travel on a Pullman car, and dally with slang and cigarettes in the smoking-room. Altogether it is a new Republic, and only those unborn shall know if it be greater.

The man of learning and odd character and humble life was quite familiar once, and not only in Hillsborough. Often he was born out of time, loving ideals of history and too severe with realities around him. In Darrel it is sought to portray a force held in fetters and covered with obscurity, yet strong to make its way and widely felt. His troubles granted, one may easily concede his character, and his troubles are, mainly, no fanciful invention. There is good warrant for them in the court record of a certain case, together with the inference of a great lawyer who lived a time in its odd mystery. The author, it should be added, has given success to a life that ended in failure. He cares not if that success be unusual should any one be moved to think it within his reach.

A man of rugged virtues and good fame once said: "The forces that have made me? Well, first my mother, second my poverty, third Felix Holt. That masterful son of George Eliot became an ideal of my youth, and unconsciously I began to live his life."

It is well that the boy in the book was nobler than any who lived in Treby Magna.

As to "the men of the dark," they have long afflicted a man living and well known to the author of this tale, who now commits it to the world hoping only that these poor children of his brain may deserve kindness if not approval.

NEW YORK CITY,
March, 1903.

CONTENTS

PRELUDE

Yonder up in the hills are men and women, white-haired, who love to tell of that time when the woods came to the door-step and God's cattle fed on the growing corn. Where, long ago, they sowed their youth and strength, they see their sons reaping, but now, bent with age, they have ceased to gather save in the far fields of memory. Every day they go down the long, well-trodden path and come back with hearts full. They are as children plucking the meadows of June. Sit with them awhile, and they will gather for you the unfading flowers of joy and love—good sir! the world is full of them. And should they mention Trove or a certain clock tinker that travelled from door to door in the olden time, send your horse to the stable and God-speed them!—it is a long tale, and you may listen far into the night.

"See the big pines there in the dale yonder?" some one will ask. "Well, Theron Allen lived there, an' across the pond, that's where the moss trail came out and where you see the cow-path—that's near the track of the little red sleigh."

Then—the tale and its odd procession coming out of the far past.

I

THE STORY OF THE LITTLE RED SLEIGH

It was in 1835, about mid-winter, when Brier Dale was a narrow clearing, and the horizon well up in the sky and to anywhere a day's journey.

Down by the shore of the pond, there, Allen built his house. To-day, under thickets of tansy, one may see the rotting logs, and there are hollyhocks and catnip in the old garden. He was from Middlebury, they say, and came west—he and his wife—in '29. From the top of the hill above Allen's, of a clear day, one could look far across the tree-tops, over distant settlements that were as blue patches in the green canopy of the forest, over hill and dale to the smoky chasm of the St. Lawrence thirty miles north. The Allens had not a child; they settled with no thought of school or neighbour. They brought a cow with them and a big collie whose back had been scarred by a lynx. He was good company and a brave hunter, this dog; and one day—it was February, four years after their coming, and the snow lay deep—he left the dale and not even a track behind him. Far and wide they went searching, but saw no sign of him. Near a month later, one night, past twelve o'clock, they heard his bark in the distance. Allen rose and lit a candle and opened the door. They could hear him plainer, and now, mingled with his barking, a faint tinkle of bells.

It had begun to thaw, and a cold rain was drumming on roof and window.

"He's crossing the pond," said Allen, as he listened. "He's dragging some heavy thing over the ice."

Soon he leaped in at the door, the little red sleigh bouncing after him. The dog was in shafts and harness. Over the sleigh was a tiny cover of sail-cloth shaped like that of a prairie schooner. Bouncing over the door-step had waked its traveller, and there was a loud voice of complaint in the little cavern of sail-cloth. Peering in, they saw only the long fur of a gray wolf. Beneath it a very small boy lay struggling with straps that held him down. Allen loosed them and took him out of the sleigh, a ragged but handsome youngster with red cheeks and blue eyes and light, curly hair. He was near four years of age then, but big and strong as any boy of five. He stood rubbing his eyes a minute, and the dog came over and licked his face, showing fondness acquired they knew not where. Mrs. Allen took the boy in her lap and petted him, but he was afraid—like a wild fawn that has just been captured —and broke away and took refuge under the bed. A long time she sat by her bedside with the candle, showing him trinkets and trying to coax him out. He ceased to cry when she held before him a big, shiny locket of silver, and soon his little hand came out to grasp it. Presently she began to reach his confidence with sugar. There was a moment of silence, then strange words came out of his hiding-place. "Anah jouhan" was all they could make of them, and they remembered always that odd combination of sounds. They gave him food, which he ate with eager haste. Then a moment of silence and an imperative call for more in some strange tongue. When at last he came out of his hiding-place, he fled from the woman. This time he sought refuge between the knees of Allen, where soon his fear gave way to curiosity, and he began to feel her face and gown. By and by he fell asleep.

They searched the sleigh and shook out the robe and blanket, finding only a pair of warm bricks.

A Frenchman worked for the Allens that winter, and the name, Trove, was of his invention.

And so came Sidney Trove, his mind in strange fetters, travelling out of the land of mystery, in a winter night, to Brier Dale.

II

THE CRYSTAL CITY AND THE TRAVELLER

The wind, veering, came bitter cold; the rain hardened to hail; the clouds, changed to brittle nets of frost, and shaken to shreds by the rough wind, fell hissing in a scatter of snow. Next morning when Allen opened his door the wind was gone, the sky clear. Brier Pond, lately covered with clear ice, lay under a blanket of snow. He hurried across the pond, his dog following. Near the far shore was a bare spot on the ice cut by one of the sleigh-runners. Up in the woods, opposite, was the Moss Trail. Sunlight fell on the hills above him. He halted, looking up at the tree-tops. Twig, branch, and trunk glowed with the fire of diamonds through a lacy necking of hoar frost. Every tree had put on a jacket of ice and become as a fountain of prismatic hues. Here and there a dead pine rose like a spire of crystal; domes of deep-coloured glass and towers of jasper were as the landmarks of a city. Allen climbed the shore, walking slowly. He could see no track of sleigh or dog or any living thing. A frosted, icy tangle of branches arched the trail—a gateway of this great, crystal city of the woods. He entered, listening as he walked. Branches of hazel and dogwood were like jets of water breaking into clear, halted drops and foamy spray above him. He went on, looking up at this long sky-window of the woods. In the deep silence he could hear his heart beating.

Irving Bacheller

"Sport," .said he to the dog, "show me the way;" but the dog only wagged his tail.

Allen returned to the house.

"Wife," said he, "look at the woods yonder. They are like the city of holy promise. 'Behold I will lay thy stones with fair colours and thy foundations with sapphires, and I will make thy windows of agate.'"

"Did you find the track of the little sleigh?" said she.

"No," he answered, "nor will any man, for all paths are hidden."

"Theron—may we keep the boy?" she inquired.

"I think it is the will of God," said Allen.

The boy grew and throve in mind and body. For a time he prattled in a language none who saw him were able to comprehend. But he learned English quickly and soon forgot the jargon of his babyhood. The shadows of mystery that fell over his coming lengthened far into his life and were deepened by others that fell across them. Before he could have told the story, all memory of whom he left or whence he came had been swept away. It was a house of riddles where Allen dwelt—a rude thing of logs and ladders and a low roof and two rooms. Yet one ladder led high to glories no pen may describe. The Allens, with this rude shelter, found delight in dreams of an eternal home whose splendour and luxury would have made them miserable here below. What a riddle was this! And then, as to the boy Sid, there was the riddle of his coming, and again that of his character, which latter was, indeed, not easy to solve. There were few books and no learning in that home. For three winters Trove tramped a trail to the schoolhouse two miles away, and had no further schooling until he was a big, blond boy of fifteen, with red cheeks, and eyes large, blue, and discerning, and hands hardened to the axe helve. He had then discovered the beauty of the woods and begun to study the wild folk that live in holes and thickets. He had a fine face. You would have called him handsome, but not they among whom he lived. With them handsome was as handsome did, and the face of a man, if it were cleanly, was never a proper cause of blame or compliment. But there was that in his soul, which even now had waked the mother's wonder and set forth a riddle none were able to solve.

III

THE CLOCK TINKER

The harvesting was over in Brier Dale. It was near dinner-time, and Allen, Trove, and the two hired men were trying feats in the dooryard. Trove, then a boy of fifteen, had outdone them all at the jumping. A stranger came along, riding a big mare with a young filly at her side. He was a tall, spare man, past middle age, with a red, smooth-shaven face and long, gray hair that fell to his rolling collar. He turned in at the gate. A little beyond it his mare halted for a mouthful of grass. The stranger unslung a strap that held a satchel to his side and hung it on the pommel.

"Go and ask what we can do for him," Allen whispered to the boy.

Trove went down the drive, looking up at him curiously.

"What can I do for you?" he inquired.

"Give me thy youth," said the stranger, quickly, his gray eyes twinkling under silvered brows.

The boy, now smiling, made no answer.

"No?" said the man, as he came on slowly. "Well, then, were thy wit as good as thy legs it would be o' some use to me."

The words were spoken with dignity in a deep, kindly tone. They were also faintly salted with Irish brogue.

He approached the men, all eyes fixed upon him with a look of inquiry.

"Have ye ever seen a drunken sailor on a mast?" he inquired of Allen,

"No."

"Well, sor," said the stranger, dismounting slowly, "I am not that. Let me consider—have ye ever seen a cocoanut on a plum tree?"

"I believe not," said Allen, laughing.

"Well, sor, that is more like me. 'Tis long since I rode a horse, an' am out o' place in the saddle."

He stood erect with dignity, a smile deepening the many lines in his face.

"Can I do anything for you?" Allen asked.

"Ay—cure me o' poverty—have ye any clocks to mend?"

"Clocks! Are you a tinker?" said Allen.

"I am, sor, an' at thy service. Could beauty, me lord, have better commerce than with honesty?"

They all surveyed him with curiosity and amusement as he

tied the mare.

All had begun to laugh. His words came rapidly on a quick undercurrent of good nature. A clock sounded the stroke of midday.

"What, ho! The clock," said he, looking at his watch. "Thy time hath a lagging foot, Marry, were I that slow, sor, I'd never get to Heaven."

"Mother," said Allen, going to the doorstep, "here is a tinker, and he says the clock is slow."

"It seems to be out of order." said his wife, coming to the step.

"Seems, madam, nay, it is," said the stranger. "Did ye mind the stroke of it?"

"No," said she.

"Marry, 'twas like the call of a dying man."

Allen thought a moment as he whittled.

"Had I such a stroke on me I'd—I'd think I was parralyzed," the stranger added.

"You'd better fix it then," said Allen.

"Thou art wise, good man," said the stranger. "Mind the two hands on the clock an' keep them to their pace or they'll beckon thee to poverty."

The clock was brought to the door-step and all gathered about him as he went to work.

"Ye know a power o' scripter," said one of the hired men.

"Scripter," said the tinker, laughing. "I do, sor, an' much of it according to the good Saint William. Have ye never read Shakespeare?"

None who sat before him knew anything of the immortal bard.

"He writ a book 'bout Dan'l Boone an' the Injuns," a hired man ventured.

"'Angels an' ministers o' grace defend us!'" the tinker exclaimed,

Trove laughed.

"I'll give ye a riddle," said the tinker, turning to him.

"How is it the clock can keep a sober face?"

"It has no ears," Trove answered.

"Right," said the old tinker, smiling. "Thou art a knowing youth. Read Shakespeare, boy—a little of him three times a day for the mind's sake. I've travelled far in lonely places and needed no other company."

"Ever in India?" Trove inquired. He had been reading of that far land.

"I was, sor," the stranger continued, rubbing a wheel. "I was five years in India, sor, an' part o' the time fighting as hard as ever a man could fight."

"Fighting!" said Trove, much interested.

"I was, sor," he asserted, oiling a pinion of the old clock.

"On which side?"

"Inside an' outside."

"With natives?"

"I did, sor; three kinds o' them,—fever, fleas, an' the divvle."

"Give us some more Shakespeare," said the boy, smiling.

The tinker rubbed his spectacles thoughtfully, and, as he resumed his work, a sounding flood of tragic utterance came out of him—the great soliloquies of Hamlet and Macbeth and Richard III and Lear and Antony, all said with spirit and appreciation. The job finished, they bade him put up for dinner.

"A fine colt!" said Allen, as they were on their way to the stable.

"It is, sor," said the tinker, "a most excellent breed o' horses."

"Where from?"

"The grandsire from the desert of Arabia, where Allah created the horse out o' the south wind. See the slender flanks of the Barbary? See her eye?"

He seemed to talk in that odd strain for the mere joy of it, and there was in his voice the God-given vanity of bird or poet.

He had caught the filly by her little plume and stood patting her forehead.

"A wonderful thing, sor, is the horse's eye," he continued. "A glance! an' they know if ye be kind or cruel. Sweet Phyllis! Her eyelids are as bows; her lashes like the beard o' the corn. Have ye ever heard the three prayers o' the horse?"

"No," said Allen.

"Well, three times a day, sor, he prays, so they say, in the desert. In the morning he thinks a prayer like this, 'O Allah! make me beloved o' me master.' At noon, 'Do well by me master that he may do well by me.' At even, 'O Allah! grant, at last, I may bear me master into Paradise.'"

"An' the Arab, sor, he looks for a hard ride an' many jumps in the last journey, an' is kind to him all the days of his life, sor, so he may be able to make it."

For a moment he led her up and down at a quick trot, her dainty feet touching the earth lightly as a fawn's.

"Thou'rt made for the hot leagues o' the great sand sea," said he, patting her head. "Ah! thy neck shall be as the bowsprit; thy dust as the flying spray."

"In one thing you are like Isaiah," said Allen, as he whittled. "The Lord God hath given thee the tongue of the learned."

"An' if he grant me the power to speak a word in season to him that is weary, I shall be content," said the tinker.

Dinner over, they came out of doors. The stranger stood filling his pipe. Something in his talk and manner had gone deep into the soul of the boy, who now whispered a moment with his father.

"Would you sell the filly?" said Allen. "My boy would like

to own her."

"What, ho, the boy! the beautiful boy! An' would ye love her, boy?" the tinker asked.

"Yes, sir," the boy answered quickly,

"An' put a ribbon in her forelock, an' a coat o' silk on her back, an', mind ye, a man o' kindness in the saddle?"

"Yes, sir."

"Then take thy horse, an' Allah grant thou be successful on her as many times as there be hairs in her skin."

"And the price?" said Allen.

"Name it, an' I'll call thee just."

The business over, the tinker called to Trove, who had led the filly to her stall,—

"You, there, strike the tents. Bring me the mare. This very day she may bear me to forgiveness."

Trove brought the mare.

"Remember," said the old man, turning as he rode away, "in the day o' the last judgment God 'll mind the look o' thy horse."

He rode on a few steps and halted, turning in the saddle.

"Thou, too, Phyllis," he called. "God 'll mind the look o' thy master; see that ye bring him safe."

The little filly began to rear and call, the mother to answer. For days she called and trembled, with wet eyes, listening for the voice that still answered, though out of hearing, far over the hills. And Trove, too, was lonely, and there was a kind of longing in his heart for the music in that voice of the stranger.

IV

THE UPHILL ROAD

For Trove it was a day of sowing. The strange old tinker had filled his heart with a new joy and a new desire. Next morning he got a ride to Hillsborough—fourteen miles—and came back, reading, as he walked, a small, green book, its thin pages covered thick with execrably fine printing, its title "The Works of Shakespeare." He read the book industriously and with keen pleasure. Allen complained, shortly, that Shakespeare and the filly had interfered with the potatoes and the corn.

The filly ceased to take food and sickened for a time after the dam left her. Trove lay in the stall nights and gave her milk sweetened to her liking. She grew strong and playful, and forgot her sorrow, and began to follow him like a dog on his errands up and down the farm. Trove went to school in the autumn—"Select school," it was called. A two-mile journey it was, by trail, but a full three by the wagon road. He learned only a poor lesson the first day, for, on coming in sight of the schoolhouse, he heard a rush of feet behind him and saw his filly charging down the trail. He had to go back with her and lose the day, a thought dreadful to him, for now hope was high, and school days few and precious. At first he was angry. Then he sat among the ferns, covering his face and sobbing with sore resentment. The little filly stood over him and rubbed her silky muzzle on his neck, and kicked up her heels in play as he pushed her back. Next morning he put her behind a fence, but she went over it with the ease of a wild deer and came bounding after him. When, at last, she was shut in the box-stall he could hear her calling, half a mile away, and it made his heart sore. Soon after, a moose treed him on the trail and held him there for quite half a day. Later he had to help thrash and was laid up with the measles. Then came rain and flooded flats that turned him off the trail. Years after he used to say that work and weather, and sickness and distance, and even the beasts of the field and wood, resisted him in the way of learning.

He went to school at Hillsborough that winter. His time, which Allen gave him in the summer, had yielded some forty-five dollars. He hired a room at thirty-five cents a week. Mary Allen bought him a small stove and sent to him, in the sleigh, dishes, a kettle, chair, bed, pillow, and quilt, and a supply of candles.

She surveyed him proudly, as he was going away that morning in December,

"Folks may call ye han'some," she said. "They'd like to make fool of ye, but you go on 'bout yer business an' act as if ye didn't hear."

He had a figure awkward, as yet, but fast shaping to comeliness. Long, light hair covered the tops of his ears and fell to his collar. His ruddy cheeks were a bit paler that morning; the curve in his lips a little drawn; his blue eyes had begun to fill and the dimple in his chin to quiver, slightly, as he kissed her who had been as a mother to him. But he went away laughing.

Many have seen the record in his diary of those lank and busy days. The Saturday of his first week at school he wrote as follows:—

"Father brought me a small load of wood and a sack of potatoes yesterday, so, after this, I shall be able to live cheaper. My expenses this week have been as follows:—

Rent	35 cents
Corn meal	14 "
Milk	20 "
Bread	8 "
Beef bone	5 "
Honey	5 "
Four potatoes,	about 1"
	88 cents.

"Two boys who have a room on the same floor got through the week for 75 cents apiece, but they are both undersized and don't eat as hearty. This week I was tempted by the sight of honey and was fool enough to buy a little which I didn't need. I have some meal left and hope next week to get through for 80 cents. I wish I could have a decent necktie, but conscience doth make cowards of us all. I have committed half the first act of 'Julius Caesar.'"

And yet, with pudding and milk and beef bone and four potatoes and "Julius Caesar" the boy was cheerful.

"Don't like meat any more—it's mostly poor stuff anyway," he said to his father, who had come to see him.

"Sorry—I brought down a piece o' venison," said Allen.

"Well, there's two kinds o' meat," said the boy; "what ye can have, that's good, an' what ye can't have, that ain't worth havin'."

He got a job in the mill for every Saturday at 75 cents a day, and soon thereafter was able to have a necktie and a pair of fine boots, and a barber, now and then, to control the length of his hair.

Trove burnt the candles freely and was able but never brilliant in his work that year, owing, as all who knew him agreed, to great modesty and small confidence. He was a kindly, big-hearted fellow, and had wit and a knowledge of animals and of woodcraft that made him excellent company. That schoolboy diary has been of great service to all with a wish to understand him. On a faded leaf in the old book one may read as follows:—

"I have received letters in the handwriting of girls, unsigned. They think they are in love with me and say foolish things. I know what they're up to. They're the kind my mother spoke of—the kind that set their traps for a fool, and when he's caught they use him for a thing to laugh at. They're not going to catch me.

"Expenses for seven days have been $1.14. Clint McCormick spent 60 cents to take his girl to a show and I had to help him through the week. I told him he ought to love Caesar less and Rome more."

Then follows the odd entry without which it is doubtful if the history of Sidney Trove could ever have been written. At least only a guess would have been possible, where now is certainty. And here is the entry:—

"Since leaving home the men of the dark have been very troublesome. They wake me about every other night and sometimes I wonder what they mean."

Now an odd thing had developed in the mystery of the boy. Even before he could distinguish between reality and its shadow that we see in dreams, he used often to start up with a loud cry of fear in the night. When a small boy he used to explain it briefly by saying, "the men in the dark." Later he used to say, "the men outdoors in the dark." At ten years of age he went off on a three days' journey with the Allens. They put up in a tavern that had many rooms and stairways and large windows. It was a while after his return of an evening, before candle-light, when a gray curtain of dusk had dimmed the windows, that he first told the story, soon oft repeated and familiar, of "the men in the dark"—at least he went as far as he knew.

"I dream," he was wont to say in after life, "that I am listening in the still night alone—I am always alone. I hear a sound in the silence, of what I cannot be sure. I discover then, or seem to, that I stand in a dark room and tremble, with great fear, of what I do not know. I walk along softly in bare feet—I am so fearful of making a noise. I am feeling, feeling, my hands out in the dark. Presently they touch a wall and I follow it and then I discover that I am going downstairs. It is a long journey. At last I am in a room where I can see windows, and, beyond, the dim light of the moon. Now I seem to be wrapped in fearful silence. Stealthily I go near the door. Its upper half is glass, and beyond it I can see the dark forms of men. One is peering through with face upon the pane; I know the other is trying the lock, but I hear no sound. I am in a silence like that of the grave. I try to speak. My lips move, but, try as I may, no sound comes out of them. A sharp terror is pricking into me, and I flinch as if it were a knife-blade. Well, sir, that is a thing I cannot understand. You know me—I am not a coward. If I were really in a like scene fear would be the least of my emotions;

but in the dream I tremble and am afraid. Slowly, silently, the door opens, the men of the dark enter, wall and windows begin to reel. I hear a quick, loud cry, rending the silence and falling into a roar like that of flooding waters. Then I wake, and my dream is ended—for that night."

Now men have had more thrilling and remarkable dreams, but that of the boy Trove was as a link in a chain, lengthening with his life, and ever binding him to some event far beyond the reach of his memory.

V

AT THE SIGN O' THE DIAL

It was Sunday and a clear, frosty morning of midwinter. Trove had risen early and was walking out on a long pike that divided the village of Hillsborough and cut the waste of snow, winding over hills and dipping into valleys, from Lake Champlain to Lake Ontario. The air was cold but full of magic sun-fire. All things were aglow—the frosty roadway, the white fields, the hoary forest, and the mind of the beholder. Trove halted, looking off at the far hills. Then he heard a step behind him and, as he turned, saw a tall man approaching at a quick pace. The latter had no overcoat. A knit muffler covered his throat, and a satchel hung from a strap on his shoulder.

"What ho, boy!" said he, shivering. "'I'll follow thee a month, devise with thee where thou shalt rest, that thou may'st hear of us, an' we o' thee.' What o' thy people an' the filly?"

"All well," said Trove, who was delighted to see the clock tinker, of whom he had thought often. "And what of you?"

"Like an old clock, sor—a weak spring an' a bit slow. But, praise God! I've yet a merry gong in me. An' what think you, sor, I've travelled sixty miles an' tinkered forty clocks in the week gone."

"I think you yourself will need tinkering."

"Ah, but I thank the good God, here is me home," the old man remarked wearily.

"I'm going to school here," said Trove, "and hope I may see you often."

"Indeed, boy, we'll have many a blessed hour," said the tinker. "Come to me shop; we'll talk, meditate, explore, an' I'll see what o'clock it is in thy country."

They were now in the village, and, halfway down its main thoroughfare, went up a street of gloom and narrowness between dingy workshops. At one of them, shaky, and gray with the stain of years, they halted. The two lower windows in front were dim with dirt and cobwebs. A board above them was the rude sign of Sam Bassett, carpenter. On the side of the old shop was a flight of sagging, rickety stairs. At the height of a man's head an old brass dial was nailed to the gray boards. Roughly lettered in lampblack beneath it were the words, "Clocks Mended." They climbed the shaky stairs to a landing, supported by long braces, and whereon was a broad door, with latch and keyhole in its weathered timber.

"All bow at this door," said the old tinker, as he put his long iron key in the lock. "It's respect for their own heads, not for mine," he continued, his hand on the eaves that overhung below the level of the door-top.

They entered a loft, open to the peak and shingles, with a window in each end. Clocks, dials, pendulums, and tiny cogwheels of wood and brass were on a long bench by the street window. Thereon, also, were a vice and tools. The room was

Irving Bacheller

cleanly, with a crude homelikeness about it. Chromos and illustrated papers had been pasted on the rough, board walls.

"On me life, it is cold," said the tinker, opening a small stove and beginning to whittle shavings, "'Cold as a dead man's nose.' Be seated, an' try—try to be happy."

There was an old rocker and two small chairs in the room.

"I do not feel the cold," said Trove, taking one of them.

"Belike, good youth, thou hast the rose of summer in thy cheeks," said the old man.

"And no need of an overcoat," the boy answered, removing the one he wore and passing it to the tinker. "I wish you to keep it, sir."

"Wherefore, boy? 'Twould best serve me on thy back."

"Please take it," said Trove. "I cannot bear to think of you shivering in the cold. Take it, and make me happy."

"Well, if it keep me warm, an' thee happy, it will be a wonderful coat," said the old man, wiping his gray eyes.

Then he rose and filled the stove with wood and sat down, peering at Trove between the upper rim of his spectacles and the feathery arches of silvered hair upon his brows.

"Thy coat hath warmed me heart already—thanks to the good God!" said he, fervently. "Why so kind?"

"If I am kind, it is because I must be," said the boy. "Who were my father and mother, I never knew. If I meet a man who is in need, I say to myself, 'He may be my father or my brother, I must be good to him;' and if it is a woman, I cannot help thinking that, maybe, she is my mother or my sister. So I should have to be kind to all the people in the world if I were to meet them."

"Noble suspicion! by the faith o' me fathers!" said the old man, thoughtfully, rubbing his long nose. "An' have ye thought further in the matter? Have ye seen whither it goes?"

"I fear not."

"Well, sor, under the ancient law, ye reap as ye have sown, but more abundantly. I gave me coat to one that needed it more, an' by the goodness o' God I have reaped another an' two friends. Hold to thy course, boy, thou shalt have friends an' know their value. An' then thou shalt say, 'I'll be kind to this man because he may be a friend;' an' love shall increase in thee, an' around thee, an' bring happiness. Ah, boy! in the business o' the soul, men pay thee better than they owe. Kindness shall bring friendship, an' friendship shall bring love, an' love shall bring happiness, an' that, sor, that is the approval o' God. What speculation hath such profit? Hast thou learned to think?"

"I hope I have," said the boy.

"Prithee—think a thought for me. What is the first law o' life?"

There was a moment of silence.

"Thy pardon, boy," said the venerable tinker, filling a clay pipe and stretching himself on a lounge. "Thou art not long out o' thy clouts. It is, 'Thou shalt learn to think an' obey.' Consider how man and beast are bound by it. Very well— think thy way up. Hast thou any fear?"

The old man was feeling his gray hair, thoughtfully.

"Only the fear o' God," said the boy, after a moment of hesitation.

"Well, on me word, I am full sorry," said the tinker. "Though mind ye, boy, fear is an excellent good thing, an' has done a work in the world. But, hear me, a man had two horses the same age, size, shape, an' colour, an' one went for fear o' the whip, an' the other went as well without a whip in the wagon. Now, tell me, which was the better horse?"

"The one that needed no whip."

"Very well!" said the old man, with emphasis. "A man had two sons, an' one obeyed him for fear o' the whip, an' the other, because he loved his father, an' could not bear to grieve him. Tell me again, boy, which was the better son?"

"The one that loved him," said the boy.

"Very well! very well!" said the old man, loudly. "A man had two neighbours, an' one stole not his sheep for fear o' the law, an' the other, sor, he stole them not, because he loved his neighbour. Now which was the better man?"

"The man that loved him."

"Very well! very well! and again very well!" said the tinker, louder than before. "There were two kings, an' one was feared, an' the other, he was beloved; which was the better king?"

"The one that was beloved."

"Very well! and three times again very well!" said the old

man, warmly. "An' the good God is he not greater an' more to be loved than all kings? Fear, boy, that is the whip o' destiny driving the dumb herd. To all that fear I say 'tis well, have fear, but pray that love may conquer it. To all that love I say, fear only lest ye lose the great treasure. Love is the best thing, an' with too much fear it sickens. Always keep it with thee—a little is a goodly property an' its revenoo is happiness. Therefore, be happy, boy—try ever to be happy."

There was a moment of silence broken by the sound of a church bell.

"To thy prayers," said the clock tinker, rising, "an' I'll to mine. Dine with me at five, good youth, an' all me retinoo—maids, warders, grooms, attendants—shall be at thy service."

"I'll be glad to come," said the boy, smiling at his odd host.

"An' see thou hast hunger."

"Good morning, Mr.—?" the boy hesitated.

"Darrel—Roderick Darrel—" said the old man, "that's me name, sor, an' ye'll find me here at the Sign o' the Dial."

A wind came shrieking over the hills, and long before evening the little town lay dusky in a scud of snow mist. The old stairs were quivering in the storm as Trove climbed them.

"Welcome, good youth," said the clock tinker, shaking the boy's hand as he came in. "Ho there! me servitors. Let the feast be spread," he called in a loud voice, stepping quickly to the stove that held an upper deck of wood, whereon were dishes. "Right Hand bring the meat an' Left Hand the potatoes an' Quick Foot give us thy help here."

He suited his action to the words, placing a platter of ham and eggs in the centre of a small table and surrounding it with hot roast potatoes, a pot of tea, new biscuit, and a plate of honey.

"Ho! Wit an' Happiness, attend upon us here," said he, making ready to sit down.

Then, as if he had forgotten something, he hurried to the door and opened it.

"Care, thou skeleton, go hence, and thou, Poverty, go also, and see thou return not before cock-crow," said he, imperatively.

"You have many servants," said Trove.

"An' how may one have a castle without servants? Forsooth, boy, horses an' hounds, an' lords an' ladies have to be attended to. But the retinoo is that run down ye'd think me home a hospital. Wit is a creeping dotard, and Happiness he is in poor health an' can barely drag himself to me table, an' Hope is a tippler, an' Right Hand is getting the palsy. Alack! me best servant left me a long time ago."

"And who was he?"

"Youth! lovely, beautiful Youth! but let us be happy. I would not have him back—foolish, inconstant Youth! dreaming dreams an' seeing visions. God love ye, boy! what is thy dream?"

This rallying style of talk, in which the clock tinker indulged so freely, afforded his young friend no little amusement. His tongue had long obeyed the lilt of classic diction; his thought came easy in Elizabethan phrase. The slight Celtic brogue served to enhance the piquancy of his talk. Moreover he was really a man of wit and imagination.

"Once," said the boy, after a little hesitation, "I thought I should try to be a statesman, but now I am sure I would rather write books."

"An' what kind o' books, pray?"

"Tales."

"An' thy merchandise be truth, capital!" exclaimed the tinker. "Hast thou an ear for tales?"

"I'm very fond of them."

"Marry, I'll tell thee a true tale, not for thy ear only but for thy soul, an' some day, boy, 'twill give thee occupation for thy wits."

"I'd love to hear it," said the boy.

The pendulums were ever swinging like the legs of a procession trooping through the loft, some with quick steps, some with slow. Now came a sound as of drums beating. It was for the hour of eight, and when it stopped the tinker began.

"Once upon a time," said he, as they rose from the table and the old man went for his pipe, "'twas long ago, an' I had then the rose o' youth upon me, a man was tempted o' the devil an' stole money—a large sum—an' made off with it. These hands o' mine used to serve him those days, an' I remember he was a man comely an' well set up, an', I think, he had honour an' a good heart in him."

The old man paused.

"I should not think it possible," said Trove, who was at the age of certainty in his opinions and had long been trained to the uncompromising thought of the Puritan. "A man who steals can have no honour in him."

"Ho! Charity," said the clock tinker, turning as if to address one behind him. "Sweet Charity! attend upon this boy. Mayhap, sor," he continued meekly. "God hath blessed me with little knowledge o' what is possible. But I speak of a time before guilt had sored him. He was officer of a great bank—let us say—in Boston. Some thought him rich, but he lived high an' princely, an' I take it, sor, his income was no greater than his needs. It was a proud race he belonged to— grand people they were, all o' them—with houses an' lands an' many servants. His wife was dead, sor, an' he'd one child—a little lad o' two years, an' beautiful. One day the boy went out with his nurse, an' where further nobody knew. He never came back. Up an' down, over an' across they looked for him, night an' day, but were no wiser, A month went by an' not a sight or sign o' him, an' their hope failed. One day the father he got a note,—I remember reading it in the papers, sor,—an' it was a call for ransom money—one hundred thousand dollars."

"Kidnapped!" Trove exclaimed with much interest.

"He was, sor," the clock tinker resumed. "The father he was up to his neck in trouble, then, for he was unable to raise the money. He had quarrelled with an older brother whose help would have been sufficient. Well, God save us all! 'twas the old story o' pride an' bitterness. He sought no help o' him. A year an' a half passes an' a gusty night o' midwinter the bank burns. Books, papers, everything is destroyed. Now the poor man has lost his occupation. A week more an' his good name is gone; a month an' he's homeless. A whisper goes down the long path o' gossip. Was he a thief an' had he burned the record of his crime? The scene changes, an' let me count the swift, relentless years."

The old man paused a moment, looking up thoughtfully.

"Well, say ten or mayhap a dozen passed—or more or less it matters little. Boy an' man, where were they? O the sad world, sor! To all that knew them they were as people buried in their graves. Think o' this drowning in the flood o' years— the stately ships sunk an' rotting in oblivion; some word of it, sor, may well go into thy book."

The tinker paused a moment, lighting his pipe, and after a puff or two went on with the tale.

"It is a winter day in a great city—there are buildings an' crowds an' busy streets an' sleet'in the bitter wind. I am there,—an' me path is one o' many crossing each other like— well, sor, like lines on a slate, if thou were to make ten thousand o' them an' both eyes shut. I am walking slowly, an' lo! there is the banker. I meet him face to face—an ill-clad, haggard, cold, forgotten creature. I speak to him."

"'The blessed Lord have mercy on thee,' I said."

"'For meeting thee?' said the poor man. 'What is thy name?'"

"'Roderick Darrel.'"

"'An' I,' said he, sadly, 'am one o' the lost in hell. Art thou the devil?'"

"'Nay, this hand o' mine hath opened thy door an' blacked thy boots for thee often,' said I. 'Dost thou not remember?'"

Irving Bacheller

"'Dimly—it was a long time ago,' he answered."

"We said more, sor, but that is no part o' the story. Very well! I went with him to his lodgings,—a little cold room in a garret,—an' there alone with me he gave account of himself. He had shovelled, an' dug, an' lifted, an' run errands until his strength was low an' the weight of his hand a burden. What hope for him—what way to earn a living!

"'Have courage, man,' I said to him. 'Thou shalt learn to mend clocks. It's light an' decent work, an' one may live by it an' see much o' the world.'"

"There was an old clock, sor, in a heap o' rubbish that lay in a corner. I took it apart, and soon he saw the office of each wheel an' pinion an' the infirmity that stopped them an' the surgery to make them sound. I tarried long in the great city, an' every evening we were together in the little room. I bought him a kit o' tools an' some brass, an' we would shatter the clockworks an' build them up again until he had skill, sor, to make or mend.

"'Me good friend,' said he, one evening after we had been a long time at work, 'I wish thou could'st teach me how to mend a broken life. For God's sake, help me! I am fainting under a great burden.'"

"'What can I do?' said I to him."

"Then, sor, he went over his story with me from beginning to end. It was an impressive, a sacred confidence. Ah, boy, it would be dishonour to tell thee his name, but his story, that I may tell thee, changing the detail, so it may never add a straw to his burden. I shall quote him in substance only, an' follow the long habit o' me own tongue.

"'Well, ye remember how me son was taken,' said he. 'I could not raise the ransom, try as I would. Now, large sums were in me keeping an' I fell. I remember that day. Ah! man, the devil seemed to whisper to me. But, God forgive! it was for love that I fell. Little by little I began to take the money I must have an' cover its absence. I said to meself, some time I'll pay it back—that ancient sophistry o' the devil. When me thieving had gone far, an' near its goal, the bank burned. As God's me witness I'd no hand in that. I weighed the chances an' expected to go to prison—well, say for ten years, at least. I must suffer in order to save the boy, an' was ready for the sacrifice. Free again, I would help him to return the money. That burning o' the records shut off the prison, but opened the fire o' hell upon me. Half a year had gone by, an' not a word from the kidnappers. I took a note to the place appointed,—a hollow log in the woods, a bit east of a certain bridge on the public highway twenty miles out o' the city,— but no answer,—not a word,—not a line up to this moment. They must have relinquished hope an' put the boy to death.'"

"'In that old trunk there under the bed is a dusty, moulding, cursed heap o' money done up in brown paper an' tied with a string. It is a hundred thousand dollars, an' the price o' me soul.'"

"'An' thou in rags an' a garret,' said I."

"'An' I in rags an' hell,' said he, sor, looking down at himself."

"He drew out the trunk an' showed me the money, stacks of it, dirty, an' stinking o' damp mould."

"'There it is,' said he, 'every dollar I stole is there. I brought it with me an' over these hundreds o' miles I could hear the tongue o' gossip. Every night as I lay down I could hear the whispering of all the people I ever knew. I could see them shake their heads. Then came this locket o' gold.'"

"A beautiful, shiny thing it was, an' he took out of it a little strand o' white hair an' read these words cut in the gleaming case:—

"'Here are silver an' gold,
The one for a day o' remembrance between thee an' dishonour,
The other for a day o' plenty between thee an' want.'"

"It was an odd thought an' worth keeping, an' often I have repeated the words. The silvered hair, that was for remembrance; an' the gold he might sell and turn it into a day o' plenty.

"'In the locket was a letter,' said the poor man. 'Here it is,' an' he held it in the light o' the candle. 'See, it is signed "mother."'"

"An' he read from the letter words o' sorrow an' bitter shame, an' firm confidence in his honour,"

"'It ground me to the very dust,' he went on. 'I put the money in that bundle, every dollar. I could not return it, an' so confirm the disgrace o' her an' all the rest. I could not use it, for if I lived in comfort they would ask—all o' them— whence came his money? For their sake I must walk in poverty all me days. An' I went to work at heavy toil, sor, as became a poor man. As God's me judge I felt a pride in rags an' the horny hand.'"

The tinker paused a moment in which all the pendulums seemed to quicken pace, tick lapping upon tick, as if trying to get ahead of each other.

"Think of it, boy," Darrel continued. "A pride in rags an' poverty. Bring that into thy book an' let thy best thinking bear upon it. Show us how patch an' tatter were for the poor man as badges of honour an' success.

"'I thought to burn the money,' me host went on. 'But no, that would have robbed me o' one great possibility—that o' restoring it. Some time, when they were dead, maybe, an' I could suffer alone, I would restore it, or, at least, I might see a way to turn it into good works. So I could not be quit o' the money. Day an' night these slow an' heavy years it has been me companion, cursing an' accusing me."

"'I lie here o' nights thinking. In that heap o' money I seem to hear the sighs an' sobs o' the poor people that toiled to earn it. I feel their sweat upon me, an' God! this heart o' mine is crowded to bursting with the despair o' hundreds. An', betimes, I hear the cry o' murder in the cursed heap as if there were some had blood upon it. An' then I dream it has caught fire beneath me an' I am burning raw in the flame.'"

The tinker paused again, crossing the room and watching the swing of a pendulum.

"Boy, boy," said he, returning to his chair, "think' o' that complaining, immovable heap lying there like the blood of a murder. An' thy reader must feel the toil an' sweat an' misery an' despair that is in a great sum, an' how it all presses on the heart o' him that gets it wrongfully.

"'Well, sor,' the poor fellow continued, 'now an' then I met those had known me, an' reports o' me poverty went home. An' those dear to me sent money, the sight o' which filled me with a mighty sickness, an' I sent it back to them. Long ago, thank God! they ceased to think me a thief, but only crazy. Tell me, man, what shall I do with the money? There be those living I have to consider, an' those dead, an' those unborn.'"

"'Hide it,' said I, 'an' go to thy work an' God give thee counsel.'"

Man and boy rose from the table and drew up to the little stove.

"Now, boy," said the clock tinker, leaning toward him with knitted brows, "consider this poor thief who suffered so for his friends. Think o' these good words, 'Greater love hath no man than this, that he lay down his life for his friends.' If thou should'st ever write of it, thy problem will be to reckon the good an' evil, an' give each a careful estimate an' him his proper rank!"

"What a sad tale!" said the boy, thoughtfully. "It's terrible to think he may be my father."

"I'd have no worry o' that, sor," said the clock tinker. "There be ten thousand—ay, more—who know not their fathers. An', moreover, 'twas long, long ago."

"Please tell me when was the boy taken," said Trove.

"Time, or name, or place, I cannot tell thee, lest I betray him," said the old man, "Neither is necessary to thy tale. Keep it with thee a while; thou art young yet an' close inshore. Wait until ye sound the further deep. Then, sor, write, if God give thee power, and think chiefly o' them in peril an' about to dash their feet upon the stones."

For a moment the clocks' ticking was like the voice of many ripples washing the shore of the Infinite. A new life had begun for Trove, and they were cutting it into seconds. He looked up at them and rose quickly and stood a moment, his thumb on the door-latch. Outside they could hear the rush and scatter of the snow.

"Poor youth!" said the old man. "Thou hast no coat—take mine. Take it, I say. It will give thee comfort an' me happiness."

He would hear no refusal, and again the coat changed owners, giving happiness to the old and comfort to the new.

Then Trove went down the rickety stairs and away in the darkness.

VI

A CERTAIN RICK MAN

Riley Brooke had a tongue for gossip, an ear for evil report, an eye for rascals. Every day new suspicions took root in him, while others grew and came to great size and were as hard to conceal as pumpkins. He had meanness enough to equip all he knew, and gave it with a lavish tongue. In his opinion Hillsborough came within one of having as many rascals in it as there were people. He had tried to bring them severally to justice by vain appeals to the law, having sued for every cause in the books, but chiefly for trespass and damages, real and exemplary. He was a money-lender, shaving notes or taking them for larger sums than he lent, with chattel mortgages for security. Foreclosure and sale were a perennial source of profit to him. He was tall and well past middle age, with a short, gray beard, a look of severity, a stoop in his shoulders, and a third wife whom nobody, within the knowledge of the townfolk, had ever seen. If he had no other to gossip with, he provided imaginary company and talked to his own ears. He thought himself a most powerful and agile man, boasting often that he still kept the vigour of his youth. On his errands in the village he often broke into an awkward gallop, like a child at play. When he slackened pace it was to shake his head solemnly, as if something had reminded him of the wickedness of the world.

"If I dared tell all I knew," he would whisper suggestively, and then proceed to tell much more than he could possibly have known. Any one of many may have started his tongue, but the shortcomings of one Ezekiel Swackhammer were for him an ever present help and provocation. If there were nothing new to talk about, there was always Swackhammer. Poor Swackhammer had done everything he ought not to have done. The good God himself was the only being that had the approval of old Riley Brooke. It was curious—that turning of his tongue from the slander of men to the praise of God. And of the goodness of the Almighty he was quite as sure as of the badness of men. Assurance of his own salvation had come to him one day when he was shearing sheep, and when, as he related often, finding himself on his knees to shear, he remained to pray. Sundays and every Wednesday evening he wore a stove-pipe hat and a long frock coat of antique and rusty aspect. On his way to church—with hospitality even for the like of him, thank God!—he walked slowly with head bent until, remembering his great agility and strength, he began to run, giving a varied exhibition of skips and jumps terminating in a sort of gallop. Once in the sacred house he looked to right and left accusingly, and aloft with encouraging applause. His God was one of wrath, vengeance, and destruction; his hell the destination of his enemies. They who resented the screw of his avarice, and pulled their thumbs away; they who treated him with contempt, and whose faults, compared to his own, were as a mound to a mountain—they were all to burn with everlasting fire, while he, on account of that happy thought the day of the sheep-shearing, was to sit forever with the angels in heaven.

"Ye're going t' heaven, I hear," said Darrel, who had repaired a clock for him, and heard complaint of his small fee.

"I am," was the spirited reply.

"God speed ye!" said the tinker, as he went away.

In such disfavour was the poor man, that all would have been glad to have him go anywhere, so he left Hillsborough.

One day in the Christmas holidays, a boy came to the door of Riley Brooke, with a buck-saw on his arm.

"I'm looking for work," said the boy, "and I'd be glad of the chance to saw your wood."

"How much a cord?" was the loud inquiry.

"Forty cents."

"Too much," said Brooke. "How much a day?"

"Six shillings."

"Too much," said the old man, snappishly. "I used to git six dollars a month, when I was your age, an' rise at four o'clock in the mornin' an' work till bedtime. You boys now-days are a lazy good-fer-nothin' lot. What's yer name?"

"Sidney Trove."

"Don't want ye."

"Well, mister," said the boy, who was much in need of money, "I'll saw your wood for anything you've a mind to give me."

"I'll give ye fifty cents a day," said the old man.

Trove hesitated. The sum was barely half what he could earn, but he had given his promise, and fell to. Riley Brooke spent half the day watching and urging him to faster work. More than once the boy was near quitting, but kept his good nature and a strong pace. When, at last, Brooke went away, Trove heard a sly movement of the blinds, and knew that other eyes were on the watch. He spent three days at the job—laming, wearisome days, after so long an absence from heavy toil.

"Wal, I suppose y& want money," Brooke snapped, as the boy came to the door. "How much?"

"One dollar and a half."

"Too much, too much; I won't pay it."

"That was the sum agreed upon."

"Don't care, ye hain't earned no dollar 'n a half. Here, take that an' clear out;" having said which, Brooke tossed some money at the boy and slammed the door in his face. Trove counted the money—it was a dollar and a quarter. He was sorely tempted to open the door and fling it back at him, but wisely kept his patience and walked away. It was the day before Christmas. Trove had planned to walk home that evening, but a storm had come, drifting the snow deep, and he had to forego the visit. After supper he went to the Sign of the Dial. The tinker was at home in his odd little shop and gave him a hearty welcome. Trove sat by the fire, and told of the sawing for Riley Brooke.

"God rest him!" said the tinker, thoughtfully puffing his pipe. "What would happen, think ye, if a man like him were let into heaven?"

"I cannot imagine," said the boy.

"Well, for one thing," said the tinker, "he'd begin to look for chattels, an' I do fear me there'd soon be many without harps."

"What is one to do with a man like that?" Trove inquired.

"Only this," said the tinker; "put him in thy book. He'll make good history. But, sor, for company he's damnably poor."

"It's a new way to use men," said Trove.

"Nay, an old way—a very old way. Often God makes an example o' rare malevolence an' seems to say, 'Look, despise, and be anything but this.' Like Judas and Herod he is an excellent figure in a book. Put him in thine, boy."

"And credit him with full payment?" the boy asked.

"Long ago, praise God, there was a great teacher," said the old man. "It is a day to think of Him. Return good for evil—those were His words. We've never tried it, an' I'd like to see how it may work. The trial would be amusing if it bore no better fruit."

"What do you propose?"

"Well, say we take him a gift with our best wishes," said the tinker.

"If I can afford it," the boy replied.

The tinker answered quickly: "Oh, I've always a little for a Christmas, an' I'll buy the gifts. Ah, boy, let's away for the gifts. We'll—we'll punish him with kindness."

They went together and bought a pair of mittens and a warm

muffler for Riley Brooke and walked to his door with them and rapped upon it. Brooke came to the door with a candle.

"What d'ye want?" he demanded.

"To wish you Merry Christmas and present you gifts," said Trove.

The old man raised his candle, surveying them with surprise and curiosity.

"What gifts?" he inquired in a milder tone.

"Well," said the boy, "we've brought you mittens and a muffler."

"Ha! ha! Yer consciences have smote ye," said Brooke, "Glory to God who brings the sinner to repentance!"

"And fills the bitter cup o' the ungrateful," said the tinker. And they went away.

"I'd like to bring one other gift," said Darrel.

"What's that?"

"God forgive me! A rope to hang him. But mind thee, boy, we are trying the law o' the great teacher, and let us see if we can learn to love this man."

"Love Riley Brooke?" said Trove, doubtfully.

"A great achievement, I grant thee," said the tinker. "For if we can love him, we shall be able to love anybody. Let us try and see what comes of it."

A man was waiting for Darrel at the foot of the old stairs—a tall man, poorly dressed, whom Trove had not seen before, and whom, now, he was not able to see clearly in the darkness.

"The mare is ready," said Darrel. "Tis a dark night."

He to whom the tinker had spoken made no answer.

"Good night," said the tinker, turning. "A Merry Christmas to thee, boy, an' peace an' plenty."

"I have peace, and you have given me plenty to think about," said Trove.

On his way home the boy thought of the stranger at the stairs, wondering if he were the other tinker of whom Darrel had told him. At his lodging he found a new pair of boots with only the Christmas greeting on a card.

"Well," said Trove, already merrier than most of far better fortune, "he must have been somebody that knew my needs."

VII

DARREL OF THE BLESSED ISLES

The clock tinker was off in the snow paths every other week. In more than a hundred homes, scattered far along road lines of the great valley, he set the pace of the pendulums. Every winter the mare was rented for easy driving and Darrel made his journeys afoot. Twice a day Trove passed the little shop, and if there were a chalk mark on the dial, he bounded upstairs to greet his friend. Sometimes he brought another boy into the rare atmosphere of the clock shop—one, mayhap, who needed some counsel of the wise old man.

Spring had come again. Every day sowers walked the hills and valleys around Hillsborough, their hands swinging with a godlike gesture that summoned the dead to rise; everywhere was the odour of broken field or garden. Night had come again, after a day of magic sunlight, and soon after eight o'clock Trove was at the door of the tinker with a schoolmate.

"How are you?" said Trove, as Darrel opened the door.

"Better for the sight o' you," said the old man, promptly. "Enter Sidney Trove and another young gentleman."

The boys took the two chairs offered them in silence.

"Kind sor," the tinker added, turning to Trove, "thou hast thy cue; give us the lines."

"Pardon me," said the boy. "Mr. Darrel, my friend Richard Kent."

"Of the Academy?" said Darrel, as he held to the hand of Kent.

"Of the Academy," said Trove.

"An', I make no doubt, o' good hope," the tinker added. "Let me stop one o' the clocks—so I may not forget the hour o' meeting a new friend."

Darrel crossed the room and stopped a pendulum.

"He would like to join this night-school of ours," Trove answered.

"Would he?" said the tinker. "Well, it is one o' hard lessons. When ye come t' multiply love by experience, an' subtract vanity an' add peace, an' square the remainder, an' then divide by the number o' days in thy life—it is a pretty problem, an' the result may be much or little, an' ye reach it—"

He paused a moment, thoughtfully puffing the smoke.

"Not in this term o' school," he added impressively.

All were silent a little time.

"Where have you been?" Trove inquired presently.

"Home," said the old man.

There was a puzzled look on Trove's face.

"Home?" he repeated with a voice of inquiry.

"I have, sor," the clock tinker went on. "This poor shelter is not me home—it's only for a night now an' then. I've a grand house an' many servants an' a garden, sor, where there be flowers—lovely flowers—an' sunlight an' noble music. Believe me, boy, 'tis enough to make one think o' heaven."

"I did not know of it," said Trove.

"Know ye not there is a country in easy reach of us, with fair fields an' proud cities an' many people an' all delights, boy, all delights? There I hope thou shalt found a city thyself an' build it well so nothing shall overthrow it—fire, nor flood, nor the slow siege o' years."

"Where?" Trove inquired eagerly.

"In the Blessed Isles, boy, in the Blessed Isles. Imagine the infinite sea o' time that is behind us. Stand high an' look back over its dead level. King an' empire an' all their striving multitudes are sunk in the mighty deep. But thou shalt see rising out of it the Blessed Isles of imagination. Green—forever green are they—and scattered far into the dim distance. Look! there is the city o' Shakespeare—Norman towers and battlements and Gothic arches looming above the sea. Go there an' look at the people as they come an' go. Mingle with them an' find good company—merry-hearted folk a-plenty, an' God knows I love the merry-hearted! Talk with them, an' they will teach thee wisdom. Hard by is the Isle o' Milton, an' beyond are many—it would take thee years to visit them. Ah, sor, half me time I live in the Blessed

Isles. What is thy affliction, boy?"

He turned to Kent—a boy whose hard luck was proverbial, and whose left arm was in a sling.

"Broke it wrestling," said the boy.

"Kent has bad luck," said Trove. "Last year he broke his leg."

"Obey the law, or thou shalt break the bone o' thy neck," said Darrel, quickly.

"I do obey the law," said Trent.

"Ay—the written law," said the clock tinker, "an' small credit to thee. But the law o' thine own discovery,—the law that is for thyself an' no other,—hast thou ne'er thought of it? Ill luck is the penalty o' law-breaking. Therefore study the law that is for thyself. Already I have discovered one for thee, an' it is, 'I have not limberness enough in me bones, so I must put them in no unnecessary peril.' Listen, I'll read thee me own code."

The clock tinker rose and got his Shakespeare, ragged from long use, and read from a fly-leaf, his code of private law, to wit:—

"Walk at least four miles a day."

"Eat no pork and be at peace with thy liver."

"Measure thy words and cure a habit of exaggeration."

"Thine eyes are faulty—therefore, going up or down, look well to thy steps."

"Beware of ardent spirits, for the curse that is in thy blood. It will turn thy heart to stone."

"In giving, remember Darrel."

"Bandy no words with any man."

"Play at no game of chance."

"Think o' these things an' forget thyself."

"Now there is the law that is for me alone," Darrel continued, looking up at the boys. "Others may eat pork or taste the red cup, or dally with hazards an' suffer no great harm—not I. Good youths, remember, ill luck is for him only that is ignorant, neglectful, or defiant o' private law."

"But suppose your house fall upon you," Trove suggested.

"I speak not o' common perils," said the tinker. "But enough—let's up with the sail. Heave ho! an' away for the Blessed Isles. Which shall it be?"

He turned to a rude shelf, whereon were books,—near a score,—some worn to rags.

"What if it be yon fair Isle o' Milton?" he inquired, lifting an old volume.

"Let's to the Isle o' Milton," Trove answered.

"Well, go to one o' the clocks there, an' set it back," said the tinker.

"How much?" Trove inquired with a puzzled look.

"Well, a matter o' two hundred years," said Darrel, who was now turning the leaves. "List ye, boy, we're up to the shore an' hard by the city gates. How sweet the air o' this enchanted isle!

"'And west winds with musky wing
Down the cedarn alleys fling
Nard and cassia's balmy smells.'"

He quoted thoughtfully, turning the leaves. Then he read the shorter poems,—a score of them,—his voice sounding the noble music of the lines. It was revelation for those raw youths and led them high. They forgot the passing of the hours and till near midnight were as those gone to a strange country. And they long remembered that night with Darrel of the Blessed Isles.

VIII

DUST OF DIAMONDS IN THE HOUR-GLASS

The axe of Theron Allen had opened the doors of the wilderness. One by one the great trees fell thundering and were devoured by fire. Now sheep and cattle were grazing on the bare hills. Around the house he left a thicket of fir trees that howled ever as the wind blew, as if "because the mighty were spoiled." Neighbours had come near; every summer great rugs of grain, vari-hued, lay over hill and dale.

Allen bad prospered, and begun to speculate in cattle. Every year late in April he went to Canada for a drove and sent them south—a great caravan that filled the road for half a mile or more, tramping wearily under a cloud of dust. He sold a few here and there, as the drove went on—a far journey, often, to the sale of the last lot.

The drove came along one morning about the middle of May, 1847. Trove met them at the four corners on Caraway Pike. Then about sixteen years of age, he made his first long journey into the world with Allen's drove. He had his time that summer and fifty cents for driving. It was an odd business, and for the boy full of new things.

A man went ahead in a buckboard wagon that bore

provisions. One worked in the middle and two behind. Trove was at the heels of the first section. It was easy work after the cattle got used to the road and a bit leg weary. They stopped them for water at the creeks and rivers; slowed them down to browse or graze awhile at noontime; and when the sun was low, if they were yet in a land of fences, he of the horse and wagon hurried on to get pasturage for the night.

That first day some of the leaders had begun to wander and make trouble. For that reason Trove was walking beside the buckboard in front of the drove.

"We'll stop to-night on Cedar Hill," said the boss, about mid-afternoon. "Martha Vaughn has got the best pasture and the prettiest girl in this part o' the country. If you don't fall in love with that girl, you ought t' be licked."

Now Trove had no very high opinion of girls. Up there in Brier Dale he had seen little of them. At the red schoolhouse, even, they were few and far from his ideal. And they were a foolish lot there in Hillsborough, it seemed to him—all save two or three who were, he owned, very sweet and beautiful; but he had seen how they tempted other boys to extravagance, and was content with a sly glance at them now and then.

"I don't ever expect to fall in love," said Trove, confidently.

"Wal, love is a thing that always takes ye by surprise," the other answered. "Mrs. Vaughn is a widow, an' we generally stop there the first day out. She's a poor woman, an' it gives her a lift."

They came shortly to the little weather-stained house of the widow. As they approached, a girl, with arms bare to the elbow, stood looking at them, her hand shading her eyes.

"Co' boss! Co' boss! Co' boss!" she was calling, in a sweet, girlish treble.

Trove came up to the gate, and presently her big, dark eyes were looking into his own. That very moment he trembled before them as a reed shaken by the wind. Long after then, he said that something in her voice had first appealed to him. Her soft eyes were, indeed, of those that quicken the hearts of men. It is doubtful if there were, in all the world, a lovelier thing than that wild flower of girlhood up there in the hills. She was no dream of romance, dear reader. In one of the public buildings of a certain capital her portrait has been hanging these forty years, and wins, from all who pass it, the homage of a long look. But Trove said, often, that she was never quite so lovely as that day she stood calling the cows—her shapely, brown face aglow with the light of youth, her dark hair curling on either side as it fell to her shoulders.

"Good day," said he, a little embarrassed.

"Good day," said she, coolly, turning toward the house.

Trove was now in the midst of the cattle. Suddenly a dog rushed upon them, and they took fright. For a moment the boy was in danger of being trampled, but leaped quickly to the backs of the cows and rode to safety. After supper the men sat talking in the stable door, beyond which, on the hay, they were to sleep that night. But Trove stood a long time with the girl, whose name was Polly, at the little gate of the widow.

They seemed to meet there by accident. For a moment they were afraid of each other. After a little hesitation Polly picked a sprig of lilac. He could see a tremble in her hand as she gave it to him, and he felt his own blushes.

Irving Bacheller

"Couldn't you say something?" she whispered with a smile.

"I—I've been trying to think of something," he stammered.

"Anything would do," said the girl, laughing, as she retreated a step or two and stood with an elbow leaning on the board fence. She had on her best gown.

It was a curious interview, the words of small account, the silences full of that power which has been the very light of the world. If there were only some way of reporting what followed the petty words,—swift arrows of the eye, lips trembling with the peril of unuttered thought, faces lighting with sweet discovery or darkening with doubt,—well, the author would have better confidence.

Their glances met—the boy hesitated.

"I—don't think you look quite as lovely in that dress," he ventured.

A shadow of disappointment came into her face, and she turned away. The boy was embarrassed. He had taken a misstep. She turned impatiently and gave him a glance from head to foot.

"But you're lovely enough now," he ventured again.

There was a quick movement of her lips, a flicker of contempt in her eyes. It seemed an age before she answered him.

"Flatterer!" said she, presently, looking down and jabbing the fence top with a pin. "I suppose you think I'm very homely."

"I always mean what I say."

"Then you'd better be careful—you might spoil me." She smiled faintly, turning her face away.

"How so?"

"Don't you know," said she, seriously, "that when a girl thinks she's beautiful she's spoiled?"

Their blushes had begun to fade; their words to come easier.

"Guess I'm spoilt, too," said the boy, looking away thoughtfully. "I don't know what to say—but sometime, maybe, you will know me better and believe me." He spoke with some dignity.

"I know who you are," the girl answered, coming nearer and looking into his eyes. "You're the boy that came out of the woods in a little red sleigh."

"How did you know?" Trove inquired; for he was not aware that any outside his own home knew it.

"A man told us that came with the cattle last year. And he said you must belong to very grand folks."

"And how did he know that?"

"By your looks."

"By my looks?"

"Yes, I—I suppose he thought you didn't look like other boys around here." She was now plying the pin very attentively.

"I must be a very curious-looking boy."

"Oh, not very," said she, looking at him thoughtfully. "I—I—well I shall not tell you what I think," She spoke decisively.

She had begun to blush again.

Their eyes met, and they both looked away, smiling. Then a moment of silence.

"Don't you like brown?" She was now looking down at her dress, with a little show of trouble in her eyes.

"I liked the brown of your arms," he answered.

The pin stopped; there was a puzzled look in her face.

"I'm afraid it's a very homely dress, anyway," said she, looking down upon it, as she moved her foot impatiently.

Her mother came out of doors. "Polly," said she, "you'd better go over to the post-office."

"May I go with her?" Trove inquired.

"Ask Polly," said the widow Vaughn, laughing.

"May I?" he asked.

Polly turned away smiling. "If you care to," said she, in a low voice.

"You must hurry and not be after dark," said the widow.

They went away, but only the moments hurried. They that read here, though their heads be gray and their hearts heavy, will understand; for they will remember some little space of time, with seconds flashing as they went, like dust of diamonds in the hour-glass.

"Don't you remember how you came in the little red sleigh?" she asked presently.

"No."

"I think it's very grand," said she. "It's so much like a story."

"Do you read stories?"

"All I can get. I've been reading 'Greytower.'"

"I read it last winter," said the boy. "What did you like best in it?"

"I'm ashamed to tell you," said she, with a quick glance at him.

"Please tell me."

"Oh, the love scenes, of course," said she, looking down with a sigh, and a little hesitation.

"He was a fine lover."

"I've something in my eye," said she, stopping.

"Perhaps I can get it," said he; "let me try."

"I'm afraid you'll hurt me," said she, looking up with a smile.

"I'll be careful."

He lifted her face a little, his fingers beneath her pretty chin.

Then, taking her long, dark lashes between thumb and finger, he opened the lids.

"You are hurting," said she, soberly; and now the lashes were trying to pull free.

"I can see it," said he.

"It must be a bear—you look so frightened."

"It's nothing to be afraid of," said the boy.

"Well, your hands tremble," said she, laughing.

"There," he answered, removing a speck of dust with his handkerchief.

"It is gone now, thank you," said Polly, winking.

She stood close to him, and as she spoke her lips trembled. He could delay no longer with a subject knocking at the gate of speech.

"Do you believe in love at first sight?" he asked.

She turned, looking up at him seriously. Her lips parted in a smile that showed her white teeth. Then her glance fell. "I shall not tell you that," said she, in a half whisper.

"I hope we shall meet again," he said,

"Do you?" said she, glancing up at him shyly.

"Yes."

"Well, if I were you and wanted to see a girl,—I'd—I'd come

and see her."

"What if you didn't know whether she was willing or not?" he asked.

"I'd take my chances," said she, soberly.

There were pauses in which their souls went far beyond their words and seemed to embrace each other fondly with arms of the spirit invisible and resistless. And whatever was to come, in that hour the great priest of Love in the white robe of innocence had made them one. The air about them was full of strange delight, They were in deep dusk as they neared the house. For one moment of long-remembered joy she let him put his arm about her waist, but when he kissed her cheek she drew herself away.

They walked a little time in silence.

"I am no flirt," she whispered presently. Neither spoke for a moment.

Then she seemed to feel and pity his emotion. Something slowed the feet of both.

"There," she whispered; "you may kiss my hand if you care to."

He kissed the pretty hand that was offered to him, and her whisper seemed to ring in the dusky silence like the dying rhythm of a bell.

IX

DROVE AND DROVERS

A little after daybreak they went on with the cows. For half a mile or more until the little house had sunk below the hill crest Trove was looking backward. Now and ever after he was to think and tarry also in the road of life and look behind him for the golden towers of memory. The drovers saw a change in Trove and flung at him with their stock of rusty, ancestral witticisms. But Thurst Tilly had a way of saying and doing quite his own,

"Never see any one knocked so flat as you was," said he. "Ye didn't know enough t' keep ahead o' the cattle. I declare I thought they'd trample ye 'fore ye could git yer eye unsot."

Trove made no answer.

"That air gal had a mighty power in her eye," Thurst went on. "When I see her totin' you off las' night I says t' the boys, says I, 'Sid is goin' t' git stepped on. He ain't never goin' t' be the same boy ag'in.'"

The boy held his peace, and for days neither ridicule nor excitement—save only for the time they lasted—were able to bring him out of his dream.

That night they came to wild country, where men and cattle lay down to rest by the roadway—a thing Trove enjoyed. In the wagon were bread and butter and boiled eggs and tea and doughnuts and cake and dried herring. The men built fires and made tea and ate their suppers, and sang, as the night fell, those olden ballads of the frontier—"Barbara Allen," "Bonaparte's Dream," or the "Drover's Daughter."

For days they were driving in the wild country. At bedtime each wound himself in a blanket and lay down to rest, beneath a rude lean-to if it were raining, but mostly under the stars. On this journey Trove got his habit of sleeping, out-of-doors in fair weather. After it, save in midwinter, walls seemed to weary and roofs to smother him. The drove began to low at daybreak, and soon they were all cropping the grass or browsing in the briers. Then the milking, and breakfast over a camp fire, and soon after sunrise they were all tramping in the road again.

It was a pleasant journey—the waysides glowing with the blue of violets, the green of tender grass, the thick-sown, starry gold of dandelions. Wild fowl crossed the sky in wedge and battalion, their videttes out, their lines now firm, now wheeling in a long curve to take the path of the wind. Every thicket was a fount of song that fell to silence when darkness came and the low chant of the marshes.

When they came into settled country below the big woods they began selling. At length the drove was reduced to one section; Trove following with the helper named Thurston Tilly, familiarly known as "Thurst."

He was a tall, heavy, good-natured man, distinguished for fat, happiness, and singular aptitudes. He had lifted a barrel of salt by the chimes and put it on a wagon; once he had eaten two mince pies at a meal; again he had put his heel six inches above his head on a barn door, and, any time, he could wiggle one ear or both or whistle on his thumb. At every lodging place he had left a feeling of dread and relief as well as a perennial topic of conversation. At every inn he added something to his stock of fat and happiness. Then, often, he seemed to be overloaded with the latter and would sit and shake his head and roar with laughter, now and then giving out a wild yell. He had a story of which no one had ever heard the finish. He began it often, but, somehow, never got to the end. He always clung to the lapel of his hearer's coat as if in fear of losing him, and never tried his tale but once on the same pair of ears. Having got his inspiration he went in quest of his hearer, and having hitched him, as it were, by laying hold of his elbow or coat collar, began the tale. It was like pouring molasses on a level place—it moved slowly and spread and got nowhere in particular. At first his manner was slow, dignified, and confidential, changing to fit his emotion. He whispered, he shouted, he laughed, he looked sorrowful, he nudged the stranger in his abdomen, he glared upon him, eye close to eye, he shook him by the shoulder, and slowly wore him out. Some endured long and were patient, but soon or late all began to back and dodge, and finally broke away, and seeing the hand of the narrator reach for them, dodged quickly and, being pursued, ran. Often this odd chase took them around trees and stumps and buildings, the stranger escaping, frequently, through some friendly door which he could lock or hold fast. Then Thurst, knocking loudly, gave out a wild yell or two, peered in at the nearest window, and came at last to his chair, sorrowful and much out of breath, his tale unfinished. There was in the man a saving element of good nature, and no one ever got angry with him. At each new attempt be showed a grimmer determination to finish, but even there, in a land of strong and patient men, not one, they used to say, had ever the endurance to hear the end of that unfinished tale.

It was not easy to dispose of cattle in the southern counties that year, but they found a better market as they bore west, and were across the border of Ohio when the last of the drove were sold. That done, Trove and Thurst Tilly took the main road to Cleveland, whence they were to return home by steamboat.

It led them into woods and by stumpy fields and pine-odoured hamlets. The first day of their walk was rainy, and they went up a toteway into thick timber and built a fire and kept dry and warm until the rain ceased. That evening they fell in with emigrants on their way to the far west.

The latter were camped on the edge of a wood, near the roadway, and cooking supper as the two came along. Being far from a town, Trove and Tilly were glad to accept the hospitality of the travellers.

They had come to the great highway of travel from east to west. Every day it was cut by wagons of the mover over-loaded with Lares and Penates, with old and young, enduring hardships and the loss of home and old acquaintance for hope of better fortune.

A man and wife and three boys were the party, travelling with two wagons. They were bound for Iowa and, being heavy loaded, were having a hard time. All sat on a heap of boughs in the firelight after supper.

"It's a long, long road to Iowa, father," said the woman.

"It'll soon be over," said he, with a tone of encouragement.

"I've been thinking all day of the lilacs and the old house," said she.

They looked in silence at the fire a moment.

"We're a bit homesick," said the man, turning to Trove, "an' no wonder. It's been hard travelling, an' we've broke down every few miles. But we'll have better luck the rest o' the journey."

Evidently his cheerful courage had been all that kept them going.

"Lost all we had in the great fire of '35," said he, thought-fully. "I went to bed a rich man, but when I rose in the morning I had not enough to pay a week's board. Everything had been swept away."

"A merchant?" Trove inquired.

"A partner in the great Star Mill on East River," said the man. "I could have got a fortune for my share—at least a hundred thousand dollars—and I had worked hard for it."

"And were you not able to succeed again?"

"No," said the traveller, sadly, shaking his head. "If some time you have to lose all you possess. God grant you still have youth and a strong arm. I tried—that is all—I tried."

The boy looked up at him, his heart touched. The man was near sixty years of age; his face had deep lines in it; his voice the dull ring of loss, and failure, and small hope. The woman covered her face and began to sob.

"There, mother," said the man, touching her head; "we'd better forget. I'll never speak of that again—never. We're going to seek our fortune. Away in the great west we'll seek our fortune."

His effort to be cheerful was perhaps the richest colour of that odd scene there in the still woods and the firelight.

"We're going to take a farm in the most beautiful country in the world. It's easy to make money there."

"If you've no objection I'd like to go with you," said Thurst Tilly. "I'm a good farmer."

"Can you drive a team?" said the man.

"Drove horses all my life," said Thurst; whereupon they made a bargain.

Trove and Tilly went away to the brook for water while the travellers went to bed in their big, covered wagon. Trove lay down with his blanket on the boughs, reading over the indelible record of that day. And he said, often, as he thought of it, years after, that the saddest thing in all the world is a man of broken courage.

X

AN ODD MEETING

They were up betimes in the morning, and Trove ate hastily from his own store and bade them all good-by and made off, for he had yet a long road to travel.

That day Trove fell in with a great, awkward country boy, slouching along the road on his way to Cleveland. He was an odd figure, with thick hair of the shade of tow that burst out from under a slouch hat and muffled his neck behind; his coat was thread-bare and a bit too large; his trousers of satinet fell loosely far enough to break joints with each bootleg; the dusty cowhide gave his feet a lonely and arid look. He carried a bundle tied to a stick that lay on his left shoulder. They met near a corner, nodded, and walked on a while together in silence. For a little time they surveyed each other curiously. Then each began to quicken the pace.

"Maybe you think you can walk the fastest," said he of the long hair.

They were going a hot pace, their free arms flying. Trove bent to his work stubbornly. They both began to tire and slow up. The big boy looked across at the other and laughed loudly.

"Wouldn't give up if ye broke a leg, would ye?" said he.

"Not if I could swing it," said Trove.

"Goin' t' Cleveland?"

"Yes; are you?"

"Yes. I'm goin' t' be a sailor," said the strange boy.

"Goin' off on the ocean?" Trove inquired with deep interest.

"Yes; 'round the world, maybe. Then I'll come back an' go t' school—if I don't git wrecked like Robi'son Crusoe."

"My stars!" said Trove, with a look of awe.

"Like t' go?" the other inquired.

"Guess I would!"

"Better stay t' home; it's a hard life." This with an air of parental wisdom.

"I've read 'Robi'son Crusoe,'" said Trove, as if it were some excuse.

"So 've I; an' Grimshaw's 'Napoleon,' an' Weems's 'Life o' Marion,' an' 'The Pirates' Book,' an' the Bible."

"I've got half through the Bible," said Trove.

"Who slew Absolum?" the other inquired doubtfully.

Trove remembered the circumstances, but couldn't recall the name.

They sat down to rest and eat luncheon.

"You going to be a statesman?" Trove inquired.

"No; once I thought I'd try t' go t' Congress, but I guess I'd rather go t' sea. What you goin' t' be?"

"I shall try to be an author," said Trove.

"Why, if I was you, I'd go into politics," said the other. "Ye might be President some day, no telling. Do ye know how t' chop er hoe er swing a scythe?"

"Yes."

"Wal, then, if ye don't ever git t' be President, ye won't have t' starve. I saw an author one day."

"You did?"

"He was an awful-lookin' cuss," said the other, with a nod of affirmation.

The strange boy took another bite of bread and butter.

"Wrote dime novels an' drank whisky an' wore a bearskin vest," he added presently.

"Do you know the Declaration of Independence?"

"No."

"I do," said the strange boy, and gave it word for word.

They chatted and tried tricks and spent a happy hour there by the roadside. It was an hour of pure democracy—neither knew even the name of the other so far.

They got to Cleveland late in the afternoon.

"Now keep yer hand on yer wallet," said the strange boy, as they were coming into the city. "I've got three dollars an' seventy-five cents in mine, an' I don't propose t' have it took away from me."

Trove went to a tavern, the other to stay with friends. Near noon next day both boys met on the wharf, where Trove was to board a steamboat.

"Got a job?" Trove inquired.

"No," said the other, with a look of dejection. "I tried, an' they cursed an' damned me awful. I got away as quick as I could. Dunno but I'll have t' go back an' try t' be a statesman er something o' that kind. Guess it's easier than goin' t' sea. Give me yer name an' address, an' maybe I'll write ye a letter."

Trove complied.

"Please give me yours," said he.

"It's James Abram Garfield, Orange, O.," said the other.

Then they spoke a long good-by.

XI

THE OLD RAG DOLL

The second week of September Trove went down the hills again to school, with food and furniture beside him in the great wagon. He had not been happy since he got home. Word of that evening with the pretty "Vaughn girl" had come to the ears of Allen.

"You're too young for that, boy," said he, the day Trove came. "You must promise me one thing—that you'll keep away from her until you are eighteen."

In every conviction Allen was like the hills about him—there were small changes on the surface, but underneath they were ever the same rock-boned, firm, unmoving hills.

"But I'm in love with her," said the boy, with dignity. "It is more than I can bear. I tell you, sir, that I regard the young lady with—with deep affection." He had often a dignity of phrase and manner beyond his years.

"Then it will last," said Allen. "You're only a boy, and for a while I know what is best for you."

Trove had to promise, and, as that keen edge of his feeling

wore away, doubted no more the wisdom of his father. He wrote Polly a letter, quaint with boyish chivalry and frankness—one of a package that has lain these many years in old ribbons and the scent of lavender.

He went to the Sign of the Dial as soon as he got to Hillsborough that day. Darrel was at home, and a happy time it was, wherein each gave account of the summer. A stranger sat working at the small bench. Darrel gave him no heed, chatting as if they were quite alone.

"And what is the news in Hillsborough?" said Trove, his part of the story finished.

"Have ye not heard?" said Darrel, in a whisper. "Parson Hammond hath swapped horses."

Trove began to laugh.

"Nay, that is not all," said the tinker, his pipe in hand. "Deacon Swackhammer hath smitten the head o' Brooke. Oh, sor, 'twas a comedy. Brooke gave him an ill-sounding word. Swackhammer removed his coat an' flung it down. 'Deacon, lie there,' said he. Then each began, as it were, to bruise the head o' the serpent. Brooke—poor man!—he got the worst of it. An' sad to tell! his wife died the very next day."

"Of what?" Trove inquired,

"Marry, I do not know; it may have been joy," said the tinker, lighting his pipe. "Ah, sor, Brooke is tough. He smites the helping hand an' sickens the heart o' kindness. I offered him help an' sympathy, an' he made it all bitter with suspicion o' me. I turned away, an' said I to meself, 'Darrel, thy head is soft—a babe could brain thee with a lady's fan.'"

Darrel puffed his pipe in silence a little time.

"Every one hates Brooke," said Trove.

"Once," said Darrel, presently, "a young painter met a small animal with a striped back, in the woods. They exchanged compliments an' suddenly the painter ran, shaking his head. As he came near his own people, they all began to flee before him. He followed them for days, an' every animal in the woods ran as he came near. By an' by he stopped to rest. Then he looked down at himself an' spat, sneeringly. When, after weeks o' travel, he was at length admitted to the company of his kind, they sat in judgment on him.

"'Tell us,' said one, 'what evil hath befallen thee?'"

"'Alas!' said the poor cat, 'I met a little creature with a striped back.'"

"'A little creature! an' thee so put about?' said another, with great contempt."

"'Ay; but he hath a mighty talent,' said the sad painter. 'Let him but stand before thee, an' he hath spoiled the earth, an' its people, an' thou would'st even flee from thyself. But in fleeing thou shalt think thyself on the way to hell.'"

For a moment Darrel shook with silent laughter. Then he rose and put his pipe on the shelf.

"Well, I'd another chance to try the good law on him," said Darrel, presently. "In July he fell sick o' fever, an' I delayed me trip to nurse him. At length, when he was nearly well, an' I had come to his home one evening, the widow Glover met me at his door.

"'If ye expect money fer comin' here, ye better go on 'bout yer business,' Brooke shouted from the bedroom. 'I don't need ye any more, an' I'll send yc a bushel o' potatoes by 'n by. Good day.'"

"Not a word o' thanks!" the tinker exclaimed. "Wrath o' God! I fear there is but one thing would soften him."

"And what is that?"

"A club," said Darrel. "But God forgive me! I must put away anger. Soon it went about that Brooke was to marry the widow. All were delighted, for each party would be in the nature of a punishment. God's justice! they did deserve each other."

Darrel shook with happiness, and relighted his pipe.

"Mayhap ye've seen the dear lady," Darrel went on. "She is large, bony, quarrelsome—a weaver of some fifty years— neither amiable nor fair to look upon. Every one knows her—a survivor o' two husbands an' many a battle o' high words.

"'Is it a case o' foreclosure, Brooke?' says I to him one day in the road."

"'No, sor,' he snaps out; 'I had a little mortgage on her furniture, but I'm going t' marry her for a helpmeet. She is a great worker an' neat an' savin'.'"

"'An' headstrong,' says I. 'Ye must have patience with her.'"

"'I can manage her,' said Brooke. 'The first morning after we are married I always say to my wife, "Here's the breeches; now if ye want 'em, take 'em, an' I'll put on the dress."'"

"He looked wise, then, as if 'twere a great argument."

"'Always?' says I. 'God bless thee, 'tis an odd habit.'"

"Well, the boast o' Brooke went from one to another an' at last to the widow's ear. They say a look o' firmness an' resolution came into her face, an' late in August they were married of an evening at the home o' Brooke. Well, about then, I had been having trouble."

"Trouble?" said Trove.

"It was another's trouble—that of a client o' mine, a poor woman out in the country. Brooke had a mortgage on her cattle, an' she could not pay, an' I undertook to help her. I had some money due me, but was unable to put me hand on it. That day before the wedding I went to the old sinner."

"'Brooke, I came to see about the Martha Vaughn mortgage,' says I."

"Martha Vaughn!" said Trove, turning quickly.

"Yes, one o' God's people," said the tinker.

"Ye may have seen her?"

"I have seen her," said Trove.

"'At ten o'clock to-morrow I shall foreclose,' says Brooke, waving his fist."

"'Give her a little time—till the day after to-morrow,—man, it is not much to ask,' says I."

"'Not an hour,' says he; an' I came away."

Darrel rose and put on his glasses and brought a newspaper and gave it to the boy.

"Read that," said he, his finger on the story, "an' see what came of it."

The article was entitled "A Rag Doll—The Story of a Money-lender whose Name, let us say, is Brown."

After some account of the marriage and of bride and groom, the story went on as follows:—

"At midnight the charivari was heard—a noisy beating of pans and pots in the door-yard of the unhappy groom, who flung sticks of wood from the window, and who finally dispersed the crowd with an old shotgun. Bright and early next day came the milkman—a veteran of the war of 1812— who, agreeably with his custom, sounded the call of boots and saddles on his battered bugle at Brown's door. But none came to open it. The noon hour passed with no sign of life in the old house.

"'Suthin' hes happened over there,' said his nearest neighbour, peering out of the window. 'Mebbe they've fit an' disabled each other.'"

"'You'd better go an' rap on the door,' said his wife."

"He started, halting at his gate and looking over at the house of mystery. While he stood there, the door of the money-lender opened a little, and a head came out beckoning for help. He hurried to the door, that swung open as he came near it.

"'Heavens!' said he, 'What is the matter?'"

"Brown stood behind the door, in a gown of figured calico, his feet bare, his shock of gray hair dishevelled. The gown was a poor fit, stopping just below the knees.

"'That woman!' he gasped, sinking into a chair and making an angry gesture with his fist. 'That woman has got every pair o' breeches in the house.'"

"His wife appeared in the rusty, familiar garments of the money-lender."

"'He tried to humble me this morning,' said she, 'an' I humbled him. He began to order me around, an' I told him I wouldn't hev it. "Then," says he, "you better put on the breeches an' I'll put on the dress." "Very well," says I, and grabbed the breeches, an' give him the dress. I know ye, Brown; ye'll never abuse me.'"

"'I'll get a divorce—I'll have the law on ye,' said the old man, angrily, as he walked the floor in his gown of calico."

"'Go on,' said she. 'Go to the lawyer now.'"

"'Will ye git me a pair o' breeches?'"

"'No; I took yer offer, an' ye can't have 'em 'til ye've done the work that goes with the dress. Come, now, I want my dinner.'"

"'I can't find a stitch in the house,' said he, turning to his neighbour. 'I wish ye'd bring me some clothes.'"

"The caller made no reply, but came away smiling, and told of Brown's dilemma."

"'It's good for him,' said the neighbour's wife. 'Don't ye take him any clothes. He's bullied three wives to death, an' now I'm glad he's got a wife that can bully him.'"

"Brown waited long, but no help arrived. The wife was firm and he very hungry. She called him 'wife'—a title not calculated to soothe a man of his agility and vigour. He galloped across the room at her, yelling as he brandished a poker. She quickly took it away and drove him into a corner. He had taken up the poker and now seemed likely to perish by it. Then, going to the stove with this odd weapon, she stuck its end in the fire, and Brown had no sooner flung a wash-basin across the room at her head than she ran after him with the hot poker. Then, calling for help, he ran around the stove and out of doors like a wild man, his dress of calico and his long hair flying in the breeze. Pedestrians halted, men and women came out of their homes. The bare feet of the money-lender were flying with great energy.

"'She's druv him crazy,' a man shouted."

"'An' knocked the socks off him,' said another."

"'Must have been tryin' t' make him into a rag doll,' was the comment of a third."

"'Brown, if yer goin' t' be a womern,' said one, as they surrounded him, 'ye'd ought to put on a longer dress. Yer enough t' scare a hoss.'"

"Brown was inarticulate with anger."

"A number of men judging him insane, seized and returned him to his punishment. They heard the unhappy story with loud laughter."

"'You'd better give up an' go to the kitchen. Brown,' said one

Irving Bacheller

of them; and there are those who maintain that he got the dinner before he got the trousers."

"Well, God be praised!" said Darrel, when Trove had finished reading the story; "Brooke was unable to foreclose that day, an' the next was Sunday, an' bright an' early on Monday morning I paid the debt."

"Mrs. Vaughn has a daughter," said Trove, blushing.

"Ay; an' she hath a pretty redness in her lip," said Darrel, quickly, "an' a merry flash in her eye. Thou hast yet far to go, boy. Look not upon her now, or she will trip thee. By an' by, boy, by an' by."

There was an odd trait in Darrel. In familiar talk he often made use of "ye"—a shortened you—in speaking to those of old acquaintance. But when there was man or topic to rouse him into higher dignity it was more often "thee" or "thou" with him. Trove made no answer and shortly went away.

In certain court records one may read of the celebrated suit for divorce which enlivened the winter of that year in the north country. It is enough to quote the ringing words of one Colonel Jenkins, who addressed the judge as follows:—

"Picture to yourself, sir, this venerable man, waking from his dream of happiness to be robbed of his trousers—the very insignia of his manhood. Picture him, sir, sitting in calico and despair, mingled with hunger and humiliation. Think of him being addressed as 'wife.' Being called 'wife,' sir, by this woman he had taken to his heart and home. That, your Honour, was ingratitude sharper than a serpent's tooth. Picture him driven from his fireside in skirts,—the very drapery of humiliation,—skirts, your Honour, that came barely to the knees and left his nether limbs exposed to the autumnal breeze and the ridicule of the unthinking. Sir, it is for you to say how far the widow may go in her oppression. If such conduct is permitted, in God's name, who is safe?"

"May it please your Honour," said the opposing lawyer, "having looked upon these pictures of the learned counsel, it is for you to judge whether you ever saw any that gave you greater joy. They are above all art, your Honour. In the galleries of memory there are none like them—none so charming, so delightful. If I were to die to-morrow, sir, I should thank God that my last hour came not until I had seen these pictures of Colonel Jenkins; and it may be sir, that my happiness would even delay the hand of death. My only regret is that mine is the great misfortune of having failed to witness the event they portray. Sir, you have a great responsibility, for you have to judge whether human law may interfere with the working of divine justice. It was the decree of fate, your Honour, following his own word and action, that this man should become as a rag doll in the hands of a termagant. I submit to you that Providence, in the memory of the living, has done no better job."

A tumult of applause stopped him, and he sat down.

Brooke was defeated promptly, and known ever after as "The Old Rag Doll."

XII

THE SANTA CLAUS OF CEDAR HILL

Christmas Eve had come and the year of 1850. For two weeks snow had rushed over the creaking gable of the forest above Martha Vaughn's, to pile in drifts or go hissing down the long hillside. A freezing blast had driven it to the roots of the stubble and sown it deep and rolled it into ridges and whirled it into heaps and mounds, or flung it far in long waves that seemed to plunge, as if part of a white sea, and break over fence and roof and chimney in their downrush. Candle and firelight filtered through frosty panes and glowed, dimly, under dark fathoms of the snow sheet now flying full of voices. Mrs. Vaughn opened her door a moment to peer out. A great horned owl flashed across the light beam with a snap and rustle of wings and a cry "oo-oo-oo," lonely, like that, as if it were the spirit of darkness and the cold wind. Mrs. Vaughn started, turning quickly and closing the door.

"Ugh! what a sound," said Polly. "It reminds me of a ghost story."

"Well," said the widow, "that thing belongs to the only family o' real ghosts in the world."

"What was it?" said a small boy. There were Polly and three children about the fireplace.

"An air cat," said she, shivering, her back to the fire. "They go 'round at night in a great sheet o' feathers an' rustle it, an' I declare they do cry lonesome. Got terrible claws, too!"

"Ever hurt folks?" one of the boys inquired.

"No; but they're just like some kinds o' people—ye want to let 'em alone. Any one that'll shake hands with an owl would be fool enough to eat fish-hooks. They're not made for friendship—those owls."

"What are they made for?" another voice inquired.

"Just to kill," said she, patting a boy's head tenderly. "They're Death flying round at night—the angel o' Death for rats an' rabbits an' birds an' other little creatures. Once,—oh, many years ago,—it seemed so everything was made to kill. Men were like beasts o' prey, most of 'em; an' they're not all gone yet. Went around day an' night killing. I declare they must have had claws. Then came the Prince o' Peace."

"What did he do to 'em, mother?" said Paul—a boy of seven.

"Well, he began to cut their claws for one thing," said the mother. "Taught 'em to love an' not to kill. Shall I read you the story—how he came in a manger?"

"B'lieve I'd rather hear about Injuns," said the boy.

"We shall hear about them too," the mother added. "They're like folks o' the olden time. They make a terrible fuss; but they've got to hold still an' have their claws cut."

Presently she sat down by a table, where there were candles, and began reading aloud from a county paper. She read anecdotes of men, remarkable for their success and piety, and an account of Indian fighting, interrupted, as a red man lifted his tomahawk to slay, by the rattle of an arrow on the buttery door.

It was off the cross-gun of young Paul. He had seen everything in the story and had taken aim at the said Indian just in the nick of time.

She read, also, the old sweet story of the coming of the Christ Child.

"Some say it was a night like this," said she, as the story ended.

Paul had listened, his thin, sober face glowing.

"I'll bet Santa Claus was good to him," said he. "Brought him sleds an' candy an' nuts an' raisins an' new boots an' everything."

"Why do you think so?" asked his mother, who was now reading intently.

"'Cos he was a good boy. He wouldn't cry if he had to fill the wood box; would he, mother?"

That query held a hidden rebuke for his brother Tom.

"I do not know, but I do not think he was ever saucy or spoke a bad word."

"Huh!" said Tom, reflectively; "then I guess he never had no mustard plaster put on him."

The widow bade him hush.

"Er never had nuthin' done to him, neither," the boy continued, rocking vigorously in his little chair.

"Mustn't speak so of Christ," the mother added.

"Wal," said Paul, rising, "I guess I'll hang up my stockin's."

"One'll do, Paul," said his sister Polly, with a knowing air.

"No, 'twon't," the boy insisted. "They ain't half 's big as yours. I'm goin' t' try it, anyway, an' see what he'll do to 'em."

He drew off his stockings and pinned them carefully to the braces on the back of a chair.

"Well, my son," said Mrs. Vaughn, looking over the top of her paper, "it's bad weather; Santa Claus may not be able to get here."

"Oh, yes, he can," said the boy, confidently, but with a little quiver of alarm in his voice. "I'm sure he'll come. He has a team of reindeers. 'An' the deeper the snow the faster they go.'"

Soon the others bared their feet and hung their stockings on four chairs in a row beside the first.

Then they all got on the bed in the corner and pulled a quilt over them to wait for Santa Claus. The mother went on with her reading as they chattered.

Sleep hushed them presently. But for the crackling of the fire, and the push and whistle of the wind, that room had become as a peaceful, silent cave under the storm.

Irving Bacheller

The widow rose stealthily and opened a bureau drawer. The row of limp stockings began to look cheerful and animated. Little packages fell to their toes, and the shortest began to reach for the floor. But while they were fat in the foot they were still very lean in the leg.

Her apron empty, Mrs. Vaughn took her knitting to the fire, and before she began to ply the needles, looked thoughtfully at her hands. They had been soft and shapely before the days of toil. A frail but comely woman she was, with pale face, and dark eyes, and hair prematurely white.

She had come west—a girl of nineteen—with her young husband, full of high hopes. That was twenty-one years ago, and the new land had poorly kept its promise.

And the children—"How many have you?" a caller had once inquired. "Listen," said she, "hear 'em, an' you'd say there were fifteen, but count 'em an' they're only four."

The low, weathered house and sixty acres were mortgaged. Even the wilderness had not wholly signed off its claim. Every year it exacted tribute, the foxes taking a share of her poultry, and the wild deer feeding on her grain.

A little beggar of a dog, that now lay in the firelight, had offered himself one day, with cheerful confidence, and been accepted. Small, affectionate, cowardly, irresponsible, and yellow, he was in the nature of a luxury, as the widow had once said. He had a slim nose, no longer than a man's thumb, and ever busy. He was a most prudent animal, and the first day found a small opening in the foundation of the barn through which he betook himself always at any sign of danger. He soon buried his bones there, and was ready for a siege if, perchance, it came. One blow or even a harsh word sent him to his refuge in hot haste. He had learned early that the ways of hired men were full of violence and peril. Hospitality and affection had won his confidence but never deprived him of his caution.

Presently there came a heavy step and a quick pull at the latch-string. An odd figure entered in a swirl of snow—a real Santa Claus, the mystery and blessing of Cedar Hill. For five years, every Christmas Eve, in good or bad weather, he had come to four little houses on the Hill, where, indeed, his coming had been as a Godsend. Whence he came and who he might be none had been able to guess. He never spoke in his official capacity, and no citizen of Faraway had such a beard or figure as this man. Now his fur coat, his beard, and eyebrows were hoary with snow and frost. Icicles hung from his mustache around the short clay pipe of tradition. He lowered a great sack and brushed the snow off it. He had borne it high on his back, with a strap at each shoulder.

The sack was now about half full of things. He took out three big bundles and laid them on the table. They were evidently for the widow herself, who quickly stepped to the bedside.

"Come, children," she whispered, rousing them; "here is Santa Claus."

They scrambled down, rubbing their eyes. Polly took the hands of the two small boys and led them near him. Paul drew his hand away and stood spellbound, eyes and mouth open. He watched every motion of the good Saint, who had come to that chair that held the little stockings. Santa Claus put a pair of boots on it. They were copper-toed, with gorgeous front pieces of red morocco at the top of the leg. Then, as if he had some relish of a joke, he took them up, looked them over thoughtfully, and put them in the sack again, whereupon the boy Paul burst into tears. Old Santa Claus, shaking with silent laughter, replaced them in the

Irving Bacheller

chair quickly,

As if to lighten the boy's heart he opened a box and took out a mouth-organ. He held it so the light sparkled on its shiny side. Then he put his pipe in his pocket and began to dance and play lively music. Step and tune quickened. The bulky figure was flying up and down above a great clatter of big boots, his head wagging to keep time. The oldest children were laughing, and the boy Paul, he began to smile in the midst of a great sob that shook him to the toes. The player stopped suddenly, stuffed the instrument in a stocking, and went on with his work. Presently he uncovered a stick of candy long as a man's arm. There were spiral stripes of red from end to end of it. He used it for a fiddle-bow, whistling with terrific energy and sawing the air. Then he put shawls and tippets and boots and various little packages on the other chairs.

At last he drew out of the sack a sheet of pasteboard, with string attached, and hung it on the wall. It bore the simple message, rudely lettered in black, as follows:—

"Mery Crismus. And Children i have the
honnor to remane, Yours Respec'fully
SANDY CLAUS."

His work done, he swung the pack to his shoulders and made off as they all broke the silence with a hearty "Thank you, Santa Claus!"

They listened a moment, as he went away with a loud and merry laugh sounding above the roar of the wind. It was the voice of a big and gentle heart, but gave no other clew. In a moment cries of delight, and a rustle of wrappings, filled the room. As on wings of the bitter wind, joy and good fortune had come to them, and, in that little house, had drifted deep as the snow without.

The children went to their beds with slow feet and quick pulses. Paul begged for the sacred privilege of wearing his new boots to bed, but compromised on having them beside his pillow. The boys went to sleep at last, with all their treasures heaped about them. Tom shortly rolled upon the little jumping-jack, that broke away and butted him in the face with a loud squawk. It roused the boy, who promptly set up a defence in which the stuffed hen lost her tail-feathers and the jumping-jack was violently put out of bed. When the mother came to see what had happened, order had been restored—the boys were both sleeping.

It was an odd little room under bare shingles above stairs. Great chests, filled with relics of another time and country, sat against the walls. Here and there a bunch of herbs or a few ears of corn, their husks braided, hung on the bare rafters. The aroma of the summer fields—of peppermint, catnip, and lobelia—haunted it. Chimney and stovepipe tempered the cold. A crack in the gable end let in a sift of snow that had been heaping up a lonely little drift on the bare floor. The widow covered the boys tenderly and took their treasures off the bed, all save the little wooden monkey, which, as if frightened by the melee, had hidden far under the clothes. She went below stairs to the fire, which every cold day was well fed until after midnight, and began to enjoy the sight of her own gifts. They were a haunch of venison, a sack of flour, a shawl, and mittens. A small package had fallen to the floor. It was neatly bound with wrappings of blue paper. Under the last layer was a little box, the words "For Polly" on its cover. It held a locket of wrought gold that outshone the light of the candles. She touched a spring, and the case opened. Inside was a lock of hair, white as her own. There were three lines cut in the glowing metal, and she read them over and over again:—

Irving Bacheller

"Here are silver and gold,
The one for a day of remembrance between thee and
dishonour,
The other for a day of plenty between thee and want."

She went to her bed, presently, where the girl lay sleeping, and, lifting dark masses of her hair, kissed a ruddy cheek. Then the widow stood a moment, wiping her eyes.

XIII

A CHRISTMAS ADVENTURE

Long before daylight one could hear the slowing of the wind. Its caravan now reaching eastward to mid-ocean was nearly passed. Scattered gusts hurried on like weary and belated followers. Then, suddenly, came a silence in which one might have heard the dust of their feet falling, their shouts receding in the far woodland. The sun rose in a clear sky above the patched and ragged canopy of the woods—a weary multitude now resting in the still air.

The children were up looking for tracks of reindeer and breaking paths in the snow. Sunlight glimmered in far-flung jewels of the Frost King. They lay deep, clinking as the foot sank in them. At the Vaughn home it was an eventful day. Santa Claus—well, he is the great Captain that leads us to the farther gate of childhood and surrenders the golden key. Many ways are beyond the gate, some steep and thorny; and some who pass it turn back with bleeding feet and wet eyes, but the gate opens not again for any that have passed. Tom had got the key and begun to try it. Santa Claus had winked at him with a snaring eye, like that of his aunt when she had sugar in her pocket, and Tom thought it very foolish. The boy had even felt of his greatcoat and got a good look at his boots and trousers. Moreover, when he put his pipe away,

Irving Bacheller

Tom saw him take a chew of tobacco—an abhorrent thing if he were to believe his mother.

"Mother," said he, "I never knew Santa Claus chewed tobacco."

"Well, mebbe he was Santa Claus's hired man," said she.

"Might 'a' had the toothache," Paul suggested, for Lew Allen, who worked for them in the summer time, had an habitual toothache, relieved many times a day by chewing tobacco.

Tom sat looking into the fire a moment.

Then he spoke of a matter Paul and he had discussed secretly.

"Joe Bellus he tol' me Santa Claus was only somebody rigged up t' fool folks, an' hadn't no reindeers at all."

The mother turned away, her wits groping for an answer.

"Hadn't ought 'a' told mother, Tom," said Paul, with a little quiver of reproach and pity. "'Tain't so, anyway—we know 'tain't so."

He was looking into his mother's face.

"'Tain't so," Paul repeated with unshaken confidence.

"Mus'n't believe all ye hear," said the widow, who now turned to the doubting Thomas.

And that very moment Tom was come to the last gate of childhood, whereon are the black and necessary words, "Mus'n't believe all ye hear."

The boys in their new boots were on the track of a painter. They treed him, presently, at the foot of the stairs.

"How'll we kill him?" one of them inquired.

"Just walk around the tree once," said the mother, "an' you'll scare him to death. Why don't ye grease your boots?"

"'Fraid it'll take the screak out of 'em," said Paul, looking down thoughtfully at his own pair.

"Well," said she, "you'll have me treed if you keep on. No hunter would have boots like that. A loud foot makes a still gun."

That was her unfailing method of control—the appeal to intelligence. Polly sat singing, thoughtfully, the locket in her hand. She had kissed the sacred thing and hung it by a ribbon to her neck and bathed her eyes in the golden light of it and begun to feel the subtle pathos in its odd message. She was thinking of the handsome boy who came along that far May-day with the drove, and who lately had returned to be her teacher at Linley School. Now, he had so much dignity and learning, she liked him not half so well and felt he had no longer any care for her. She blushed to think how she had wept over his letter and kissed it every day for weeks. Her dream was interrupted, presently, by the call of her brother Tom. Having cut the frost on a window-pane, he stood peering out. A man was approaching in the near field. His figure showed to the boot-top, mounting hills of snow, and sank out of sight in the deep hollows. It looked as if he were walking on a rough sea. In a moment he came striding over the dooryard fence on a pair of snowshoes.

"It's Mr. Trove, the teacher," said Polly, who quickly began to shake her curls.

As the door swung open all greeted the young man. Loosening his snow-shoes, he flung them on the step and came in, a foxtail dangling from his fur cap.

He shook hands with Polly and her mother, and lifted Paul to the ceiling. "Hello, young man!" said he. "If one is four, how many are two?"

"If you're speaking of new boots," said the widow, "one is at least fifteen."

The school teacher made no reply, but stood a moment looking down at the boy.

"It's a cold day," said Polly.

"I like it," said the teacher, lifting his broad shoulders and smiting them with his hands. "God has been house cleaning. The dome of the sky is all swept and dusted. There isn't a cobweb anywhere. Santa Claus come?"

"Yes," said the younger children, who made a rush for their gifts and laid them on chairs before him.

"Grand old chap!" said he, staring thoughtfully at the flannel cat in his hands. "Any idea who it is?"

"Can't make out," said Mrs. Vaughn; "very singular man."

"Generous, too," the teacher added. "That's the best cat I ever saw, Tom. If I had my way, the cats would all be made of flannel. Miss Polly, what did you get?"

"This," said Polly, handing him the locket.

"Beautiful!" said he, turning it in his hand. "Anything inside?"

Polly showed him how to open it. He sat a moment or more looking at the graven gold.

"Strange!" said he, presently, surveying the wrought cases,

Mrs. Vaughn was now at his elbow.

"Strange?" she inquired.

"Well, long ago," said he, "I heard of one like it. Some time it may solve the mystery of your Santa Claus."

An ear of the teacher had begun to swell and redden.

"Should have pulled my cap down," said he, as the widow spoke of it. "Frost-bitten years ago, and if I'm out long in the cold, I begin to feel it."

"Must be very painful," said Polly, as indeed it was.

"No," said he, with a little squint as he touched the aching member. "It's good—I rather like it. I wouldn't take anything for that ear. It—it—" He hesitated, as if trying to recall the advantages of a chilled ear. "Well, I shouldn't know I had any ears if it weren't for that one. Come, Paul, put on your cap an' mittens. We'll take a sack and get some green boughs for your mother."

He put on snow-shoes, wrapped the boy snugly in a shawl, and, seating him on a snowboat, made off, hauling it with a rope over white banks and hollows toward the big timber. The dog, Bony, came along with them, wallowing to his ears and barking merrily. Since morning the sun had begun to warm the air, and a light breeze had risen. The boy sat bracing on a rope fastened before and looped around him. As they went along he was oversown with sparkling crystals.

They made his cheeks tingle, and almost took his breath as he went plunging into steep hollows. Often he tipped over and sank in the white deep. Then Trove hauled him out, brushed him a little, and set him back on the boat again. Snow lay deep and level in the woods—a big, white carpet, seamed with tiny tracks and figured with light and shadow. Trove stopped a moment, looking up at the forest roof. They could hear a baying of hounds in the far valley. Down the dingle near them a dead leaf was drumming on a bough—a clock of the wood telling the flight of seconds. Above, they could hear the low creak of brace and rafter and great waves of the upper deep sweeping over and breaking with a loud wash on reefs of evergreen. The little people of this odd winter land had begun to make roads from tree to tree and from thicket to thicket. A partridge had broken out of her cave, and they followed the track of her snow-shoes down the side-hill to a little brook. Under its ice roof they could hear the tinkling water. Above them the brook fell from a rock shelf, narrow and high as a man's head. The fall was muted to a low murmur under its vault of ice.

"Come, Paul," said Trove, as he lifted the small boy; "here's a castle of King Frost. There are thousands in his family, and he's many castles. Building new ones every day somewhere. Goes north in the spring, and when he moves out they begin to rot and tumble."

He cleared a space for the boy to stand upon. Then he brushed away the snow blanket flung loosely over the vault of ice. A wonderful bit of masonry stood exposed. Near its centre were two columns, large and rugose, each tapering to a capital and cornice. Between them was a deep lattice of crystal. Some bars were clear, some yellow as amber, and all were powdered over with snow, ivory-white. Under its upper part they could see a grille of frostwork, close-wrought, glistening, and white. It was the inner gate of the castle, and each ray of light, before entering, had to pay a toll of its warmth. On either side was a rough wall of ice, with here and there a barred window. The snow cleared away, they could hear the song of falling water. The teacher put his ear to the ice wall. Then he called the boy.

"Listen," said he; "it's the castle bell." Indeed, the whole structure rang like a bell, if one put his ear down to hear it.

"See!" said he, presently, stirring a heap of tiny crystals in his palm. "Here are the bricks he builds with, and the water of the brook is his mortar."

Near the bank was an opening partly covered with snow. It led to a cavern behind the ice curtain under the rock floor of the brook above.

The teacher took off his snow-shoes. In a moment they had crawled through and were crouching on a frosty bed of pebbles. A warm glow lit the long curtain of ice. Beams of sunlight fell through windows oddly mullioned with icicles and filtered in at the lattice of crystal. They jewelled the grille of frostwork and flung a sprinkle of gold on the falling water. The breath of the waterfall, rising out of bubbles, filled its castle with the very wine of life. The narrow hall rang with its music.

"See the splendour of a king's home," said the teacher, his eyes brimming.

The boy, young as he was, had seen and felt the beauty and mystery of the place, and never forgot it.

"See how it sifts the sunlight to take the warmth out of it," the teacher continued. "Warmth is poison to the King, and every ray of light is twisted and turned upside down to see if he has any in his pocket."

They could now hear a loud baying on the hill above.

As they turned to listen, a young fox leaped in at the hole and, as he saw them, checked a foot in the air. He was panting, his tongue out, and blood was dripping from his long fur at the shoulder. He turned, stilling his breath a little as the hounds came near. Then he trembled,—a pitiful sight,—for he was near spent and between two perils.

"Come—poor fellow!" said the teacher, stroking him gently.

The fox ran aside, shaking with fear, his foot lifted appealingly. With a quick movement the teacher caught him by the nape of his neck and thrust him into the sack. The leader now had his nose in the hole.

"Back there!" Trove shouted, kicking at him.

In a moment he had rolled a heavy stone to the hole and made it too small for the hounds to enter. Half a dozen of them were now baying outside.

"We'll give him air," said the teacher, as he cut a hole in the sack and tied it. "Don't know how we'll get him out of here alive. They'd be all over me like a pack of wolves."

He stood a moment thinking. Bony had wriggled away from Paul and begun to bark loudly.

"I've an idea," said the teacher, as he cut the foxtail from his cap. Then he rubbed it in the blood and spittle of the fox and tied it to the stub tail of Bony. The dog's four feet were scented in the same manner. The smell of them irked him sorely. His hair rose, and his head fell with a sense of injury.

He made a rush at his new tail and was rudely stopped.

"He's fresh, and they'll not be able to catch him," said the young man, as Paul protested. "Wouldn't hurt anything but the tail if they did."

Then breaking the ice curtain, as far from the hole as possible, he gave Bony a spank and flung him out on the snow above with a loud "go home." The pack saw him and scrambled up the bank in full cry. He had turned for a glance at his new tail, but seeing the pack rush at him started up the hillside with a yelp of fear and the energy of a wildcat. When the two came out of the cavern they saw him leaping like a rabbit in the snow, his hair on end, his brush flying, and the hounds in full pursuit.

"My stars! See that dog run," said the teacher, laughing, as he put on his snow-shoes. "He don't intend to be caught with such a tail and smell on him."

He put the sack over his shoulder.

"All aboard, Paul," said he; "now we can go home in peace."

Coming down out of the woods, they saw a pack of hounds digging at one side of the stable. Bony had gone to his refuge under the barn floor.

As he entered, one of them had evidently caught hold of his new tail, and the pack had torn it in shreds. Two hunters came along shortly, and, after a talk with the teacher, took their dogs away. But for three days Bony came not forth and was seen no more of men, save only when he crept to the hole for a lap of water and to seize a doughnut from the hand of Paul, whereupon he retired promptly.

"He ain't going to take any chances," said the widow, laughing.

When at last he came forth, it was with a soft step and new resolutions. And a while later, when Trove heard Darrel say that caution was the only friend of weakness, he understood him perfectly.

"Not every brush has a fox on it," said the widow, and the words went from lip to lip until they were a maxim of those country-folk.

And Trove was to think of it when he himself was like the poor dog that wore a fox's tail.

XIV

A DAY AT THE LINLEY SCHOOLHOUSE

A remarkable figure was young Sidney Trove, the new teacher in District No. 1. He was nearing nineteen years of age that winter.

"I like that," he said to the trustee, who had been telling him of the unruly boys—great, hulking fellows that made trouble every winter term. "Trouble—it's a grand thing I—but I'm not selfish, and if I find any, I'll agree to divide it with the boys. I don't know but I'll be generous and let them have the most of it. If they put me out of the schoolhouse, I'll have learned something."

The trustee looked at the six feet and two inches of bone and muscle that sat lounging in a chair—looked from end to end of it.

"What's that?" he inquired, smiling.

"That I've no business there," said young Mr. Trove.

"I guess you'll dew," said the trustee. "Make 'em toe the line; that's all I got t' say."

Irving Bacheller

"And all I've got to do is my best—I don't promise any more," the other answered modestly, as he rose to leave.

Linley School was at the four corners in Pleasant Valley,—a low, frame structure, small and weathered gray. Windows, with no shade, or shutter, were set, two on a side, in perfect apposition. A passing traveller could see through them to the rocky pasture beyond. Who came there for knowledge, though a fool, was dubbed a "scholar." It was a word sharply etched in the dialect of that region. If one were to say *skollur-r-r*, he might come near it. Every winter morning the scholar entered a little vestibule which was part of the woodshed. He passed an ash barrel and the odour of drying wood, hung cap and coat On a peg in the closet, lifted the latch of a pine door, and came into the schoolroom. If before nine, it would be noisy with shout and laughter, the buzz of tongues, the tread of running feet. Big girls, in neat aprons, would be gossiping at the stove hearth; small boys would be chasing each other up and down aisles and leaping the whittled desks of pine; little girls, in checked flannel, or homespun, would be circling in a song play; big boys would be trying feats of strength that ended in loud laughter. So it was, the first morning of that winter term in 1850. A tall youth stood by the window. Suddenly he gave a loud "sh—h—h!" Running feet fell silently and halted; words begun with a shout ended in a whisper. A boy making caricatures at the blackboard dropped his chalk, that now fell noisily. A whisper, heavy with awe and expectation, flew hissing from lip to lip—"The teacher!" There came a tramping in the vestibule, the door-latch jumped with a loud rattle, and in came Sidney Trove. All eyes were turned upon him. A look of rectitude, dovelike and too good to be true, came over many faces.

"Good morning!" said the young man, removing his cap, coat, and overshoes. Some nodded, dumb with timidity. Only a few little ones had the bravery to speak up, as they gave back the words in a tone that would have fitted a golden text. He came to the roaring stove and stood a moment, warming his hands. A group of the big boys were in a corner whispering. Two were sturdy and quite six feet tall,—the Beach boys.

"Big as a bull moose," one whispered,

"An' stouter," said another.

The teacher took a pencil from his pocket and tapped the desk.

"Please take your seats," said he.

All obeyed. Then he went around with the roll and took their names, of which there were thirty-four.

"I believe I know your name," said Trove, smiling, as he came to Polly Vaughn.

"I believe you do," said she, glancing up at him, with half a smile and a little move in her lips that seemed to ask, "How could you forget me?"

Then the teacher, knowing the peril of her eyes, became very dignified as he glanced over the books she had brought to school. He knew it was going to be a hard day. For a little, he wondered if he had not been foolish, after all, in trying a job so difficult and so perilous. If he should be thrown out of school, he felt sure it would ruin him—he could never look Polly in the face again. As he turned to begin the work of teaching, it seemed to him a case of do or die, and he felt the strength of an ox in his heavy muscles.

The big boys had settled themselves in a back corner side by side—a situation too favourable for mischief. He asked them to take other seats. They complied sullenly and with hesitation. He looked over books, organized the school in classes, and started one of them on its way. It was the primer class, including a half dozen very small boys and girls. They shouted each word in the reading lesson, laboured in silence with another, and gave voice again with unabated energy. In their pursuit of learning they bayed like hounds. Their work began upon this ancient and informing legend, written to indicate the shout and skip of the youthful student:—

The—sun—is—up—and—it—is—day—day?—day.

"You're afraid," the teacher began after a little. "Come up here close to me."

They came to his chair and stood about him. Some were confident, others hung back suspicious and untamed.

"We're going to be friends," said he, in a low, gentle voice. He took from his pocket a lot of cards and gave one to each.

"Here's a story," he continued. "See—I put it in plain print for you with pen and ink. It's all about a bear and a boy, and is in ten parts. Here's the first chapter. Take it home with you to-night—"

He stopped suddenly. He had turned in his chair and could see none of the boys. He did not move, but slowly took off a pair of glasses he had been wearing.

"Joe Beach," said he, coolly, "come out here on the floor."

There was a moment of dead silence. That big youth—the terror of Linley School—was now red and dumb with amazement. His deviltry had begun, but how had the teacher seen it with his back turned?

"I'll think it over," said the boy, sullenly.

The teacher laid down his book, calmly, walked to the seat of the young rebel, took him by the collar and the back of the neck, tore him out of the place where his hands and feet were clinging like the roots of a tree, dragged him roughly to the aisle and over the floor space, taking part of the seat along, and stood him to the wall with a bang that shook the windows. There was no halting—it was all over in half a minute.

"You'll please remain there," said he, coolly, "until I tell you to sit down."

He turned his back on the bully, walked slowly to his chair, and opened his book again.

"Take it home with you to-night," said he, continuing his talk to the primer class. "Spell it over, so you won't have to stop long between words. All who read it well to-morrow will get another chapter."

They began to study at home. Wonder grew, and pleasure came with labour as the tale went on.

He dismissed the primer readers, calling the first class in geography. As they took their places he repaired the broken seat, a part of which had been torn off the nails. The fallen rebel stood leaning, his back to the school. He had expected help, but the reserve force had failed him.

"Joe Beach—you may take your seat," said the teacher, in a kind of parenthetical tone.

Irving Bacheller

"Geography starts at home," he continued, beginning the recitation. "Who can tell me where is the Linley schoolhouse?"

A dozen hands went up.

"You tell," said he to one.

"It's here," was the answer.

"Where's here?"

A boy looked thoughtful.

"Nex' t' Joe Linley's cow-pastur'," he ventured presently,

"Will you tell us?" the teacher asked, looking at a bright-eyed girl.

"In Faraway, New York," said she, glibly.

"Tom Linley, I'll take that," said the teacher, in a lazy tone. He was looking down at his book. Where he sat, facing the class, he could see none of the boys without turning. But he had not turned. To the wonder of all, up he spoke as Tom Linley was handing a slip of paper to Joe Beach. There was a little pause. The young man hesitated, rose, and walked nervously down the aisle.

"Thank you," said the teacher, as he took the message and flung it on the fire, unread. "Faraway, New York;" he continued on his way to the blackboard as if nothing had happened.

He drew a circle, indicating the four points of the compass on it. Then he mapped the town of Faraway and others, east, west, north, and south of it. So he made a map of the county and bade them copy it. Around the county in succeeding lessons he built a map of the state. Others in the middle group were added, the structure growing, day by day, until they had mapped the hemisphere.

At the Linley schoolhouse something had happened. Cunning no sooner showed its head than it was bruised like a serpent, brawny muscles had been easily outdone, boldness had grown timid, conceit had begun to ebb. A serious look had settled upon all faces. Every scholar had learned one thing, learned it well and quickly—it was to be no playroom.

There was a recess of one hour at noon. All went for their dinner pails and sat quietly, eating bread and butter followed by doughnuts, apples, and pie.

The young men had walked to the road. Nothing had been said. They drew near each other. Tom Linley looked up at Joe Beach. In his face one might have seen a cloud of sympathy that had its silver lining of amusement.

"Powerful?" Tom inquired, soberly.

"What?" said Joe.

"Powerful?" Tom repeated.

"Powerful! Jiminy crimps!" said Joe, significantly.

"Why didn't ye kick him?"

"Kick him?"

"Yes."

"Kick *him*?

"Kick *him*."

"Huh! dunno," said Joe, with a look of sadness turning into contempt.

"Scairt?" the other inquired.

"Scairt? Na—a—w," said Joe, scornfully.

"What was ye, then?"

"Parr'lyzed—seems so."

There was an outbreak of laughter.

"You was goin' t' help," said Joe, addressing Tom Linley.

A moment of silence followed.

"*You* was goin' t' help," the fallen bully repeated, with large emphasis on the pronoun.

"Help?" Tom inquired, sparring for wind as it were.

"Yes, help."

"You was licked 'fore I had time."

"Didn't dast—that's what's the matter—didn't dast," said big Joe, with a tone of irreparable injury.

"Wouldn't 'a' been nigh ye fer a millyun dollars," said Tom, soberly.

"Why not?"

"'Twant safe; that's why."

"'Fraid o' him! ye coward!"

"No; 'fraid o' you."

"Why?"

"'Cos if one o' yer feet had hit a feller when ye come up ag'in that wall," Tom answered slowly, "there wouldn't 'a' been nuthin' left uv him."

All laughed loudly.

Then there was another silence. Joe broke it after a moment of deep thought.

"Like t' know how he seen me," said he.

"'Tis cur'us," said another.

"Guess he's one o' them preformers like they have at the circus—" was the opinion of Sam Beach. "See one take a pig out o' his hat las' summer."

"'Tain't fair 'n' square," said Tom Linley; "not jest eggzac'ly."

"Gosh! B'lieve I'll run away," said Joe, after a pause. "Ain' no fun here for me."

"Better not," said Archer Town; "not if ye know when yer well off."

"Why not?"

"Wal, he'd see ye wherever ye was an' do suthin' to ye," said

Archer. "Prob'ly he's heard all we been sayin' here."

"Wal, I ain't said nuthin' I'm 'shamed of," said Sam Beach, thoughtfully.

A bell rang, and all hurried to the schoolhouse. The afternoon was uneventful. Those rough-edged, brawny fellows had become serious. Hope had died in their breasts, and now they looked as if they had come to its funeral. They began to examine their books as one looks at a bitter draught before drinking it. In every subject the teacher took a new way not likely to be hard upon tender feet. For each lesson he had a method of his own. He angled for the interest of the class and caught it. With some a term of school had been as a long sickness, lengthened by the medicine of books and the surgery of the beech rod. They had resented it with ingenious deviltry. The confusion of the teacher and some incidental fun were its only compensations. The young man gave his best thought to the correction of this mental attitude. Four o'clock came at last—the work of the day was over. Weary with its tension all sat waiting the teacher's word. For a little he stood facing them.

"Tom Linley and Joe Beach," said he, in a low voice, "will you wait a moment after the others have gone? School's dismissed."

There was a rush of feet and a rattle of dinner pails. All were eager to get home with the story of that day—save the two it had brought to shame. They sat quietly as the others went away. A deep silence fell in that little room. Of a sudden it had become a lonely place.

The teacher damped the fire and put on his overshoes.

"Boys," said he, drawing a big silver watch, "hear that watch ticking. It tells the flight of seconds. You are—eighteen, did you say? They turn boys into oxen here in this country; just a thing of bone and muscle, living to sweat and lift and groan. Maybe I can save you, but there's not a minute to lose. With you it all depends on this term of school. When it's done you'll either be ox or driver. Play checkers?"

Tom nodded.

"I'll come over some evening, and we'll have a game. Good night!"

XV

THE TINKER AT LINLEY SCHOOL

Every seat was filled at the Linley School next morning. The tinker had come to see Trove and sat behind the big desk as work began.

"There are two kinds of people," said the teacher, after all were seated—"those that command—those that obey. No man is fit to command until he has learned to obey—he will not know how. The one great thing life has to teach you is—obey. There was a young bear once that was bound to go his own way. The old bear told him it wouldn't do to jump over a precipice, but, somehow, he couldn't believe it and jumped. 'Twas the last thing he ever did. It's often so with the young. Their own way is apt to be rather steep and to end suddenly. There are laws everywhere,—we couldn't live without them,—laws of nature, God, and man. Until we learn the law and how to obey it, we must go carefully and take the advice of older heads. We couldn't run a school without laws in it—laws that I must obey as well as you. I must teach, and you must learn. The two first laws of the school are teach and learn—you must help me to obey mine; I must help you to obey yours. And we'll have as much fun as possible, but we must obey."

Then Trove invited Darrel to address the school.

"Dear children," the tinker began with a smile, "I mind ye're all looking me in the face, an' I do greatly fear ye. I fear I may say something ye will remember, an' again I fear I may not. For when I speak to the young—ah! then it seems to me God listens. I heard the teacher speaking o' the law of obedience. Which o' ye can tell me who is the great master— the one ye must never disobey?"

"Yer father," said one of the boys.

"Nay, me bright lad, one o' these days ye may lose father an' mother an' teacher an' friend. Let me tell a story, an' then, mayhap, ye'll know the great master. Once upon a time there was a young cub who thought his life a burden because he had to mind his mother. By an' by a bullet killed her, an' he was left alone. He wandered away, not knowing' what to do, and came near the land o' men. Soon he met an old bear.

"'Foolish cub! Why go ye to the land o' men?' said the old bear. 'Thy legs are not as long as me tail. Go home an' obey thy mother.'"

"'But I've none to obey,' said the young bear; an' before he could turn, a ball came whizzing over a dingle an' ripped into his ham. The old bear had scented danger an' was already out o' the way. The cub made off limping, an' none too quickly. They followed him all day, an' when night came he was the most weary an' bedraggled bear in the woods. But he stopped the blood an' went away on a dry track in the morning. He came to a patch o' huckleberries that day and began to help himself. Then quick an' hard he got a cuff on the head that tore off an ear and knocked him into the bushes. When he rose there stood the old bear. "'Ah, me young cub,' said he, 'ye'll have a master now.'"

Irving Bacheller

"'An' no more need o' him,' said the young bear, shaking his bloody head."

"'Nay, ye will prosper,' said the old bear. 'There are two ways o' learning,—by hearsay an' by knocks. Much ye may learn by knocks, but they are painful. There be two things every one has to learn,—respect for himself; respect for others. Ye'll know, hereafter, in the land o' men a bear has to keep his nose up an' his ears open—because men hurt. Ye'll know better, also, than to feed on the ground of another bear—because he hurts. Now, were I a cub an' had none to obey, I'd obey meself. Ye know what's right, do it; ye know what's wrong, do it not.'"

"'One thing is sure,' said the young bear, as he limped away; 'if I live, there'll not be a bear in the woods that'll take any better care of himself.'"

"Now the old bear knew what he was talking about. He was, I maintain, a wise an' remarkable bear. We learn to obey others, so that by an' by we may know how to obey ourselves. The great master of each man is himself. By words or by knocks ye will learn what is right, and ye must do it. Dear children, ye must soon be yer own masters. There be many cruel folk in the world, but ye have only one to fear—yerself. Ah! ye shall find him a hard man, for, if he be much offended, he will make ye drink o' the cup o' fire. Learn to obey yerselves, an' God help ye."

Thereafter, many began to look into their own hearts for that fearful master, and some discovered him.

XVI

A RUSTIC MUSEUM

That first week Sidney Trove went to board at the home of "the two old maids," a stone house on Jericho Road, with a front door rusting on idle hinges and blinds ever drawn. It was a hundred feet or more from the highway, and in summer there were flowers along the path from its little gate and vines climbing to the upper windows. In winter its garden was buried deep under the snow. One family—the Vaughns—came once in awhile to see "the two old maids." Few others ever saw them save from afar. A dressmaker came once a year and made gowns for them, that were carefully hung in closets but never worn. To many of their neighbours they were as dead as if they had been long in their graves. Tales of their economy, of their odd habits, of their past, went over hill and dale to far places. They had never boarded the teacher and were put in a panic when the trustee came to speak of it.

"He's a grand young man," said he; "good company—and you'll enjoy it."

They looked soberly at each other. According to tradition, one was fifty-four the other fifty-five years of age. An exclamation broke from the lips of one. It sounded like the letter *y* whispered quickly.

"Y!" the other answered.

"It might make a match," said Mr. Blount, the trustee, smiling.

"Y! Samuel Blount!" said the younger one, coming near and smiting him playfully on the elbow. "You stop!"

Miss Letitia began laughing silently. They never laughed aloud.

"If he didn't murder us," said Miss S'mantha, doubtfully.

"Nonsense," said the trustee; "I'll answer for him."

"Can't tell what men'll do," she persisted weakly. "When I was in Albany with Alma Haskins, a man came 'long an' tried t' pass the time o' day with us. We jes' looked t'other way an' didn't preten' t' hear him. It's awful t' think what might 'a' happened."

She wiped invisible tears with an embroidered handkerchief. The dear lady had spent a good part of her life thinking of that narrow escape.

"If he wa'n't too partic'lar," said Miss Letitia, who had been laughing at this maiden fear of her sister.

"If he would mind his business, we—we might take him for one week," said Miss S'mantha. She glanced inquiringly at her sister.

Letitia and S'mantha Tower, "the two old maids," had but one near relative—Ezra Tower, a brother of the same neighbourhood.

There were two kinds of people in Faraway,—those that Ezra Tower spoke to and those he didn't. The latter were of the majority. As a forswearer of communication he was unrivalled. His imagination was a very slaughter-house, in which all who crossed him were slain. If they were passing, he looked the other way and never even saw them again. Since the probate of his father's will both sisters were of the number never spoken to. He was a thin, tall, sullen, dry, and dusty man. Dressed for church of a Sunday, he looked as if he had been stored a year in some neglected cellar. His broadcloth had a dingy aspect, his hair and beard and eyebrows the hue of a cobweb. He had a voice slow and rusty, a look arid and unfruitful. Indeed, it seemed as if the fires of hate and envy had burned him out.

The two old maids, feeling the disgrace of it and fearing more, ceased to visit their neighbours or even to pass their own gate. Poor Miss S'mantha fell into the deadly mire of hypochondria. She often thought herself very ill and sent abroad for every medicine advertised in the county paper. She had ever a faint look and a thin, sickly voice. She had the man-fear,—a deep distrust of men,—never ceasing to be on her guard. In girlhood, she had been to Albany, Its splendour and the reckless conduct of one Alma Haskins, companion of her travels, had been ever since a day-long perennial topic of her conversation. Miss Letitia was more amiable. She had a playful, cheery heart in her, a mincing and precise manner, and a sweet voice. What with the cleaning, dusting, and preserving, they were ever busy. A fly, driven hither and thither, fell of exhaustion if not disabled with a broom. They were two weeks getting ready for the teacher. When, at last, he came that afternoon, supper was ready and they were nearly worn out.

"Here he is!" one whispered suddenly from a window. Then, with a last poke at her hair, Miss Letitia admitted the teacher. They spoke their greeting in a half whisper and stood near, waiting timidly for his coat and cap.

"No, thank you," said he, taking them to a nail. "I can do my own hanging, as the man said when he committed suicide."

Miss S'mantha looked suspicious and walked to the other side of the stove. Impressed by the silence of the room, much exaggerated by the ticking of the clock, Sidney Trove sat a moment looking around him. Daylight had begun to grow dim. The table, with its cover of white linen, was a thing to give one joy. A ruby tower of jelly, a snowy summit of frosted cake, a red pond of preserved berries, a mound of chicken pie, and a corduroy marsh of mince, steaming volcanoes of new biscuit, and a great heap of apple fritters, lay in a setting of blue china. They stood a moment by the stove,—the two sisters,—both trembling in this unusual publicity. Miss Letitia had her hand upon the teapot.

"Our tea is ready," said she, presently, advancing to the table. She spoke in a low, gentle tone.

"This is grand!" said he, sitting down with them. "I tell you, we'll have fun before I leave here."

They looked up at him and then at each other, Letitia laughing silently, S'mantha suspicious. For many years fun had been a thing far from their thought.

"Play checkers?" he inquired.

"Afraid we couldn't," said Miss Letitia, answering for both.

"Old Sledge?"

She shook her head, smiling.

"I don't wish to lead you into recklessness," the teacher remarked, "but I'm sure you wouldn't mind being happy."

Miss S'mantha had a startled look.

"In—in a—proper way," he added. "Let's be joyful. Perhaps we could play 'I spy.'"

"Y!" they both exclaimed, laughing silently.

"Never ate chicken pie like that," he added in all sincerity. "If I were a poet, I'd indite an ode 'written after eating some of the excellent chicken pie of the Misses Tower.' I'm going to have some like it on my farm."

In reaching to help himself he touched the teapot, withdrawing his hand quickly.

"Burn ye?" said Miss S'mantha.

"Yes; but I like it!" said he, a bit embarrassed. "I often go and—and put my hand on a hot teapot if I'm having too much fun."

They looked up at him, puzzled.

"Ever slide down hill?" he inquired, looking from one to the other, after a bit of silence.

"Oh, not since we were little!" said Miss Letitia, holding her biscuit daintily, after taking a bite none too big for a bird to manage.

"Good fun!" said be. "Whisk you back to childhood in a

jiffy. Folks ought to slide down hill more'n they do. It isn't a good idea to be always climbing."

"'Fraid we couldn't stan' it," said Miss S'mantha, tentatively. Under all her man-fear and suspicion lay a furtive recklessness.

"Y, no!" the other whispered, laughing silently.

The pervading silence of that house came flooding in between sentences. For a moment Trove could hear only the gurgle of pouring tea and the faint rattle of china softly handled. When he felt as if the silence were drowning him, he began again:—

"Life is nothing but a school. I'm a teacher, and I deal in rules. If you want to kill misery, load your gun with pleasure."

"Do you know of anything for indigestion?" said Miss S'mantha, charging her sickly voice with a firmness calculated to discourage any undue familiarity.

"Just the thing—a sure cure!" said he, emphatically.

"Come high?" she inquired.

"No, it's cheap and plenty."

"Where do you send?"

"Oh!" said he; "you will have to go after it."

"What is it called ?"

"Fun," said the teacher, quickly; "and the place to find it is out of doors. It grows everywhere on my farm. I'd rather have a pair of skates than all the medicine this side of China."

She set down her teacup and looked up at him. She was beginning to think him a fairly safe and well-behaved man, although she would have been more comfortable if he had been shut in a cage.

"If I had a pair o' skates," said she, faintly, with a look of inquiry at her sister, "I dunno but I'd try 'em."

Miss Letitia began to laugh silently.

"I'd begin with overshoes," said the teacher, "A pair of overshoes and a walk on the crust every morning before breakfast; increase the dose gradually."

The two old maids were now more at ease with their guest. His kindly manner and plentiful good spirits had begun to warm and cheer them. Miss S'mantha even cherished a secret resolve to slide if the chance came.

After tea Sidney Trove, against their protest, began to help with the dishes. Miss S'mantha prudently managed to keep the stove between him and her. A fire and candles were burning in the parlour. He asked permission, however, to stay where he could talk with them. Tunk Hosely, the man of all work, came in for his supper. He was an odd character. Some, with a finger on their foreheads, confided the opinion that he was "a little off." All agreed he was no fool—in a tone that left it open to argument. He had a small figure and a big squint. His perpetual squint and bristly, short beard were a great injustice to him. They gave him a look severer than he deserved. A limp and leaning shoulder complete the inventory of external traits. Having eaten, he set a candle in the old barn lantern.

"Wal, mister," said he, when all was ready, "come out an' look at my hoss."

The teacher went with him out under a sky bright with stars to the chill and gloomy stable.

"Look at me," said Tunk, holding up the lantern as he turned about. "Gosh all fish-hooks! I'm a wreck."

"What's the matter?" Sidney Trove inquired.

"All sunk in—right here," Tunk answered impressively, his hand to his chest.

"How did it happen?"

"Kicked by a boss; that's how it happened," was the significant answer. "Lord! I'm all shucked over t' one side—can't ye see it?"

"A list t' sta'b'rd—that's what they call it, I believe," said the teacher.

"See how I limp," Tunk went on, striding to show his pace. "Ain't it awful!"

"How did that happen?"

"Sprung my ex!" he answered, turning quickly with a significant look. "Thrown from a sulky in a hoss race an' sprung my ex. Lord! can't ye see it?"

The teacher nodded, not knowing quite how to take him.

"Had my knee unsot, too," he went on, lifting his knee as he turned the light upon it. "Jes' put yer finger there," said he, indicating a slight protuberance. "Lord! it's big as a bog spavin."

He had planned to provoke a query, and it came.

"How did you get it?"

"Kicked ag'in," said Tunk, sadly. "Heavens! I've had my share o' bangin'. Can't conquer a skittish hoss without sufferin' some—not allwus. Now, here's a boss," he added, as they walked to a stall. "He ain't much t' look at, but—"

He paused a moment as he neared the horse—a white and ancient palfrey. He stood thoughtfully on "cocked ankles," every leg in a bandage, tail and mane braided,

"Get ap, Prince," Tunk shouted, as he gave him a slap. Prince moved aside, betraying evidence of age and infirmity.

"But—" Tunk repeated with emphasis.

"Ugly?" the teacher queried.

"Ugly!" said Tunk, as if the word were all too feeble for the fact in hand. "Reg'lar hell on wheels!—that's what he is. Look out! don't git too nigh him. He ain't no conscience—that hoss ain't."

"Is he fast?"

"Greased lightnin'!" said Tunk, shaking his head. "Won twenty-seven races."

"You're a good deal of a horseman, I take it." said the teacher.

"Wal, some," said he, expectorating thoughtfully. "But I don't have no chance here. What d'ye 'spect of a man livin,' with them ol' maids ?"

He seemed to have more contempt than his words would carry.

"Every night they lock me upstairs," he continued with a look of injury; "they ain't fit fer nobody t' live with. Ain't got no hoss but that dummed ol' plug."

He had forgotten his enthusiasm of the preceding moment. His intellect was a museum of freaks. Therein, Vanity was the prodigious fat man, Memory the dwarf, and Veracity the living skeleton. When Vanity rose to show himself, the others left the stage.

Tunk's face had become suddenly thoughtful and morose. In truth, he was an arrant and amusing humbug. It has been said that children are all given to lying in some degree, but seeing the folly of it in good time, if, indeed, they are not convinced of its wickedness, train tongue and feeling into the way of truth. The respect for truth that is the beginning of wisdom had not come to Tunk. He continued to lie with the cheerful inconsistency of a child. The' hero of his youth had been a certain driver of trotting horses, who had a limp and a leaning shoulder. In Tunk, the limp and the leaning shoulder were an attainment that had come of no sudden wrench. Such is the power of example, he admired, then imitated, and at last acquired them. One cannot help thinking what graces of character and person a like persistency would have brought to him. But Tunk had equipped himself with horsey heroism, adorning it to his own fancy. He had never been kicked, he had never driven a race or been hurled from a sulky at full speed. Prince, that ancient palfrey, was the most harmless of all creatures, and would long since have been put out of misery but for the tender consideration of his owners. And Tunk—well, they used to say of him, that if he had been truthful, he couldn't have been alive.

"Sometime," Trove thought, "his folly may bring confusion upon wise heads."

XVII

AN EVENT IN THE RUSTIC MUSEUM

Sidney Trove sat talking a while with Miss Letitia. Miss S'mantha, unable longer to bear the unusual strain of danger and publicity, went away to bed soon after supper. Tunk Hosely came in with a candle about nine.

"Wal, mister," said he, "you ready t' go t' bed?"

"I am," said Trove, and followed him to the cold hospitality of the spare room, a place of peril but beautifully clean. There was a neat rag carpet on the floor, immaculate tidies on the bureau and wash table, and a spotless quilt of patchwork on the bed. But, like the dungeon of mediaeval times, it was a place for sighs and reflection, not for rest. Half an inch of frost on every window-pane glistened in the dim light of the candle.

"As soon as they unlock my door, I'll come an' let ye out in the mornin'," Tunk whispered.

"Are they going to lock me in?"

"Wouldn't wonder," said Tunk, soberly.

"What can ye 'spect from a couple o' dummed ol' maids like them?"

There was a note of long suffering in his half-whispered tone,

"Good night, mister," said he, with a look of dejection. "Orter have a nightcap, er ye'll git hoar-frost on yer hair."

Trove was all a-shiver in the time it took him to undress, and his breath came out of him in spreading shafts of steam. Sheets of flannel and not less than half a dozen quilts and comfortables made a cover, under which the heat of his own blood warmed his body. He became uncomfortably aware of the presence of his head and face, however. He could hear stealthy movements beyond the door, and knew they were barricading it with furniture. Long before daylight a hurried removal of the barricade awoke him. Then he heard a rap at the door, and the excited voice of Tunk.

"Say, mister! come here quick," it called.

Sidney Trove leaped out of bed and into his trousers. He hurried through the dark parlour, feeling his way around a clump of chairs and stumbling over a sofa. The two old maids were at the kitchen door, both dressed, one holding a lighted candle. Tunk Hosely stood by the door, buttoning suspenders with one hand and holding a musket in the other. They were shivering and pale. The room was now cold.

"Hear that!" Tunk whispered, turning to the teacher.

They all listened, hearing a low, weird cry outside the door.

"Soun's t' me like a raccoon," Miss S'mantha whispered thoughtfully.

"Or a lamb," said Miss Letitia.

"Er a painter," Tunk ventured, his ear turning to catch the sound.

"Let's open the door," said Sidney Trove, advancing.

"Not me," said Tunk, firmly, raising his gun.

Trove had not time to act before they heard a cry for help on the doorstep. It was the voice of a young girl. He opened the door, and there stood Mary Leblanc—a scholar of Linley School and the daughter of a poor Frenchman. She came in lugging a baby wrapped in a big shawl, and both crying.

"Oh, Miss Tower," said she; "pa has come out o' the woods drunk an' has threatened to kill the baby. Ma wants to know if you'll keep it here to-night."

The two old maids wrung their hands with astonishment and only said "y!"

"Of course we'll keep it," said Trove, as he took the baby,

"I must hurry back," said the girl, now turning with a look of relief.

Tunk shied off and began to build a fire; Miss S'mantha sat down weeping, the girl ran away in the darkness, and Trove put the baby in Miss Letitia's arms.

"I'll run over to Leblanc's cabin," said he, getting his cap and coat. "They're having trouble over there."

He left them and hurried off on his way to the little cabin.

Loud cries of the baby rang in that abode of silence. It began to kick and squirm with determined energy. Poor Miss Letitia had the very look of panic in her face. She clung to the fierce little creature, not knowing what to do. Miss S'mantha lay back in a fit of hysterics. Tunk advanced bravely, with brows knit, and stood looking down at the baby.

"Lord! this is awful!" said he. Then a thought struck him. "I'll git some milk," he shouted, running into the buttery.

The baby thrust the cup away, and it fell noisily, the milk streaming over a new rag carpet.

"It's sick; I'm sure it's sick," said Miss Letitia, her voice trembling. "S'mantha, can't you do something?"

Miss S'mantha calmed herself a little and drew near.

"Jes' like a wil'cat," said Tunk, thoughtfully. "Powerful, too," he added, with an effort to control one of the kicking legs.

"What shall we do?" said Miss Letitia.

"My sister had a baby once," said Tunk, approaching it doubtfully but with a studious look.

He made a few passes with his hand in front of the baby's face. Then he gave it a little poke in the ribs, tentatively. The effect was like adding insult to injury.

"If 'twas mine," said Tunk, "which I'm glad it ain't—I'd rub a little o' that hoss liniment on his stummick,"

The two old maids took the baby into their bedroom. It was an hour later when Trove came back. Tunk sat alone by the kitchen fire. There was yet a loud wail in the bedroom.

"What's the news?" said Tunk, who met him at the door.

"Drunk, that's all," said Trove. "I took this bottle, sling-shot, and bar of iron away from him. The woman thought I had better bring them with me and put them out of his way."

He laid them on the floor in a corner.

"I got him into bed," he continued, "and then hid the axe and came away. I guess they're all right now. When I left he had begun to snore."

"Wal,—we ain't all right," said Tunk, pointing to the room. "If you can conquer that thing, you'll do well. Poor Miss Teeshy!" he added, shaking his head.

"What's the matter with her?" Trove inquired.

"Kicked in the stummick 'til she dunno where she is," said Tunk, gloomily.

He pulled off his boots.

"If she don't go lame t'morrer, I'll miss my guess," he added. "She looks a good deal like Deacon Haskins after he had milked the brindle cow."

He leaned back, one foot upon the stove-hearth. Shrill cries rang in the old house.

"'Druther 'twould hev been a painter," said Tunk, sighing.

"Why so?"

"More used to 'em," said Tunk, sadly.

They listened a while longer without speaking.

"Ye can't drive it, ner coax it, ner scare it away, ner do nuthin' to it," said Tunk, presently.

He rose and picked up the things Trove had brought with him. "I'll take these to the barn," said he; "they'd have a fit—if they was t' see 'em. What be they?"

"I do not know what they are," said Trove.

"Wal!" said Tunk. "They're queer folks—them Frenchmen. This looks like an iron bar broke in two in the middle."

He got his lantern, picked up the bottle, the sling-shot, and the iron, and went away to the barn.

Trove went to the bedroom door and rapped, and was admitted. He went to work with the baby, and soon, to his joy, it lay asleep on the bed. Then he left the room on tiptoe, and a bit weary.

"A very full day!" he said to himself.

"Teacher, counsellor, martyr, constable, nurse—I wonder what next!"

And as he went to his room, he heard Miss S'mantha say to her sister, "I'm thankful it's not a boy, anyway."

XVIII

A DAY OF DIFFICULTIES

All were in their seats and the teacher had called a class. Carlt Homer came in.

"You're ten minutes late," said the teacher.

"I have fifteen cows to milk," the boy answered.

"Where do you live?"

"'Bout a mile from here, on the Beach Plains."

"What time do you begin milking?"

"'Bout seven o'clock."

"I'll go to-morrow morning and help you," said the teacher. "We must be on time—that's a necessary law of the school."

At a quarter before seven in the morning, Sidney Trove presented himself at the Homers'. He had come to help with the milking, but found there were only five cows to milk.

"Too bad your father lost so many cows—all in a day," said

he. "It's a great pity. Did you lose anything?"

"No, sir."

"Have you felt to see?"

The boy put his hand in his pocket.

"Not there—it's an inside pocket, way inside o' you. It's where you keep your honour and pride."

"Wal," said the boy, his tears starting, "I'm 'fraid I have."

"Enough said—good morning," the teacher answered as he went away.

One morning a few days later the teacher opened his school with more remarks.

"The other day," said he, "I spoke of a thing it was very necessary for us to learn. What was it?"

"To obey," said a youngster.

"Obey what?" the teacher inquired.

"Law," somebody ventured.

"Correct; we're studying law—every one of us—the laws of grammar, of arithmetic, of reading, and so on. We are learning to obey them. Now I am going to ask you what is the greatest law in the world?"

There was a moment of silence. Then the teacher wrote these words in large letters on the blackboard; "Thou shalt not lie."

"There is the law of laws," said the teacher, solemnly. "Better never have been born than not learn to obey it. If you always tell the truth, you needn't worry about any other law. Words are like money—some are genuine, some are counterfeit. If a man had a bag of counterfeit money and kept passing it, in a little while nobody would take his money. I knew a man who said he killed four bears at one shot. There's some that see too much when they're looking over their own gun-barrels. Don't be one of that kind. Don't ever kill too many bears at a shot."

After that, in the Linley district, a man who lied was said to be killing too many bears at a shot.

Good thoughts spread with slow but sure contagion. There were some who understood the teacher. His words went home and far with them, even to their graves, and how much farther who can say? They went over the hills, indeed, to other neighbourhoods, and here they are, still travelling, and going now, it may be, to the remotest corners of the earth. The big boys talked about this matter of lying and declared the teacher was right.

"There's Tunk Hosely," said Sam Price. "Nobody'd take his word for nuthin'."

"'Less he was t' say he was a fool out an' out," another boy suggested.

"Dunno as I'd b'lieve him then," said Sam. "Fer I'd begin t' think he knew suthin'."

A little girl came in, crying, one day.

"What is the trouble?" said the teacher, tenderly, as he leaned over and put his arm around her.

"My father is sick," said the child, sobbing.

"Very sick?" the teacher inquired.

For a moment she could not answer, but stood shaken with sobs.

"The doctor says he can't live," said she, brokenly.

A solemn stillness fell in the little schoolroom. The teacher lifted the child and held her close to his broad breast a moment.

"Be brave, little girl," said he, patting her head gently. "Doctors don't always know. He may be better to-morrow."

He took the child to her seat, and sat beside her and whispered a moment, his mouth close to her ear. And what he said, none knew, save the girl herself, who ceased to cry in a moment but never ceased to remember it.

A long time he sat, with his arm around her, questioning the classes. He seemed to have taken his place between her and the dark shadow.

Joe Beach had been making poor headway in arithmetic.

"I'll come over this evening, and we'll see what's the trouble. It's all very easy," the teacher said.

He worked three hours with the young man that evening, and filled him with high ambition after hauling him out of his difficulty.

But of all difficulties the teacher had to deal with, Polly Vaughn was the greatest. She was nearly perfect in all her studies, but a little mischievous and very dear to him. "Pretty;" that is one thing all said of her there in Faraway, and they said also with a bitter twang that she loved to lie abed and read novels. To Sidney Trove the word "pretty" was inadequate. As to lying abed and reading novels, he was free to say that he believed in it.

"We get very indignant about slavery in the south," he used to say; "but how about slavery on the northern farms? I know people who rise at cock-crow and strain their sinews in heavy toil the livelong day, and spend the Sabbath trembling in the lonely shadow of the Valley of Death. I know a man who whipped his boy till he bled because he ran away to go fishing. It's all slavery, pure and simple."

"In the sweat of thy face shalt thou eat bread till thou return unto the ground," said Ezra Tower.

"If God said it, he made slaves of us all," said young Trove. "When I look around here and see people wasted to the bone with sweat and toil, too weary often to eat the bread they have earned, when I see their children dying of consumption from excess of labour and pork fat, I forget the slaves of man and think only of these wretched slaves of God."

But Polly was not of them the teacher pitied. She was a bit discontented; but surely she was cheerful and well fed. God gave her beauty, and the widow saw it, and put her own strength between the curse and the child. Folly had her task every day, but Polly had her way, also, in too many things, and became a bit selfish, as might have been expected. But there was something very sweet and fine about Polly. They were plain clothes she wore, but nobody save herself and mother gave them any thought. Who, seeing her big, laughing eyes, her finely modelled face, with cheeks pink and dimpled, her shapely, white teeth, her mass of dark hair, crowning a form tall and straight as an arrow, could see anything but the merry-hearted Polly?

"Miss Vaughn, you will please remain a few moments after school," said the teacher one day near four o'clock. Twice she had been caught whispering that day, with the young girl who sat behind her. Trove had looked down, stroking his little mustache thoughtfully, and made no remark. The girl had gone to work, then, her cheeks red with embarrassment.

"I wish you'd do me a favour, Miss Polly," said the teacher, when they were alone.

She blushed deeply, and sat looking down as she fussed with her handkerchief. She was a bit frightened by the serious air of that big young man.

"It isn't much," he went on. "I'd like you to help me teach a little. To-morrow morning I shall make a map on the blackboard, and while I am doing it I'd like you to conduct the school. When you have finished with the primer class I'll be ready to take hold again."

She had a puzzled look.

"I thought you were going to punish me," she answered, smiling.

"For what?" he inquired.

"Whispering," said she.

"Oh, yes! But you have read Walter Scott, and you know ladies are to be honoured, not punished. I shouldn't know how to do such a thing. When you've become a teacher you'll see I'm right about whispering. May I walk home with you?"

Polly had then a very serious look. She turned away, biting her lip, in a brief struggle for self-mastery.

"If you care to," she whispered.

They walked away in silence.

"Do you dance?" she inquired presently.

"No, save attendance on your pleasure," said he. "Will you teach me?"

"Is there anything I can teach you?" She looked up at him playfully.

"Wisdom," said he, quickly, "and how to preserve blue-berries, and make biscuit like those you gave us when I came to tea. As to dancing, well—I fear 'I am not shaped for sportive tricks.'"

"If you'll stay this evening," said she, "we'll have some more of my blueberries and biscuit, and then, if you care to, we'll try dancing."

"You'll give me a lesson?" he asked eagerly.

"If you'd care to have me."

"Agreed; but first let us have the blueberries and biscuit," said he, heartily, as they entered the door. "Hello, Mrs. Vaughn, I came over to help you eat supper. I have it all planned. Paul is to set the table, I'm to peel the potatoes and fry the pork, Polly is to make the biscuit and gravy and put the kettle on. You are to sit by and look pleasant."

"I insist on making the tea," said Mrs. Vaughn, with amusement.

"Shall we let her make the tea?" he asked, looking thoughtfully at Polly.

"Perhaps we'd better," said she, laughing.

"All right; we'll let her make the tea—we don't have to drink it."

"You," said the widow, "are like Governor Wright, who said to Mrs. Perkins, 'Madam, I will praise your tea, but hang me if I'll drink it.'"

"I'm going to teach the primer class in the morning," said Polly, as she filled the tea-kettle.

"Look out, young man," said Mrs. Vaughn, turning to the teacher. "In a short time she'll be thinking she can teach you."

"I get my first lesson to-night," said the young man. "She's to teach me dancing."

"And you've no fear for your soul?"

"I've more fear for my body," said he, glancing down upon his long figure. "I've never lifted my feet save for the purpose of transportation. I'd like to learn how to dance because Deacon Tower thinks it wicked and I've learned that happiness and sin mean the same thing in his vocabulary."

"I fear you're a downward and backsliding youth," said the widow.

"You know what Ezra Tower said of Ebenezer Fisher, that he was 'one o' them mush-heads that didn't believe in hell'? Are you one o' that kind?" Proclaimers of liberal thought were at work there in the north.

"Since I met Deacon Tower I'm sure it's useful and necessary. He's got to have some place for his enemies. If it were not for hell, the deacon would be miserable here and, maybe, happy hereafter."

"It's a great hope and comfort to him," said the widow, smiling.

"Well, God save us all!" said Trove, who had now a liking for both the phrase and philosophy of Darrel. They had taken chairs at the table.

"Tom," said he, "we'll pause a moment, while you give us the fourth rule of syntax."

"Correct," said he, heartily, as the last word was spoken. "Now let us be happy."

"Paul," said the teacher, as he finished eating, "what is the greatest of all laws?"

"Thou shalt not lie," said the boy, promptly.

"Correct," said Trove; "and in the full knowledge of the law, I declare that no better blueberries and biscuit ever passed my lips."

Supper over, Polly disappeared, and young Mr. Trove helped with the dishes. Soon Polly came back, glowing in her best gown and slippers.

"Why, of all things! What a foolish child!" said her mother. For answer Polly waltzed up and down the room, singing gayly.

She stopped before the glass and began to fuss with her ribbons. The teacher went to her side.

"May I have the honour, Miss Vaughn," Said he, bowing politely. "Is that the way to do?"

"You might say, 'Will you be my pardner,'" said she, mimicking the broad dialect of the region.

"I'll sacrifice my dignity, but not my language," said he. "Let us dance and be merry, for to-morrow we teach."

"If you'll watch my feet, you'll see how I do it," said she; and lifting her skirt above her dainty ankles, glided across the floor on tiptoe, as lightly as a fawn at play. But Sidney Trove was not a graceful creature. The muscles on his lithe form, developed in the school of work or in feats of strength at which he had met no equal, were untrained in all graceful trickery. He loved dancing and music and everything that increased the beauty and delight of life, but they filled him with a deep regret of his ignorance.

"Hard work," said he, breathing heavily, "and I don't believe I'm having as much fun as you are."

The small company of spectators had been laughing with amusement.

"Reminds me of a story," said the teacher. "'What are all the animals crying about?' said one elephant to another. 'Why, don't you know?—it's about the reindeer,' said the other elephant; 'he's dead. Never saw anything so sad in my life.

He skipped so, and made a noise like that, and then he died.' The elephant jumped up and down, trying the light skip of the reindeer and gave a great roar for the bleat of the dying animal, 'What,' said the first elephant, 'did he skip so, and cry that way?' And he tried it. 'No, not that way but this way,' said the other; and he went through it again. By this time every animal in the show had begun to roar with laughter. 'What on earth are you doing?' said the rhinoceros. 'It's the way the reindeer died,' said one of the elephants.

"'Never saw anything so funny,' said the rhinoceros; 'if the poor thing died that way, it's a pity he couldn't repeat the act.'"

"'This is terrible,' said the zebra, straining at his halter. 'The reindeer is dead, and the elephants have gone crazy.'"

"Sidney Trove," said the teacher, as he was walking away that evening, "you'll have to look out for yourself. You're a teacher and you ought to be a man—you must be a man or I'll have nothing more to do with you."

XIX

AMUSEMENT AND LEARNING

There was much doing that winter in the Linley district. They were a month getting ready for the school "exhibition." Every home in the valley and up Cedar Hill rang with loud declamations. The impassioned utterances of James Otis, Daniel Webster, and Patrick Henry were heard in house, and field, and stable. Every evening women were busy making costumes for a play, while the young rehearsed their parts. Polly Vaughn, editor of a paper to be read that evening, searched the countryside for literary talent. She found a young married woman, who had spent a year in the State Normal School, and who put her learning at the service of Polly, in a composition treating the subject of intemperance. Miss Betsey Leech sent in what she called "a piece" entitled "Home." Polly, herself, wrote an editorial on "Our Teacher," and there was hemming and hawing when she read it, declaring they all had learned much, even to love him. Her mother helped her with the alphabetical rhymes, each a couplet of sentimental history, as, for example:—

"A is for Alson, a jolly young man,
He'll marry Miss Betsey, they say, if he can."

They trimmed the little schoolhouse with evergreen and

Irving Bacheller

erected a small stage, where the teacher's desk had been. Sheets were hung, for curtains, on a ten-foot rod.

A while after dark one could hear a sound of sleigh-bells in the distance. Away on drifted pike and crossroad the bells began to fling their music. It seemed to come in rippling streams of sound through the still air, each with its own voice. In half an hour countless echoes filled the space between them, and all were as one chorus, wherein, as it came near, one could distinguish song and laughter.

Young people from afar came in cutters and by the sleigh load; those who lived near, afoot with lanterns. They were a merry company, crowding the schoolhouse, laughing and whispering as they waited for the first exhibit. Trove called them to order and made a few remarks.

"Remember," said he, "this is not our exhibition. It is only a sort of preparation for one we have planned. In about twenty years the Linley School is to give an exhibition worth seeing. It will be, I believe, an exhibition of happiness, ability, and success on the great stage of the world. Then I hope to have on the programme speeches in Congress, in the pulpit, and at the bar. You shall see in that play, if I mistake not, homes full of love and honour, men and women of fair fame. It may be you shall see, then, some whose names are known and honoured of all men."

Each performer quaked with fear, and both sympathy and approval were in the applause. Miss Polly Vaughn was a rare picture of rustic beauty, her cheeks as red as her ribbons, her voice low and sweet. Trove came out in the audience for a look at her as she read. Ringing salvos of laughter greeted the play and stirred the sleigh-bells on the startled horses beyond the door. The programme over, somebody called for Squire Town, a local pettifogger, who flung his soul and body into every cause. He often sored his knuckles on the court table and racked his frame with the violence of his rhetoric. He had a stock of impassioned remarks ready for all occasions.

He rose, walked to the centre of the stage, looked sternly at the people, and addressed them as "Fellow Citizens." He belaboured the small table; he rose on tiptoe and fell upon his heels; often he seemed to fling his words with a rapid jerk of his right arm as one hurls a pebble. It was all in praise of his "young friend," the teacher, and the high talent of Linley School.

The exhibition ended with this rare exhibit of eloquence. Trove announced the organization of a singing-school for Monday evening of the next week, and then suppressed emotion burst into noise. The Linley school-house had become as a fount of merry sound in the still night; then the loud chorus of the bells, diminishing as they went away, and breaking into streams of music and dying faint in the far woodland.

One Nelson Cartright—a jack of all trades they called him—was the singing-master. He was noted far and wide for song and penmanship. Every year his intricate flourishes in black and white were on exhibition at the county fair.

"Wal, sir," men used to say thoughtfully, "ye wouldn't think he knew beans. Why, he's got a fist bigger'n a ham. But I tell ye, let him take a pen, sir, and he'll draw a deer so nat'ral, sir, ye'd swear he could jump over a six-rail fence. Why, it is wonderful!"

Every winter he taught the arts of song and penmanship in the four districts from Jericho to Cedar Hill. He sang a roaring bass and beat the time with dignity and precision. For

　　　　Irving Bacheller

weeks he drilled the class on a bit of lyric melody, of which a passage is here given:—

"One, two, three, ready, sing," he would say, his ruler cutting the air, and all began:—

> Listen to the bird, and the maid, and the bumblebee,
> Tra, la la la la, tra, la la la la,
> Joyfully we'll sing the gladsome melody,
> Tra, la, la, la, la.

The singing-school added little to the knowledge or the cheerfulness of that neighbourhood. It came to an end the last day of the winter term. As usual, Trove went home with Polly. It was a cold night, and as the crowd left them at the corners he put his arm around her.

"School is over," said she, with a sigh, "and I'm sorry."

"For me?" he inquired.

"For myself," she answered, looking down at the snowy path.

There came a little silence crowded with happy thoughts.

"At first, I thought you very dreadful," she went on, looking up at him with a smile. He could see her sweet face in the moonlight and was tempted to kiss it.

"Why?"

"You were so terrible," she answered. "Poor Joe Beach! It seemed as if he would go through the wall."

"Well, something had to happen to him," said the teacher.

"He likes, you now, and every one likes you here. I wish we could have you always for a teacher."

"I'd be willing to be your teacher, always, if I could only teach you what you have taught me."

"Oh, dancing," said she, merrily; "that is nothing. I'll give you all the lessons you like."

"No, I shall not let you teach me that again," said he.

"Why?"

"Because your pretty feet trample on me."

Then came another silence.

"Don't you enjoy it?" she asked, looking off at the stars.

"Too much." said he. "First, I must teach you something—if I can."

He was ready for a query, if it came, but she put him off.

"I intend to be a grand lady," said she, "and, if you do not learn, you'll never be able to dance with me."

"There'll be others to dance with you," said he. "I have so much else to do."

"Oh, you're always thinking about algebra and arithmetic and those dreadful things," said she.

"No, I'm thinking now of something very different."

"Grammar, I suppose," said she, looking down.

"Do you remember the conjugations?"

"Try me," said she.

"Give me the first person singular, passive voice, present tense, of the verb to love."

"I am loved," was her answer, as she looked away.

"And don't you know—I love you," said he, quickly.

"That is the active voice," said she, turning with a smile.

"Polly," said he, "I love you as I could love no other in the world."

He drew her close, and she looked up at him very soberly.

"You love me?" she said in a half whisper.

"With all my heart," he answered. "I hope you will love me sometime."

Their lips came together.

"I do not ask you, now, to say that you love me," said the young man. "You are young and do not know your own heart."

She rose on tiptoe and fondly touched his cheek with her fingers.

"But I do love you," she whispered.

"I thank God you have told me, but I shall ask you for no promise. A year from now, then, dear, I shall ask you to promise that you will be my wife sometime."

"Oh, let me promise now," she whispered.

"Promise only that you will love me if you see none you love better."

They were slowly nearing the door. Suddenly she stopped, looking up at him.

"Are you sure you love me?" she asked.

"Yes," he whispered.

"Sure?"

"As sure as I am that I live."

"And will love me always?"

"Always," he answered.

She drew his head down a little and put her lips to his ear. "Then I shall love you always," she whispered.

Mrs. Vaughn, was waiting for them at the fireside. They sat talking a while.

"You go off to bed, Polly," said the teacher, presently. "I've something to say, and you're not to hear it."

"I'll listen," said she, laughing.

"Then we'll whisper," Trove answered.

"That isn't fair," said she, with a look of injury, as she held the candle. "Besides, you don't allow it yourself."

"Polly ought to go away to school," said he, after Polly had gone above stairs. "She's a bright girl."

"And I so poor I'm always wondering what'll happen to-morrow," said Mrs. Vaughn. "The farm has a mortgage, and it's more than I can do to pay the interest. Some day I'll have to give it up."

"Perhaps I can help you," said the young man, feeling the fur on his cap.

There was an awkward silence.

"Fact is," said the young man, a bit embarrassed, "fact is, I love Polly."

In the silence that followed Trove could hear the tick of his watch.

"Have ye spoken to her?" said the widow, with a serious look.

"I've told her frankly to-night that I love her," said he. "I couldn't help it, she was so sweet and beautiful."

"If you couldn't help it, I don't see how I could," said she. "But Polly's only a child. She's a big girl, I know, but she's only eighteen."

"I haven't asked her for any promise. It wouldn't be fair. She must have a chance to meet other young men, but, sometime, I hope she will be my wife."

"Poor children!" said Mrs. Vaughn, "you don't either of you

know what you're doing."

He rose to go.

"I was a little premature," he added, "but you mustn't blame me. Put yourself in my place. If you were a young man and loved a girl as sweet as Polly and were walking home with her on a moonlit night—"

"I presume there'd be more or less love-making," said the widow. "She is a pretty thing and has the way of a woman. We were speaking of you the other day, and she said to me: 'He is ungrateful. You can teach the primer class for him, and be so good that you feel perfectly miserable, and give him lessons in dancing, and put on your best clothes, and make biscuit for him, and then, perhaps, he'll go out and talk with the hired man.' 'Polly,' said I, 'you're getting to be very foolish.' 'Well, it comes so easy,' said she. 'It's my one talent'"

XX

AT THE THEATRE OF THE WOODS

Next day Trove went home. He took with him many a souvenir of his first term, including a scarf that Polly had knit for him, and the curious things he took from the Frenchman Leblanc, and which he retained partly because they were curious and partly because Mrs. Leblanc had been anxious to get rid of them. He soon rejoined his class at Hillsborough, having kept abreast of it in history and mathematics by work after school and over the week's end. He was content to fall behind in the classics, for they were easy, and in them his arrears gave him no terror. Walking for exercise, he laid the plan of his tale and had written some bits of verse. Of an evening he went often to the Sign of the Dial, and there read his lines and got friendly but severe criticism. He came into the shop one evening, his "Horace" under his arm.

"'*Maecenas, atavis, edite regibus*'" Trove chanted, pausing to recall the lines.

The tinker turned quickly. "'*O et presidium et duice decus meum,*'" he quoted, never stopping until he had finished She ode.

"Is there anything you do not know?" Trove inquired.

"Much," said the tinker, "including the depth o' me own folly. A man that displays knowledge hath need o' more."

Indeed, Trove rarely came for a talk with Darrel when he failed to discover something new in him—a further reach of thought and sympathy or some unsuspected treasure of knowledge. The tinker loved a laugh and would often search his memory for some phrase of bard or philosopher apt enough to provoke it. Of his great store of knowledge he made no vainer use.

Trove had been overworking; and about the middle of June they went for a week in the woods together. They walked to Allen's the first day, and, after a brief visit there, went off in the deep woods, camping on a pond in thick-timbered hills. Coming to the lilied shore, they sat down a while to rest. A hawk was sailing high above the still water. Crows began to call in the tree-tops. An eagle sat on a dead pine at the water's edge and seemed to be peering down at his own shadow. Two deer stood in a marsh on the farther shore, looking over at them. Near by were the bones of some animal, and the fresh footprints of a painter. Sounds echoed far in the hush of the unbroken wilderness.

"See, boy," said Darrel, with a little gesture of his right hand, "the theatre o' the woods! See the sloping hills, tree above tree, like winding galleries. Here is a coliseum old, past reckoning. Why, boy, long before men saw the Seven Hills it was old. Yet see how new it is—how fresh its colour, how strong its timbers! See the many seats, each with a good view, an' the multitude o' the people, yet most o' them are hidden. Ten thousand eyes are looking down upon us. Tragedies and comedies o' the forest are enacted here. Many a thrilling scene has held the stage—the spent deer swimming for his life, the painter stalking his prey or leaping on it."

"Tis a cruel part," said Trove. "He is the murderer of the play. I cannot understand why there are so many villains in its cast, Both the cat and the serpent baffle me."

"Marry, boy, the world is a great school—an' this little drama o' the good God is part of it," said Darrel. "An' the play hath a great moral—thou shalt learn to use thy brain or die. Now, there be many perils in this land o' the woods—so many that all its people must learn to think or perish by them. A pretty bit o' wisdom it is, sor. It keeps the great van moving—ever moving, in the long way to perfection. Now, among animals, a growing brain works the legs of its owner, sending them far on diverse errands until they are strong. Mind thee, boy, perfection o' brain and body is the aim o' Nature. The cat's paw an' the serpent's coil are but the penalties o' weakness an' folly. The world is for the strong. Therefore, God keep thee so, or there be serpents will enter thy blood an' devour thee—millions o' them."

"And what is the meaning of this law?"

"That the weak shall not live to perpetuate their kind," said Darrel. "Every year there is a tournament o' the sparrows. Which deserves the fair—that is the question to be settled. Full tilt they come together, striking with lance and wing. Knight strives with knight, lady with lady, and the weak die. Lest thou forget, I'll tell thee a tale, boy, wherein is the great plan. The queen bee—strongest of all her people—is about to marry.[1] A clear morning she comes out o' the palace gate—her attendants following. The multitude of her suitors throng the vestibule; the air, now still an' sweet, rings with the sound o' fairy timbrels. Of a sudden she rises into the blue sky, an' her suitors follow. Her swift wings cleave the air straight as a plummet falls. Only the strong may keep in sight o' her; bear that in mind, boy. Her suitors begin to fall wearied. Higher an' still higher the good queen wings her way. By an' by, of all that began the journey, there is but one left with her, an' he the strongest of her people. An' they are wed, boy, up in the sun-lit deep o' heaven. So the seed o' life is chosen, me fine lad."

[1 In behalf of Darrel, the author makes acknowledgment of his indebtedness to M. Maurice Maeterlinck for an account of the queen's flight in his interesting "Life of the Bee."]

They sat a little time in silence, looking at the shores of the pond.

"Have ye never felt the love passion?" said Darrel.

"Well, there's a girl of the name of Polly," Trove answered.

"Ah, Polly! she o' the red lip an' the dark eye," said Darrel, smiling. "She's one of a thousand." He clapped his hand upon his knee, merrily, and sang a sentimental couplet from an old Irish ballad.

"Have ye won her affection, boy?" he added, his hand on the boy's arm.

"I think I have."

"God love thee! I'm glad to hear it," said the old man. "She is a living wonder, boy, a living wonder, an' had I thy youth I'd give thee worry."

"Since her mother cannot afford to do it, I wish to send her away to school," said Trove.

"Tut, tut, boy; thou hast barely enough for thy own schooling."

"I've eighty-two dollars in my pocket," said Trove, proudly. "I do not need it. The job in the mill—that will feed me and pay my room rent, and my clothes will do me for another year."

"On me word, boy; I like it in thee," said Darrel; "but surely she would not take thy money."

"I could not offer it to her, but you might go there, and perhaps she would take it from you."

"Capital!" the tinker exclaimed. "I'll see if I can serve thee. Marry, good youth, I'll even give away thy money an' take credit for thy benevolence. Teacher, philanthropist, lover—I believe thou'rt ready to write."

"The plan of my first novel is complete," said Trove. "That poor thief,—he shall be my chief character,—the man of whom you told me."

"Poor man! God make thee kind to him," said the tinker. "An' thou'rt willing, I'll hear o' him to-night. When the firelight flickers,—that is the time, boy, for tales."

They built a rude lean-to, covered with bark, and bedded with fragrant boughs. Both lay in the firelight, Darrel smoking his pipe, as the night fell.

"Now for thy tale," said the tinker.

The tale was Trove's own solution of his life mystery, shrewdly come to, after a long and careful survey of the known facts. And now, shortly, time was to put the seal of truth upon it, and daze him with astonishment, and fill him with regret of his cunning. It should be known that he had never told Darrel or any one of his coming in the little red sleigh.

He lay thinking for a time after the tinker spoke. Then he began:—

"Well, the time is 1833, the place a New England city on the sea. Chapter I: A young woman is walking along a street, with a child sleeping in her arms. She is dark-skinned,—a Syrian. It is growing dusk; the street is deserted, save by her and two sailors, who are approaching her. They, too, are Syrians. One seems to strike her,—it is mere pretence, however,—and she falls. The other seizes the child, who, having been drugged, is still asleep. A wagon is waiting near. They drive away hurriedly, their captive under a blanket. The kidnappers make for the woods in New Hampshire. Officers of the law drive them far. They abandon their horse, tramping westward over trails in the wilderness, bearing the boy in a sack of sail-cloth, open at the top. They had guns and killed their food as they travelled. Snow came deep; by and by game was scarce and they had grown weary of bearing the boy on their backs. One waited in the woods with the little lad while the other went away to some town or city for provisions. He came back, hauling them in a little sleigh. It was much like those made for the delight of the small boy in every land of snow. It had a box painted red and two bobs and a little dashboard. They used it for the transportation of boy and impedimenta. In the deep wilderness beyond the Adirondacks they found a cave in one of the rock ledges. They were twenty miles from any post-office but shortly discovered one. Letters in cipher were soon passing between them and their confederates. They learned there was no prospect of getting the ransom. He they had thought rich was not able to raise the money they required or any large sum.

Two years went by, and they abandoned hope. What should they do with the boy? One advised murder, but the other defended him. It was unnecessary, he maintained, to kill a mere baby, who knew not a word of English, and would forget all in a month. And murder would only increase their peril. Now eight miles from their cave was the cabin of a settler. They passed within a mile of it on their way out and in. They had often met the dog of the settler roving after small game—a shepherd, trustful, affectionate, and ever ready to make friends. One day they captured the dog and took him to their cave. They could not safely be seen with the boy, so they planned to let the dog go home with him in the little red sleigh. Now the settler's cabin was like that of my father, on the shore of a pond. It was round, as a cup's rim, and a mile or so in diameter. Opposite the cabin a trail came to the water's edge, skirting the pond, save in cold weather, when it crossed the ice. They waited for a night when their tracks would soon disappear. Then, having made a cover of the sail-cloth sack in which they had brought the boy, and stretched it on withes, and made it fast to the sleigh box, they put the sleeping boy in the sleigh, with hot stones wrapped in paper, and a robe of fur, to keep him warm, hitched the dog to it, and came over hill and trail, to the little pond, a while after midnight. Here they buckled a ring of bells on the dog's neck and released him. He made for his home on the clear ice; the bells and his bark sounding as he ran. They at the cabin heard him coming and opened their door to dog and traveller. So came my hero in a little red sleigh, and was adopted by the settler and his wife, and reared by them with generous affection. Well, he goes to school and learns rapidly, and comes to manhood. It's a pretty story—that of his life in the big woods. But now for the love tale. He meets a young lady—sweet, tender, graceful, charming."

"A moment," said Darrel, raising his hand. "Prithee, boy,

ring down the curtain for a brief parley. Thou say'st they were Syrians—they that stole the lad. Now, tell me, hast thou reason for that?"

"Ample," said Trove. "When they took him out of the sleigh the first words he spoke were "Anah jouhan." He used them many times, and while he forgot they remembered them. Now "Anah jouhan" is a phrase of the Syrian tongue, meaning 'I am hungry.'"

"Very well!" said the old man, with emphasis, "and sailors—that is a just inference. It was a big port, and far people came on the four winds. Very well! Now, for the young lady. An' away with thy book unless I love her."

"She is from life—a simple-hearted girl, frank and beautiful and—" Trove hesitated, looking into the dying fire.

"Noble, boy, make sure o' that, an' nobler, too, than girls are apt to be. If Emulation would measure height with her, see that it stand upon tiptoes."

"So I have planned. The young man loves her. She is in every thought and purpose. She has become as the rock on which his hope is founded. Now he loves honour, too, and all things of good report. He has been reared a Puritan. By chance, one day, it comes to him that his father was a thief."

The boy paused. For a moment they heard only the voices of the night.

"He dreaded to tell her," Trove continued; "yet he could not ask her to be his wife without telling. Then the question, Had he a right to tell?—for his father had not suffered the penalty of the law and, mind you, men thought him honest."

"'Tis just," said Darrel; "but tell me, how came he to know his father was a thief?"

"That I am thinking of, and before I answer, is there more you can tell me of him or his people?"

Darrel rose; and lighting a torch of pine, stuck it in the ground. Then he opened his leathern pocket-book and took out a number of cuttings, much worn, and apparently from old newspapers. He put on his glasses and began to examine the cuttings.

"The other day," said he, "I found an account of his mother's death. I had forgotten, but her death was an odd tragedy."

And the tinker began reading, slowly, as follows:—

"'She an' her mother—a lady deaf an' feeble—were alone, saving the servants in a remote corner o' the house. A sound woke her in the still night. She lay a while listening. Was it her husband returning without his key? She rose, feeling her way in the dark and trembling with the fear of a nervous woman. Descending stairs, she came into a room o' many windows. The shades were up, an' there was dim moon-light in the room. A door, with panels o' thick glass, led to the garden walk. Beyond it were the dark forms of men. One was peering in, his face at a panel, another kneeling at the lock. Suddenly the door opened; the lady fell fainting with a loud cry. Next day the kidnapped boy was born.'"

Darrel stopped reading, put the clipping into his pocket-book, and smothered the torch.

"It seems the woman died the same day," said he.

"And was my mother," the words came in a broken voice.

Half a moment of silence followed them. Then Darrel rose slowly, and a tremulous, deep sigh came from the lips of Trove.

"Thy mother, boy!" Darrel whispered.

The fire had burnt low, and the great shadow of the night lay dark upon them. Trove got to his feet and came to the side of Darrel.

"Tell me, for God's sake, man, tell me where is my father," said he.

"Hush, boy! Listen. Hear the wind in the trees?" said Darrel.

There was a breath of silence broken by the hoot of an owl and the stir of high branches. "Ye might as well ask o' the wind or the wild owl," Darrel said. "I cannot tell thee. Be calm, boy, and say how thou hast come to know."

Again they sat down together, and presently Trove told him of those silent men who had ever haunted the dark and ghostly house of his inheritance.

"'Tis thy mother's terror,—an' thy father's house,—I make no doubt," said Darrel, presently, in a deep voice. "But, boy, I cannot tell any man where is thy father; not even thee, nor his name, nor the least thing, tending to point him out, until—until I am released o' me vow. Be content; if I can find the man, ere long, thou shalt have word o' him."

Trove leaned against the breast of Darrel, shaking with emotion. His tale had come to an odd and fateful climax.

The old man stroked his head tenderly.

"Ah, boy," said he, "I know thy heart. I shall make haste—I promise thee, I shall make haste. But, if the good God should bring thy father to thee, an' thy head to shame an' sorrow for his sin, forgive him, in the name o' Christ, forgive him. Ay, boy, thou must forgive all that trespass against thee."

"If I ever see him, he shall know I am not ungrateful," said the young man.

A while past twelve o'clock, those two, lying there in the firelight, thinking, rose like those startled in sleep. A mighty voice came booming over the still water and echoed far and wide. Slowly its words fell and rang in the great, silent temple of the woods:—

"'Though I speak with the tongues of men and of angels, and have not charity, I am become as sounding brass, or a tinkling cymbal."

"'And though I have the gift of prophecy, and understand all mysteries, and all knowledge; and though I have all faith, so that I could remove mountains, and have not charity, I am nothing."

"'And though I bestow all my goods to feed the poor, and though I give my body to be burned, and have not charity, it profiteth me nothing."

"'Charity suffereth long, and is kind; charity envieth not; charity vaunteth not itself; is not puffed up,"

"'Doth not behave itself unseemly, seeketh not her own, is not easily provoked, thinketh no evil;"

"'Beareth all things, believeth all things, hopeth all things, endureth all things."

"'Charity never faileth: but whether there be prophecies, they shall fail; whether there be tongues, they shall cease; whether there be knowledge, it shall vanish away.'"

As the last words died away in the far woodland, Trove and Darrel turned, wiping their eyes in silence. That flood of inspiration had filled them. Big thoughts had come drifting down with its current. They listened a while, but heard only the faint crackle of the fire.

"Strange!" said Trove, presently.

"Passing strange, and like a beautiful song," said Darrel.

"It may be some insane fanatic."

"Maybe, but he hath the voice of an angel," said the old man.

They passed a sleepless night and were up early, packing to leave the woods. Darrel was to go in quest of the boy's father. Within a week he felt sure he should be able to find him.

They skirted the pond, crossing a long ridge on its farther shore. At a spring of cool water in a deep ravine they halted to drink and rest. Suddenly they heard a sound of men approaching; and when the latter had come near, a voice, deep, vibrant, and musical as a harp-string, in these lines of Hamlet:—

> "'Why right; you are i' the right;
> And so without more circumstance at all,
> I hold it fit that we shake hands and part;
> You as your business and desire shall point you;
> For every man has business and desire
> Such as it is; and for mine own part

Look you, I'll go pray.'"

Then said Darrel, loudly:—

"'These are but wild and whirling words, my lord.'"

Two men, a guide in advance, came along the trail—one, a most impressive figure, tall, erect, and strong; its every move expressing grace and power.

Again the deep music of his voice, saying:—

"'I'm sorry they offend you heartily; yes, faith, heartily.'"

And Darrel rejoined, his own rich tone touching the note of melancholy in the other:—

"'There's no offence, my lord.'"

"'What Horatio is this?" the stranger inquired, offering his hand. "A player?"

"Ay, as are all men an' women," said Darrel, quickly. "But I, sor, have only a poor part. Had I thy lines an' makeup, I'd win applause."

The newcomers sat down, the man who had spoken removing his hat. Curly locks of dark hair, with now a sprinkle of silver in them, fell upon his brows. He had large brown eyes, a mouth firm and well modelled, a nose slightly aquiline, and wore a small, dark imperial—a mere tuft under his lip.

"Well, Colonel, you have paid me a graceful compliment," said he.

"Nay, man, do not mistake me rank," said Darrel.

"Indeed—what is it?"

"Friend," he answered, quickly. "In good company there's no higher rank. But if ye think me unworthy, I'll be content with 'Mister.'"

"My friend, forgive me," said the stranger, approaching Darrel. "Murder and envy and revenge and all evil are in my part, but no impertinence."

"I know thy rank, sor. Thou art a gentleman," said Darrel. "I've seen thee 'every inch a king.'"

Darrel spoke to the second period in that passage of Lear, the majesty and despair of the old king in voice and gesture. The words were afire with feeling as they came off his tongue, and all looked at him with surprise.

"Ah, you have seen me play it," said the stranger. "There's no other Lear that declares himself with that gesture."

"It is Edwin Forrest," said Darrel, as the stranger offered his hand.

"The same, and at your service," the great actor replied. "And may I ask who are you?"

"Roderick Darrel, son of a wheelwright on the river Bann, once a fellow of infinite jest, believe me, but now, alas! like the skull o' Yorick in the churchyard."

"The churchyard'" said Forrest, thoughtfully. "That to me is the saddest of all scenes. When it's over and I leave the stage, it is to carry with me an awe-inspiring thought of the end which is coming to all."

He crumbled a lump of clay in his palm.

"Dust!" he whispered, scattering it in the air.

"Think ye the dust is dead? Nay, man; a mighty power is in it," said Darrel. "Let us imagine thee dead an' turned to clay. Leave the clay to its own law, sor, an' it begins to cleanse an' purge itself. Its aim is purity, an' it never wearies. Could I live long enough, an' it were under me eye, I'd see the clay bleaching white with a wonderful purity. Then, slowly, it would begin to come clear, an' by an' by it would be clearer an' lovelier than a drop o' dew at sunrise. Lo and behold! the clay has become a sapphire. So, sor, in the waters o' time God washes the great world. In every grain o' dust the law is written, an' I may read the destiny o' the nobler part in the fate o' the meaner.

"'Imperious Forrest, dead an' turned to clay,
Might stop a hole to keep despair away.'"

"Delightful and happy man! I must know you better," said the great tragedian. "May I ask, sir, what is your calling?"

"I, sor, am a tinker o' clocks."

"A tinker of clocks!" said the other, looking at him thought-fully. "I should think it poorly suited to your talents."

"Not so. I've only a talent for happiness an' good company."

"And you find good company here?"

"Yes; bards, prophets, an' honest men. They're everywhere."

"Tell me," said Forrest, "were you not some time a player?"

"Player of many parts, but all in God's drama—fool, servant of a rich man, cobbler, clock tinker, all in the coat of a poor man. Me health failed me, sor, an' I took to wandering in the open air. Ten years ago in the city of New York me wife died, since when I have been tinkering here in the edges o' the woodland, where I have found health an' friendship an' good cheer. Faith, sor, that is all one needs, save the company o' the poets.

"'I pray an' sing an' tell old tales an' laugh
At gilded butterflies, an' hear poor rogues
Talk o' court news.'"

Trove had missed not a word nor even a turn of the eye in all that scene. After years of acquaintance with the tinker he had not yet ventured a question as to his life history. The difference of age and a certain masterly reserve in the old gentleman had seemed to discourage it. A prying tongue in a mere youth would have met unpleasant obstacles with Darrel. Never until that day had he spoken freely of his past in the presence of the young man.

"I must see you again," said the tragedian, rising. "Of those parts I try to play, which do you most like?"

"St. Paul," said Darrel, quickly. "Last night, sor, in this great theatre, we heard the voice o' the prophet. Ah, sor, it was like a trumpet on the walls of eternity. I commend to thee the part o' St. Paul. Next to that—of all thy parts, Lear."

"Lear?" said Forrest, rising. "I am to play it this autumn. Come, then, to New York. Give me your address, and I'll send for you."

"Sor," said Darrel, thoughtfully, "I can give thee much o' me love but little o' me time. Nay, there'd be trouble among the clocks. I'd be ashamed to look them in the face. Nay,—I thank thee,—but I must mind the clocks."

The great player smiled with amusement.

"Then," said he, "I shall have to come and see you play your part. Till then, sir, God give you happiness."

"Once upon a time," said Darrel, as he held the hand of the player, "a weary traveller came to the gate o' Heaven, seeking entrance.

"'What hast thou in thy heart?' said the good St. Peter.

"'The record o' great suffering an' many prayers,' said the poor man. 'I pray thee now, give me the happiness o' Heaven.'"

"'Good man, we have none to spare,' said the keeper. 'Heaven hath no happiness but that men bring. It is a gift to God and comes not from Him. Would ye take o' that we have an' bring nothing? Nay, go back to thy toil an' fill thy heart with happiness, an' bring it to me overflowing. Then shalt thou know the joy o' paradise. Remember, God giveth counsel, but not happiness.'"

"If I only had your wisdom," said Forrest, as they parted.

"Ye'd have need o' more," the tinker answered.

Trove and Darrel walked to the clearing above Faraway. At a corner on the high hills, where northward they could see smoke and spire of distant villages, each took his way,—one leading to Hillsborough, the other to Allen's.

"Good-by; an' when I return I hope to bear the rest o' thy tale," said Darrel, as they parted.

"Only God is wise enough to finish it," said the young man.

"'Well, God help us; 'tis a world to see,'" Darrel quoted, waving his hand. "If thy heart oppress thee, steer for the Blessed Isles."

XXI

ROBIN'S INN

A big maple sheltered the house of the widow Vaughn. After the noon hour of a summer day its tide of shadow began flowing fathoms deep over house and garden to the near field, where finally it joined the great flood of night. The maple was indeed a robin's inn at some crossing of the invisible roads of the air. Its green dome towered high above and fell to the gable end of the little house. Its deep and leafy thatch hid every timber of its frame save the rough column. Its trunk was the main beam, each limb a corridor, each tier of limbs a floor, and branch rose above branch like steps in a stairway. Up and down the high dome of the maple were a thousand balconies overlooking the meadow.

From its highest tier of a summer morning the notes of the bobolink came rushing off his lyre, and farther down the golden robin sounded his piccolo. But, chiefly, it was the home and refuge of the familiar red-breasted robin. The inn had its ancient customs. Each young bird, leaving his cradle, climbed his own stairway till he came out upon a balcony and got a first timid look at field and sky. There he might try his wings and keep in the world he knew by using bill and claw on the lower tiers.

At dawn the great hall of the maple rang with music, for every lodger paid his score with song. Therein it was ever cool, and clean, and shady, though the sun were hot. Its every nook and cranny was often swept and dusted by the wind. Its branches leading up and outward to the green wall were as innumerable stairways. Each separate home was out on rocking beams, with its own flicker of sky light overhead. For a time at dusk there was a continual flutter of weary wings at the lower entrance, a good night twitter, and a sound of tiny feet climbing the stairways in that gloomy hall. At last, there was a moment of gossip and then silence on every floor. There seemed to be a night-watch in the lower hall, and if any green young bird were late and noisy going up to his home, he got a shaking and probably lost a few feathers from the nape of his neck. Long before daybreak those hungry, half-clad little people of the nests began to worry and crowd their mothers. At first, the old birds tried to quiet them with caressing movements, and had, at last, to hold their places with bill and claw. As light came an old cock peered about him, stretched his wings, climbed a stairway, and blew his trumpet on the outer wall. The robin's day had begun.

Mid-autumn, when its people shivered and found fault and talked of moving, the maple tried to please them with new and brighter colours—gold, with the warmth of summer in its look; scarlet, suggesting love and the June roses. Soon it stood bare and deserted. Then what was there in the creak-and-whisper chorus of the old tree for one listening in the night? Belike it might be many things, according to the ear, but was it not often something to make one think of that solemn message: "Man that is born of a woman is of few days and full of trouble"? They who lived in that small house under the tree knew little of all that passed in the big world. Trumpet blasts of fame, thunder of rise and downfall, came faintly to them. There the delights of art and luxury were unknown. Yet those simple folk were acquainted with pleasure and even with thrilling and impressive incidents. Field and garden teemed with eventful life and hard by was the great city of the woods.

XXII

COMEDIES OF FIELD AND DOORYARD

Trove was three days in Brier Dale after he came out of the woods. The filly was now a sleek and shapely animal, past three years of age. He began at once breaking her to the saddle, and, that done, mounting, he started for Robin's Inn. He carried a game rooster in a sack for the boy Tom. All came out with a word of welcome; even the small dog grew noisy with delight Tunk Hosely, who had come to work for Mrs. Vaughn, took the mare and led her away, his shoulder leaning with an added sense of horsemanship. Polly began to hurry dinner, fussing with the table, and changing the position of every dish, until it seemed as if she would never be quite satisfied. Covered with the sacred old china and table-linen of her grandmother, it had, when Polly was done with it, a very smart appearance indeed. Then she called the boys and bade them wash their hands and faces and whispered a warning to each, while her mother announced that dinner was ready.

"Paul, what's an adjective?" said the teacher, as they sat down.

"A word applied to a noun to qualify or limit its meaning," the boy answered glibly.

"Right! And what adjective would you apply to this table?"

The boy thought a moment.

"Grand!" said he, tentatively.

"Correct! I'm going to have just such a dinner every day on my farm."

"Then you'll have to have Polly too," said Tom, innocently.

"Well, you can spare her."

"No, sir," the boy answered. "You ain't good to her; she cries every time you go away."

There was an awkward silence and the widow began to laugh and Polly and Trove to blush deeply.

"Maybe she whispered, an' he give her a talkin' to," said Paul.

"Have you heard about Ezra Tower?" said Mrs. Vaughn, shaking her head at the boys and changing the topic with shrewd diplomacy.

"Much; but nothing new," said Trove.

"Well, he swears he'll never cross the Fadden bridge or speak to anybody in Pleasant Valley."

"Why?"

"The taxes. He don't believe in improvements, and when he tried to make a speech in town-meeting they all jeered him. There ain't any one good enough for him to speak to now but himself an'—an' his Creator."

In the midst of dinner, they heard an outcry in the yard. Tom's game-cock had challenged the old rooster, and the two were leaping and striking with foot and wing. Before help came the old rooster was badly cut in the neck and breast. Tunk rescued him, and brought him to the woodshed, where Trove sewed up his wounds. He had scarcely finished when there came a louder outcry among the fowls. Looking out they saw a gobbler striding slowly up the path and leading the game-cock with a firm hold on the back of his neck. The whole flock of fowls were following. The rooster held back and came on with long but unequal strides, Never halting, the turkey led him into the full publicity of the open yard. Now the cock was lifted so his feet came only to the top of the grass; now his head was bent low, and his feet fell heavily. Through it all the gobbler bore himself with dignity and firmness. There was no show of wrath or unnecessary violence. He swung the cock around near the foot of the maple tree and walked him back and then returned with him. Half his journey the poor cock was reaching for the grass and was then lowered quickly, so he had to walk with bent knees. Again and again the gobbler walked up and down with him before the assembled flock. Hens and geese cackled loudly and clapped their wings. Applause and derision rose high each time the poor cock swung around, reaching for the grass. But the gobbler continued his even stride, deliberately, and as it seemed, thoughtfully, applying correction to the quarrelsome bird. Walking the grass tips had begun to tire those reaching legs. The cock soon straddled along with a serious eye and an open mouth. But the gobbler gave him no rest. When, at length, he released his hold, the game-cock lay weary and wild-eyed, with no more fight in him than a bunch of rags. Soon he rose and ran away and hid himself in the stable. The culprit fowl was then tried, convicted, and sentenced to the block.

Irving Bacheller

"It's the fate of all fighters that have only a selfish cause," said the teacher. He was sitting on the grass, Polly, and Tom, and Paul, beside him.

"Look here," said he, suddenly. "I'll show you another fight."

All gathered about him. Down among the grass roots an ant stood facing a big, hairy spider. The ant backed away, presently, and made a little detour, the spider turning quickly and edging toward him. The ant stood motionless, the spider on tiptoe, with daggers drawn. The big, hairy spider leaped like a lion to its prey. They could see her striking with the fatal knives, her great body quivering with fierce energy. The little ant was hidden beneath it. Some uttered a cry of pity, and Paul was for taking sides.

"Wait a moment," said the teacher, restraining his hand. The spider had begun to tremble in a curious manner.

"Look now," said Trove, with some excitement.

Her legs had begun to let go and were straightening stiff on both sides of her. In a moment she tilted sideways and lay still. They saw a twinkle of black, legs and the ant making off in the stubble. They picked up the spider's body; it was now only an empty shell. Her big stomach had been torn away and lay in little strips and chunks, down at the roots of the stubble.

"It's the end of a bit of history," said the teacher, as he tore away the curved blades of the spider and put them in Polly's palm.

"Let's see where the ant goes."

He got down upon his hands and knees and watched the little

black tiger, now hurrying for his lair. In a moment he was joined by others, and presently they came into a smooth little avenue under the grass. It took them into the edge of the meadow, around a stalk of mullen, where there were a number of webs.

"There's where she lived—this hairy old woman," said the teacher,—"up there in that tower. See her snares in the grass—four of them?"

He rapped on the stalk of mullen with a stick, peering into the dusty little cavern of silk near the top of it.

"Sure enough! Here is where she lived; for the house is empty, and there's living prey in the snares."

"What a weird old thing!" said Polly. "Can you tell us more about her?"

"Well, every summer," said Trove, "a great city grows up in the field. There are shady streets in it, no wider than a cricket's back, and millions living in nest and tower and cave and cavern. Among its people are toilers and idlers, laws and lawbreakers, thieves and highwaymen, grand folk and plain folk. Here is the home of the greatest criminal in the city of the field. See! it is between two leaves,—one serving as roof, the other as floor and portico. Here is a long cable that comes out of her sitting room and slopes away to the big snare below. Look at her sheets of silk in the grass. It's like a washing that's been hung out to dry. From each a slender cord of silk runs to the main cable. Even a fly's kick or a stroke of his tiny wing must have gone up the tower and shaken the floor of the old lady, maybe, with a sort of thunder. Then she ran out and down the cable to rush upon her helpless prey. She was an arrant highwayman,—this old lady,—a creature of craft and violence. She was no sooner married than she slew her husband—a timid thing smaller than she—and ate him at one meal. You know the ants are a busy people. This road was probably a thoroughfare for their freight,—eggs and cattle and wild rice. I'll warrant she used to lie and wait for them; and woe to the little traveller if she caught him unawares, for she could nip him in two with a single thrust of her knives. Then she, would seize the egg he bore and make off with it. Now the ants are cunning. They found her downstairs and cut her off from her home and drove her away into the grass jungle. I've no doubt she faced a score of them, but, being a swift climber, with lots of rope in her pocket, was able to get away. The soldier ants began to beat the jangle. They separated, content to meet her singly, knowing she would refuse to fight if confronted by more than one. And you know what happened to her."

All that afternoon they spent in the city of the field. The life of the birds in the great maple interested them most of all. In the evening he played checkers with Polly and told her of school life in the village of Hillsborough—the work and play of the students.

"Oh! I do wish I could go," said she, presently, with a deep sigh.

He thought of the eighty-two dollars in his pocket and longed to tell her all that he was planning for her sake.

Mrs. Vaughn went above stairs with the children.

Then Trove took Polly's hand. They looked deeply into each other's eyes a moment, both smiling.

"It's your move," said she, smiling as her glance fell.

He moved all the checkers.

There came a breath of silence, and a great surge of happiness that washed every checker off the board, and left the two with flushed faces. Then, as Mrs. Vaughn was coming downstairs, the checkers began to rattle into position.

"I won," said he, as the door opened.

"But he didn't play fair," said Folly.

"Children, I'm afraid you're playing more love than checkers," said the widow. "You're both too young to think of marriage."

Those two looked thoughtfully at the checkerboard, Polly's chin resting on her hand. She had begun to smile.

"I'm sure Mr. Trove has no such thought in his head," said she, still looking at the board.

"You're mother is right; we're both very young," said Trove.

"I believe you're afraid of her," said Polly, looking up at him with a smile.

"I'm only thinking of your welfare," said Mrs. Vaughn, gently. "Young love should be stored away, and if it keeps, why, then it's all right."

"Like preserves!" said Polly, soberly, as if she were not able to see the point.

Against the protest of Polly and her mother, Trove went to sleep in the sugar shanty, a quarter of a mile or so back in the woods. On his first trip with the drove he had developed fondness for sleeping out of doors. The shanty was a rude structure of logs, with an open front. Tunk went ahead, bearing a pine torch, while Trove followed, the blanket over his shoulder. They built a roaring fire in front of the shanty and sat down to talk.

"How have you been?" Trove inquired.

"Like t' killed me there at the ol' maids'."

"Were they rough with you?"

"No," said Tunk, gloomily.

"What then?"

"Hoss."

"Kicked?" was Trove's query.

"Lord! I should think so. Feel there."

Trove felt the same old protuberance on Tunk's leg.

"Swatted me right in the knee-pan. Put both feet on my chest, too. Lord! I'd be coughin' up blood all the while if I wa'n't careful."

"And why did you leave?"

"Served me a mean trick," said Tunk, frowning. "Letishey went away t' the village t' have a tooth drawed, an' t'other one locked me up all day in the garret chamber. Toward night I crawled out o' the window an' clim' down the lightnin' rod. An' she screamed for help an' run t' the neighbours. Scairt me half t' death. Heavens! I didn't know what I'd done!"

"Did you come down fast?" Trove inquired.

"Purty middlin' fast."

"Well, a man never ought to travel on a lightning rod."

Tunk sat in sober silence a moment, as if he thought it no proper time for levity.

"I made up my mind," said he, with an injured look, "it wa'n't goin' t' do my character no good t' live there with them ol' maids."

There was a bitter contempt in his voice when he said "ol' maids."

"I'd kind o' like t' draw the ribbons over that mare o' yourn, mister," said Tunk, presently.

"Do you think you could manage her?"

"What!" said Tunk, in a voice of both query and exclamation. "Huh! Don't I look as if I'd been used t' hosses. There ain't a bone in my body that ain't been kicked—some on 'em two or three times. Don't ye notice how I walk? Heavens, man! I hed my ex sprung 'fore I was fifteen!"

Tunk referred often and proudly to this early springing of his "ex," by which he meant probably that horse violence had bent him askew.

"Well, you shall have a chance to drive her," said Trove, spreading his blanket. "But if I'd gone through what you have, I'd keep out of danger."

"I like it," said Tunk, with emphasis. "I couldn't live without it. Danger is a good deal like chawin' terbaccer—dum nasty 'til ye git used to it. Fer me it's suthin' like strawberry short-cake and allwus was. An' nerve, man, why jes' look a' there."

He held out a hand to show its steadiness.

"Very good," Trove remarked.

"Good? Why, it's jest as stiddy as a hitchin' post, an' purty nigh as stout. Feel there," said Tunk, swelling his biceps.

"You must be very strong," said Trove, as he felt the rigid arm.

"A man has t' be in the boss business, er he ain't nowheres. If they get wicked, ye've got t' put the power to 'em."

Tunk had only one horse to care for at the widow's, but he was always in "the hoss business."

Then Tunk lit his torch and went away. Trove lay down, pulled his blanket about him, and went to sleep.

XXIII

A NEW PROBLEM

When Trove woke in the morning, a package covered with white paper lay on the blanket near his hand. He rose and picked it up, and saw his own name in a strange handwriting on the wrapper. He turned it, looking curiously at seal and superscription. Tearing it open, he found to his great surprise a brief note and a roll of money. "Herein is a gift for Mr. Sidney Trove," said the note. "The gift is from a friend unknown, who prays God that wisdom may go with it, so it prove a blessing to both."

Trove counted the money carefully. There were $3000 in bank bills. He sat a moment, thinking; then he rose, and began searching for tracks around the shanty. He found none, however, in the dead leaves which he could distinguish from those of Tunk and himself.

"It must be from my father," said he,—a thought that troubled him deeply, for it seemed to bring ill news—that his father would never make himself known.

"He must have seen me last night," Trove went on. "He must even have been near me—so near he could have touched me with his hand. If I had only wakened!"

Irving Bacheller

He put the money in his pocket and made ready to go. He would leave at once in quest of Darrel and take counsel of him. It was early, and he could see the first light of the sun, high in the tall towers of hemlock. The forest rang with bird songs. He went to the brook near by, and drank of its clear, cold water, and bathed in it. Then he walked slowly to Robin's Inn, where Mrs. Vaughn had begun building a fire. She observed the troubled look in his face, but said nothing of it then. Trove greeted her and went to the stable to feed his mare. As he neared the door he heard a loud "Whoa." He entered softly, and the big barn, that joined the stable, began to ring with noise. He heard Tunk shouting "Whoa, whoa, whoa!" at the top of his voice. Peering through, he could see the able horseman leaning back upon a pair of reins tied to a beam in front of him. His cry and attitude were like those of a jockey driving a hard race. He saw Trove, and began to slow up.

"You are a brave man—there's no doubt of it," said the teacher.

"What makes ye think so?" Tunk inquired soberly, but with a glowing eye.

"If you were not brave, you'd scare yourself to death, yelling that way."

"It isn't possible, or Tunk would have perished long ago," said the widow, who had come to feed her chickens.

"It's enough to raise the neighbours," Trove added.

"There ain't any near neighbours but them over 'n the buryin'-ground, and they must be a little uneasy," said the widow.

"Used t' drive so much in races," said Tunk, "got t' be kind of a habit with me—seems so. Ain't eggzac'ly happy less I have holt o' the ribbons every day or two. Ye know I used t' drive ol' crazy Jane. She pulled like Satan. All ye had t' do was t' lean back an' let 'er sail."

"But why do you shout that way?"

"Scares the other hosses," Tunk answered, dropping the reins and tossing his whip aside. "It's a shame I have t' fool my time away up here on a farm."

He went to work at the chores, frowning with discontent. Trove watered and fed his mare and went in to breakfast. An hour later, he bade them all good-by, and set out for Allen's. A new fear began to weigh upon him as he travelled. Was this a part of that evil sum, and had his father begun now to scatter what he had never any right to touch? Whoever brought him that big roll of money had robbed him of his peace. Even his ribs, against which it chafed as he rode along, began to feel sore. Home at last, he put up the mare and went to tell his mother that he must be off for Hillsborough.

"My son," said she, her arms about his neck, "our eyes are growing dim and for a long time have seen little of you."

"And I feel the loss," Trove answered. "I have things to do there, and shall return tonight."

"You look troubled," was her answer. "Poor boy! I pray God to keep you unspotted of the world." She was ever fearing unhappy news of the mystery—that something evil would come out of it.

As Trove rode away he took account of all he owed those

good people who had been mother and father to him. What a pleasure it would give him to lay that goodly sum in the lap of his mother and bid her spend it with no thought of economy.

The mare knew him as one may know a brother. There was in her manner some subtle understanding of his mood. Her master saw it in the poise of her head, in the shift of her ears, and in her tender way of feeling for his hand. She, too, was looking right and left in the fields. There were the scenes of a boyhood, newly but forever gone. "That's where you overtook me on the way to school," said he to Phyllis, for so the tinker had named her.

She drew at the rein, starting playfully as she heard his voice, and shaking his hand as if to say, "Oh, master, give me the rein. I will bear you swiftly to happiness."

Trove looked down at her proudly, patting the silken arch of her neck. If, as Darrel had once told him, God took note of the look of one's horses, she was fit for the last journey. Arriving at Hillsborough, he tied her in the sheds and took his way to the Sign of the Dial. Darrel was working at his little bench. He turned wearily, his face paler than Trove had ever seen it, his eyes deeper under their fringe of silvered hair.

"An' God be praised, the boy!" said he, rising quickly. "Canst thou make a jest, boy, a merry jest?"

"Not until you have told me what's the matter."

"Illness an' the food o' bitter fancy," said the tinker, with a sad face.

"Bitter fancy?"

"Yes; an' o' thee, boy. Had I gathered care in the broad fields all me life an' heaped it on thy back, I could not have done worse by thee."

Darrel put his hand upon the boy's shoulder, surveying him from head to foot.

"But, marry," he added, "'tis a mighty thigh an' a broad back."

"Have you seen my father?"

"Yes."

There was a moment of silence, and Trove began to change colour.

"And what did he say?"

"That he will bear his burden alone."

Then, for a moment, silence and the ticking of the clocks.

"And I shall never know my father?" said Trove, presently, his lips trembling. "God, sir! I insist upon it. I have a right to his name and to his shame also." The young man sank upon a chair, covering his face.

"Nay, boy, it is not wise," said Darrel, tenderly. "Take thought of it—thou'rt young. The time is near when thy father can make restitution, ay, an' acknowledge his sin before the world. All very near to him, saving thyself, are dead. Now, whatever comes, it can do thee no harm."

"But I care not for disgrace; and often you have told me that I should live and speak the truth, even though it burn me to the bone."

"So have I, boy, so have I; but suppose it burn others to the bone. It will burn thy wife; an' thy children, an' thy children's children, and them that have reared thee, an' it would burn thy father most of all."

Trove was utterly silenced. His father was bent on keeping his own disgrace.

"Mind thee, boy, the law o' truth is great, but the law o' love is greater. A lie for the sake o' love—think o' that a long time, think until thy heart is worn with all fondness an' thy soul is ready for its God, then judge it."

"But when he makes confession I shall know, and go to him, and stand by has side," the young man remarked.

"Nay, boy, rid thy mind o' that. If ye were to hear of his crime, ye'd never know it was thy father's."

"It is a bitter sorrow, but I shall make the best of it," said Trove.

"Ay, make the best of it. Thou'rt now in the deep sea, an' God guide thee."

"But I ask your help—will you read that?" said Trove, handing him the mysterious note that came with the roll of money.

"An' how much came with it?" said Darrel, as he read the lines.

"Three thousand dollars. Here they are; I do not know what to do with them."

"'Tis a large sum, an' maybe from thy father," said Darrel, looking down at tile money. "Possibly, quite possibly it is from thy father."

"And what shall I do with the money? It is cursed; I can make no use of it."

"Ah, boy, of one thing be sure; it is not the stolen money. For many years thy father hath been a frugal man—saving, ever saving the poor fruit of his toil. Nay, boy, if it come o' thy father, have no fear o' that. For a time put thy money in the bank."

"Then my father lives near me—where I may be meeting him every day of my life?"

"No," said Darrel, shaking his head. Then lifting his finger and looking into the eyes of Trove, he spoke slowly and with deep feeling. "Now that ye know his will I warn ye, boy, seek him no more. Were ye to meet him now an' know him for thy father an' yet refuse to let him pass, I'd think thee a monster o' selfish cruelty."

XXIV

BEGINNING THE BOOK OF TROUBLE

The rickety stairway seemed to creak with surprise at the slowness of his feet as Trove descended. It was circus day, and there were few in the street. Neither looking to right nor left he hurried to the bank of Hillsborough and left his money. Then, mounting his mare, he turned to the wooded hills and went away at a swift gallop. When the village lay far behind them and the sun was low, he drew rein to let the mare breathe, and turned, looking down the long stairway of the hills. In the south great green waves of timber land, rose into the sun-glow as they swept over hill and mountain. Presently he could hear a galloping horse and a faint halloo down the valley, out of which he had just come. He stopped, listening, and soon a man and horse, the latter nearly spent with fast travel, came up the pike.

"Well, by Heaven! You gave me a hard chase," said the man.

"Do you wish to see me?" Trove inquired.

"Yes—my name is Spinnel. I am connected with the bank of Hillsborough. Your name is Trove—Sidney Trove?"

"Yes, sir."

"You deposited three thousand dollars today?"

"I did."

"Well, I've come to see you and ask a few questions. I've no authority, and you can do as you like about answering."

The man pulled up near Trove and took a note-book and pencil out of his pocket.

"First, how came you by that money?" said he, with some show of excitement in his manner.

"That is my business," said Trove, coolly.

"There's more or less truth in that," said the other. "But I'll explain. Night before last the bank in Milldam was robbed, and the clerk who slept there badly hurt. Now, I've no doubt you're all right, but here's a curious fact—the sum taken was about three thousand dollars."

Trove began to change colour. He dismounted, looking up at the stranger and holding both horses by the bit.

"And they think me a thief?" he demanded.

"No," was the quick reply. "They've no doubt you can explain everything."

"I'll tell you all I know about the money," said Trove. "But come, let's keep the horses warm."

They led them and, walking slowly, Trove told of his night in the sugar-bush. Something in the manner of Spinnel slowed his feet and words. The story was finished. They stopped, turning face to face.

"It's grossly improbable," Trove suggested thoughtfully.

"Well, it ain't the kind o' thing that happens every day or two," said the other. "If you're innocent, you won't mind my looking you over a little to see if you have wounds or weapons. Understand, I've no authority, but if you wish, I'll do it."

"Glad to have you. Here's a hunting-knife, and a flint, and some bird shot," Trove answered, as he began to empty his pockets.

Spinnel examined the hunting-knife and looked carefully at each pocket.

"Would you mind taking off your coat?" he inquired.

The young man removed his coat, uncovering a small spatter of blood on a shirt-sleeve.

"There's no use going any farther with this," said the young man, impatiently. "Come on home with me, and I'll go back with you in the morning and prove my innocence."

The two mounted their horses and rode a long way in silence.

"It is possible," said Trove, presently, "that the robber was a man that knew me and, being close pressed, planned to divert suspicion."

Save that of the stranger, there was no sleep at the little house in Brier Dale that night. But, oddly, for Mary and Theron Allen it became a night of dear and lasting memories of their son. He sat long with them under the pine trees, and for the first time they saw and felt his strength and were as children before it.

"It's all a school," said he, calmly. "An' I'm just beginning to study the Book of Trouble. It's full of rather tough problems, but I'm not going to flunk or fail in it."

XXV

THE SPIDER SNARES

Trove and Spinnel were in Hillsborough soon after sunrise the morning of that memorable day. The young man rapped loudly on the broad door at the Sign of the Dial, but within all was silent. The day before Darrel had spoken of going off to the river towns, and must have started. A lonely feeling came into the boy's heart as he turned away. He went promptly to the house of the district attorney and told all he knew of the money that he had put in the bank. He recounted all that took place the afternoon of his stay at Robin's Inn—the battles of the cocks, and the spider, and how the wounded fowl had probably sprinkled his sleeve with blood. In half an hour, news of the young man's trouble had gone to every house in the village. Soon a score of his schoolmates and half the faculty were at his side—there in the room of the justice. Theron Allen arrived at nine o'clock, although at that hour two responsible men had already given a bail-bond. After dinner, Trove, a constable, and the attorney rode to Robin's Inn. The news had arrived before them, but only the two boys and Tunk were at home. The latter stood in front of the stable, looking earnestly up the road.

"Hello," said he, gazing curiously at horse and men as they came up to the door. He seemed to be eyeing the attorney with hopeful anticipation.

"Tunk," said Trove, cheerfully, "you have a mournful eye."

Tunk advanced slowly, still gazing, both hands deep in his trousers pockets.

"Ez Tower just went by," said he, with suppressed feeling. "Said you was arrested fer murder."

"I presume you were surprised."

"Wal," said he, "Ez ain't said a word before in six months."

Tunk opened the horse's mouth and stood a moment, peering thoughtfully at his teeth.

"Kind of unexpected to be spoke to by Ez Tower," he added, turning his eyes upon them with the same curious look.

The interrogation of Tunk and the two boys began immediately. The story of the fowl corroborated, the sugar-bush became an object of investigation. Milldam was ten miles away, and it was quite possible for the young man to have ridden there and back between the hour when Tunk left him and that of sunrise when he met Mrs. Vaughn at her door. Trove and Tunk Hosely went with the officers down a lane to the pasture and thence into the wood by a path they followed that night to and from the shanty. They discovered nothing new, save one remarkable circumstance that baffled Trove and renewed the waning suspicion of the men of the law. On almost a straight line from bush to barn were tracks of a man that showed plainly where they came out of the grass upon the garden soil. Now, the strange part of it lay in this fact: the boots of Sidney Trove exactly fitted the tracks. They followed the footprints carefully into the meadow-grass

Irving Bacheller

and up to the stalk of mullen. Near the top of it was the abandoned home of the spider and around it were the four snares Trove had observed, now full of prey.

"Do not disturb the grass here," said Trove, "and I will prove to you that the tracks were made before the night in question. Do you see the four webs?"

"Yes," said the attorney.

"The tracks go under them," said Trove, "and must, therefore, have been made before the webs. I will prove to you that the webs were spun before two o'clock of the day before yesterday. At that hour I saw the spinner die. See, her lair is deserted."

He broke the stalk of mullen and the cables of spider silk that led away from it, and all inspected the empty lair. Then he told of that deadly battle in the grass.

"But these webs might have been the work of another spider," said the attorney.

"It matters not," Trove insisted, "for the webs were spun at least twelve hours before the crime. One of them contains the body of a red butterfly with starred wings. We cut the wings that day, and Miss Vaughn put them in a book she was reading."

Paul brought the wings, which exactly fitted the tiny torso of the butterfly. They could discern the footprints, one of which had broken the ant's road, while another was completely covered by the butterfly snare.

"Those tracks were made before the webs—that is evident," said the attorney. "Do you know who made the tracks?"

"I do not," was the answer of the young man.

Trove remained at Robin's Inn that night, and after the men had gone he recalled a circumstance that was like a flash of lightning in the dark of his great mystery.

Once at the Sign of the Dial his friend, the tinker, had shown him a pair of new boots. He remembered they were of the same size and shape as those he wore.

"We could wear the same boots," he had remarked to Darrel.

"Had I to do such penance I should be damned," the tinker had answered. "Look, boy, mine are the larger by far. There's a man coming to see me at the Christmas time—a man o' busy feet. That pair in your hands I bought for him."

"Day before yesterday," said Tunk, that evening, "I was up in the sugar-bush after a bit o' hickory, an' I see a man there, an' I didn't have no idee who 'twas. He was tall and had white hair an' whiskers an' a short blue coat. When I first see him he was settin' on a log, but 'fore I come nigh he got up an' made off."

Although meagre, the description was sufficient. Trove had no longer any doubt of this—that the stranger he had seen at Darrel's had been hiding in the bush that day whose events were now so important.

Whoever had brought the money, he must have known much of the plans and habits of the young man, and, the night before Trove's arrival at Robin's Inn, he came, probably, to the sugar woods, where he spent the next day in hiding.

The young man was deeply troubled. Polly and her mother sat well into the night with him, hearing the story of his life, which he told in full, saving only the sin of his father. Of that he had neither the right nor the heart to tell.

"God only knows what is the next chapter," said he, at last. "It may rob me of all that I love in this world."

"But not of me," said Polly, whispering in his ear.

"I wish I were sure of that," he answered.

XXVI

THE COMING OF THE CARS

That year was one of much reckoning there in the land of the hills. A year it was of historic change and popular excitement. To begin with, a certain rich man bought a heavy cannon, which had roared at the British on the frontier in 1812, and gave it to the town of Hillsborough. It was no sooner dumped on the edge of the little park than it became a target of criticism. The people were to be taxed for the expense of mounting it—"Taxed fer a thing we ain't no more need of than a bear has need of a hair-brush," said one citizen. Those Yankees came of men who helped to fling the tea into Boston harbour, and had some hereditary fear of taxes.

Hunters and trappers were much impressed by it. They felt it over, peering curiously into the muzzle, with one eye closed.

"Ye couldn't kill nuthin' with it," said one of them.

"If I was to pick it up an' hit ye over the head with it, I guess ye wouldn't think so," said another.

Familiarity bred contempt, and by and by they began to shoot at it from the tavern steps.

The gun lay rejected and much in the way until its buyer came to his own rescue and agreed to pay for the mounting. Then came another and more famous controversy as to which way they should "p'int" the gun. Some favoured one direction, some another, and at last, by way of compliment, they "p'inted" it squarely at the house of the giver on the farther side of the park. And it was loaded to the muzzle with envy and ingratitude.

The arrest of Sidney Trove, also, had filled the town with exciting rumours, and gossip of him seemed to travel on the four winds—much of it as unkind as it was unfounded.

Then came surveyors, and promoters of the railroad, and a plan of aiding it by bonding the towns it traversed. In the beginning horror and distrust were in many bosoms. If the devil and some of his angels had come, he might, indeed, for a time, have made more converts and less excitement.

"It's a delusion an' a snare," said old Colonel Barclay in a speech. "Who wants t' whiz through the air like a bullet? God never intended men to go slidin' over the earth that way. It ain't nat'ral ner it ain't common sense. Some say it would bring more folks into this country. I say we can supply all the folks that's nec'sary. I've got fourteen in my own family. S'pose ye lived on a tremendous sidehill that reached clear to New York City, so ye could git on a sled an' scoot off like a streak o' lightnin'. Do ye think ye'd be any happier? Do ye think ye'd chop any more wood er raise a bigger crop o' potatoes? S'pose ye could scoot yer crops right down t' Albany in a day. That would be all right if 'ye was the only man that was scootin', but if there was anything t' be made by it, there'd be more than a million sleds on the way, an' ye couldn't sell yer stuff for so much as ye git here. Some day ye'd come home and ask where's Ma an' Mary, and then Sam would say, 'Why, Mary's slid down t' New York, and the last

I see o' Ma she was scootin' for Rochester.'"

Here, the record says, Colonel Barclay was interrupted by laughter and a voice.

"Wal, if there was a railroad, they could scoot back ag'in," said the voice.

"Yes," the Colonel rejoined, "but mebbe after they'd been there a while ye'd wish they couldn't. Wal, you git your own supper, an' then Sam says, says he, 'I guess I'll scoot over t' Watertown and see my gal fer a few minutes.' An' ye sit by the fire a while, rockin' the twins, an' by and by yer wife comes back. An' ye say, 'Ma, why don't ye stay t' home?' 'Wal,' says she, 'it is so splendid, and there's so much goin' on.' An' Mary, she begins t' talk as if she'd bit her tongue, an' step stylish, an' hold up her dress like that, jest as though she was steppin' over a hot griddle. Purty soon it's dizzle-dazzle an' flippity-floppity an' splendiferous and sewperb, an' the first thing ye know ye ain't knee-high to a grasshopper. Sam he comes back an' tells Ed all about the latest devilment. You hear of it; then, mebbe, ye begin to limber up an' think ye'll try it yerself. An' some morning ye'll wake up an' find yer moral character has scooted. You fellers that go t' meetin' here an' talk about resistin' temptation—if you ever git t' goin' it down there in New York City, temptation 'll have to resist you. My friends, ye don't want to make it too easy fer everybody to go somewhere else. If ye do, by an' by there won't be nobody left here but them that's too old t' scoot er a few sickly young folks who don't care fer the sinful attractions o' this world."

Who shall say that old Colonel Barclay had not the tongue of a prophet?

"An' how about the cost?" he added in conclusion, "Fellow-citizens, ye'll have to pay five cents a mile fer yer scootin', an' a tax,—a tax, fellow-citizens, to help pay the cost o' the railroad. If there's anybody here that don't feel as if he'd been taxed enough, he ought t' be taxed fer his folly."

The dread of "scooting" grew for a time, but wise men were able to overcome it.

In 1850, the iron way had come through the wilderness and begun to rend the northern hills. Some were filled with awe, learning for the first time that in the moving of mountains giant-powder was more efficient than faith. Soon it had passed Hillsborough and was finished. Everybody came to see the cars that day of the first train. The track was lined with people at every village; many with children upon arms and shoulders. They waited long, and when the iron horse came roaring out of the distance, women fell back and men rolled their quids and looked eagerly up the track. It came on with screaming whistle and noisy brakes and roaring wheels. Children began to cry with fear and men to yell with excitement. Dogs were barking wildly, and two horses ran away, dragging with them part of a picket-fence. A brown shoat came bounding over the ties and broke through the wall of people, carrying many off their feet and creating panic and profanity. The train stopped, its engine hissing. A brakeman of flashy attire, with fine leather showing to the knees, strolled off and up the platform on high heels, haughty as a prince. Confusion began to abate.

"Hear it pant," said one, looking at the engine.

"Seems so it had the heaves," another remarked thoughtfully.

"Goes like the wind," said a passenger, who had just alighted. "Jerked us ten mile in less 'n twenty minutes."

"Folks 'll have to be made o' cast iron to ride on them air cars," said another. "I'd ruther set on the tail of a threshin'-machine. It gave a slew on the turn up yender, an' I thought 'twas goin' right over Bowman's barn. It flung me up ag'in the side o' the car, an' I see stars fer a minute. 'What's happened,' says I to another chap. 'Oh, we're all right,' says he. 'Be we?' says I, an' then I see I'd lost a tooth an' broke my glasses. 'That ain't nuthin',' says he, 'I had my foot braced over ag'in that other seat, an' somebody fell back on my leg, an' I guess the knee is out o' j'int. But I'm alive, an' I ain't got no fault to find. If I ever git off this shebang, I'm goin' out in the woods somewhere an' set down an' see what kind o' shape I'm in. I guess I'm purty nigh sp'ilt, an' it cost me fifty cents t' do it.'

"'An' all yer common sense, tew,' says I."

A number got aboard, and the train started. Rip Enslow was on the rear platform, his faithful hound galloping gayly behind the train. Some one had tied him to the brake rod. Nearly a score of dogs followed, barking merrily. Rip's hound came back soon, his tongue low, his tail between his legs. A number called to him, but he seemed to know his own mind perfectly, and made for the stream and lay down in the middle of it, lapping the shallow water, and stayed there for the rest of the afternoon.

A crowd of hunters watched him.

"Looks so he'd been ketched by a bear," said one.

In half an hour Rip returned also, a shoulder out of joint, a lump on his forehead, a big rent in his trousers. He was one, of those men of whom others gather wisdom, for, after that, everybody in the land of the hills knew better than to jump off the cars or tie his hound to the rear platform.

Irving Bacheller

And dogs came to know, after a little while, that the roaring dragon was really afraid of them and would run like a very coward if it saw a dog coming across the fields. Every small cur that lived in sight of it lay in the tall grass, and when he saw the dragon coming, chased him off the farm of his master.

Among those who got off the train at Hillsborough that day was a big, handsome youth of some twenty years. In all the crowd there were none had ever seen him before. Dressed in the height of fashion, he was a figure so extraordinary that all eyes observed him as he made his way to the tavern. Trove and Polly and Mrs. Vaughn were in that curious throng on the platform, where a depot was being built.

"My! What a splendid-looking fellow," said Polly, as the stranger passed,

Trove had a swift pang of jealousy that moment. Turning, he saw Riley Brooke—now known as the "Old Rag Doll"— standing near them in a group of villagers.

"I tell you, he's a thief," the boy heard him saying, and the words seemed to blister as they fell; and ever after, when he thought of them, a great sternness lay like a shadow on his brow.

"I must go," said he, calmly turning to Polly. "Let me help you into the wagon."

When they were gone, he stood a moment thinking. He felt as if he were friendless and alone.

"You're a giant to day," said a friend, passing him; but Trove made no answer. Roused incomprehensibly, his heavy muscles had become tense, and he had an odd consciousness of their power. The people were scattering, and he walked slowly down the street. The sun was low, but he thought not of home or where he should spend the night. It was now the third day after his arrest. Since noon he had been looking for Darrel, but the tinker's door had been locked for days, according to the carpenter who was at work below. For an hour Trove walked, passing up and down before that familiar stairway, in the hope of seeing his friend. Daylight was dim when the tinker stopped by the stairs and began to feel for his key. The young man was quickly at the side of Darrel.

"God be praised!" said the latter; "here is the old Dial an' the strong an' noble Trove. I heard o' thy trouble, boy, far off on the postroad, an' I have made haste to come to thee."

XXVII

THE RARE AND COSTLY CUP

Trove had been reciting the history of his trouble and had finished with bitter words.

"Shame on thee, boy," said the tinker, as Trove sat before him with tears of anger in his eyes. "Watch yonder pendulum and say not a word until it has ticked forty times. For what are thy learning an' thy mighty thews if they do not bear thee up in time o' trouble? Now is thy trial come before the Judge of all. Up with thy head, boy, an' be acquitted o' weakness an' fear an' evil passion."

"We deserve better of him," said Trove, speaking of Riley Brooke. "When all others hated him, we were kind to the old sinner, and it has done him no good."

"Ah, but has it done thee good? There's the question," said Darrel, his hand upon the boy's arm.

"I believe it has," said Trove, with a look of surprise.

"It was thee I thought of, boy; I had never much thought o' him."

That moment Trove saw farther into the depth of Darrel's heart than ever before. It startled him. Surely, here was a man that passed all understanding.

Darrel crossed to his bench and began to wind the clocks.

"Ho, Clocks!" said he, thoughtfully. "Know ye the cars have come? Now must we look well to the long hand o' the clock. The old, slow-footed hour is dead, an' now, boy, the minute is our king."

He came shortly and sat beside the young man.

"Put away thy unhappiness," said he, gently, patting the boy's hand. "No harm shall come to thee—'tis only a passing cloud."

"You're right, and I'm not going to be a fool," said Trove. "It has all brought me one item of good fortune."

"An' that is?"

"I have discovered who is my father."

"An' know ye where he is now?" the tinker inquired.

"No; but I know it is he to whom you gave the boots at Christmas time."

"Hush, boy," said Darrel, in a whisper, his hand raised.

He crossed to the bench, returning quickly and drawing his chair in front of the young man.

"Once upon a time," he whispered, sitting down and touching the palm of his open hand with the index finger of the other, "a youth held in his hand a cup, rare an' costly, an' it was full o' happiness, an' he was tempted to drink. 'Ho, there, me youth,' said one who saw him, 'that is the happiness of another.' But he tasted the cup, an' it was bitter, an' he let it fall, an' the other lost his great possession. Now that bitter taste was ever on the tongue o' the youth, so that his own cup had always the flavour o' woe."

The tinker paused a moment, looking sternly into the face of the young man.

"I adjure thee, boy, touch not the cup of another's happiness, or it may imbitter thy tongue. But if thou be foolish an' take it up, mind ye do not drop it."

"I shall be careful—I shall neither taste nor drop it," said Trove.

"God bless thee, boy! thou'rt come to a great law—who drains the cup of another's happiness shall find it bitter, but who drains the cup of another's bitterness shall find it sweet."

A silence followed, in which Trove sat looking at the old man whose words were like those of a prophet. "I have no longer any right to seek my father," he thought. "And, though I meet him face to face, I must let him go his way."

Suddenly there came a rap at the door, and when Darrel opened it, they saw only a letter hanging to the latch. It contained these words, but no signature:—

"There'll be a bonfire and some fun to-night at twelve, in the middle of Cook's field. Messrs. Trove and Darrel are invited."

"Curious," said Darrel. "It has the look o' mischief."

"Oh, it's only the boys and a bit of skylarking," said Trove. "Let's go and see what's up—it's near the time."

The streets were dark and silent as they left the shop. They went up a street beyond the village limits and looked off in Cook's field but saw no light there. While they stood looking a flame rose and spread. Soon they could see figures in the light, and, climbing the fence, they hastened across an open pasture. Coming near they saw a score of men with masks upon their faces.

"Give him the tar and feathers," said a strange voice.

"Not if he will confess an' seek forgiveness," another answered.

"Down to your knees, man, an' make no outcry, an' see you repeat the words carefully, as I speak them, or you go home in tar and feathers."

They could hear the sound of a scuffle, and, shortly, the phrases of a prayer spoken by one voice and repeated by another.

They were far back in the gloom, but could hear each word of that which follows: "O God, forgive me—I am a liar and a hypocrite—I have the tongue of scandal and deceit—I have robbed the poor—I have defamed the good—and, Lord, I am sick—with the rottenness of my own heart. And hereafter—I will cheat no more—and speak no evil of any one—Amen."

"Now, go to your home, Riley Brooke," said the voice, "an' hereafter mind your tongue, or you shall ride a rail in tar and feathers."

They could see the crowd scatter, and some passed near

them, running away in the darkness.

"Stoop there an' say not a word," the tinker whispered, crouching in the grass.

When all were out of hearing, they started for the little shop.

"Hereafter," said Darrel, as they walked along, "God send he be more careful with the happiness of other men. I do assure thee, boy, it is bitter, bitter, bitter."

XXVIII

DARREL AT ROBIN'S INN

Trove had much to help him,—youth, a cheerful tempera-
ment, a counsellor of unfailing wisdom. Long after they were
gone he recalled the sadness and worry of those days with
satisfaction, for, thereafter, the shock of trouble was never
able to surprise and overthrow him.

After due examination he had been kept in bail to wait the
action of the grand jury, soon to meet. Now there were none
thought him guilty—save one or two afflicted with the evil
tongue. It seemed to him a dead issue and gave him no
worry. One thing, however, preyed upon his peace,—the
knowledge that his father was a thief. A conviction was ever
boring in upon him that he had no right to love Polly. A base
injustice it would be, he thought, to marry her without telling
what he had no right to tell. But he was ever hoping for some
word of his father—news that might set him free. He had
planned to visit Polly, and on a certain day Darrel was to
meet him at Robin's Inn. The young man waited, in some
doubt of his duty, and that day came—one of the late
summer—when he and Darrel went afoot to the Inn, crossing
hill and valley, as the crow flies, stopping here and there at
isles of shadow in a hot amber sea of light. They sat long to
hear the droning in the stubble and let their thought drift

Irving Bacheller

slowly as the ship becalmed.

"Some days," said Darrel, "the soul in me is like a toy skiff, tossing in the ripples of a duck pond an' mayhap stranding on a reed or lily. An' then," he added, with kindling eye and voice, "she is a great ship, her sails league long an' high, her masthead raking the stars, her hull in the infinite sea."

"Well," said Trove, sighing, "I'm still in the ripples of the duck pond."

"An' see they do not swamp thee," said Darrel, with a smile that seemed to say, "Poor weakling, your trouble is only as the ripples of a tiny pool." They went on slowly, over green pastures, halting at a brook in the woods. There, again, they rested in a cool shade of pines, Darrel lighting his pipe.

"I envy thee, boy," said the tinker, "entering on thy life-work in this great land—a country blest o' God. To thee all high things are possible. Where I was born, let a poor lad have great hope in him, an' all—ay, all—even those he loved, rose up to cry him down. Here in this land all cheer an' bid him God-speed. An' here is to be the great theatre o' the world's action. Many of high hope in the broad earth shall come, an' here they shall do their work. An' its spirit shall spread like the rising waters, ay, it shall flood the world, boy, it shall flood the world."

Trove made no reply, but he thought much and deeply of what the tinker said. They lay back a while on the needle carpet, thinking. They could hear the murmur of the brook and a woodpecker drumming on a dead tree.

"Me head is busy as yon woodpecker's," Darrel went on. "It's the soul fire in this great, free garden o' God—it's America. Have ye felt it, boy?"

"Yes; it is in your eyes and on your tongue," said Trove.

"Ah boy! 'tis only God's oxygen. Think o' the poor fools withering on cracker barrels in Hillsborough an' wearing away 'the lag end o' their lewdness.' I have no patience with the like o' them, I'd rather be a butcher's clerk an' carry with me the redolence o' ham."

In Hillsborough, where all spoke of him as an odd man of great learning, there were none, saving Trove and two or three others, that knew the tinker well, for he took no part in the roaring gossip of shop and store.

"Hath it ever occurred to thee," said Darrel, as they walked along, "that a fool is blind to his folly, a wise man to his wisdom?"

When they were through the edge of the wilderness and came out on Cedar Hill, and saw, below them, the great, round shadow of Robin's Inn, they began to hasten their steps. They could see Polly reading a book under the big tree.

"What ho! the little queen," said Darrel, as they came near, "Now, put upon her brow 'an odorous chaplet o' sweet summer buds.'"

She came to meet them in a pretty pink dress and slippers and white stockings.

"Fair lady, I bring thee flowers," said Darrel, handing her a bouquet. "They are from the great garden o' the fields."

"And I bring a crown," said Trove, as he kissed her and put a wreath of clover and wild roses on her brow.

"I thought something dreadful had happened," said Polly, with tears in her eyes. "For three days I've been dressed up waiting."

"An' a grand dress it is," said Barrel, surveying her pretty figure.

"I've nearly worn it out waiting," said she, looking down, her voice trembling.

"Tut, tut, girl—'tis a lovely dress," the tinker insisted.

"It is one my mother wore when she was a girl," said Polly, proudly. "It was made over."

"O—oh! God love thee, child!" said the tinker, in a tone of great admiration. "'Tis beautiful."

"And, you came through the woods?" said Polly.

"Through wood and field," was Trove's answer.

"I wonder you knew the way."

"The little god o' love—he shot his arrows, an' we followed them as the hunter follows the bee," said Darrel.

"It was nice of you to bring the flowers," said Polly. "They are beautiful."

"But not like those in thy cheeks, dear child. Where is the good mother?" said Darrel.

"She and the boys are gone a-berrying, and I have been making jelly. We're going to have a party to-night for your birthday."

"'An' rise up before the hoary head an' honour the face o' the old man,'" said Darrel, thoughtfully. "But, child, honour is not for them that tinker clocks."

"'Honour and fame from no condition rise,'" said Polly, who sat in a chair, knitting.

"True, dear girl! Thy lips are sweeter than the poet's thought."

"You'll turn my head;" the girl was laughing as she spoke.

"An it turn to me, I shall be happy," said the tinker, smiling, and then he began to feel the buttons on his waistcoat. "Loves me, loves me not, loves me, loves me not—"

"She loves you," said Polly, with a smile.

"She loves me, hear that, boy," said the tinker. "Ah, were she not bespoke! Well, God be praised, I'm happy," he added, filling his pipe.

"And seventy," said Polly.

"Ay, three score an' ten—small an' close together, now, as I look off at them, like a flock o' pigeons in the sky."

"What do you think?" said Polly, as she dropped her knitting. "The two old maids are coming to-night."

"The two old maids!" said Darrel; "'tis a sign an' a wonder."

"Oh, a great change has come over them," Polly went on. "It's all the work o' the teacher. You know he really coaxed them into sliding with him last winter."

"I heard of it—the gay Philander!" said Darrel, laughing merrily. "Ah! he's a wonder with the maidens!"

"I know it," said Polly, with a sigh.

Trove was idly brushing the mat of grass with a walking-stick. He loved fun, but he had no conceit for this kind of banter.

"It was one of my best accomplishments," said he, blushing. "I taught them that there was really a world outside their house and that men were not all as lions, seeking whom they might devour."

Soon the widow and her boys came, their pails full of berries.

"We cannot shake hands with you," said Mrs. Vaughn, her fingers red with the berry stain.

"Blood o' the old earth!" said Darrel. "How fares the clock?"

"It's too slow, Polly says."

"Ah, time lags when love is on the way," Darrel answered.

"Foolish child! A little while ago she was a baby, an' now she is in love."

"Ah, let the girl love," said Darrel, patting the red cheek of Polly, "an' bless God she loves a worthy lad,"

"You'd better fix the clock." said Polly, smiling. "It is too fast, now."

"So is the beat o' thy heart," Darrel answered, a merry look in his eyes, "an' the clock is keeping pace."

Trove got up, with a laugh, and went away, the boys following.

"I'm worried about him," the widow whispered. "For a long time he hasn't been himself."

"It's the trouble—poor lad! 'Twill soon be over," said Darrel, hopefully.

There were now tears in the eyes of Polly.

"I do not think he loves me any more," said she, her lips trembling.

"Speak not so, dear child; indeed he loves thee."

"I have done everything to please him," said Polly, in broken words, her face covered with her handkerchief.

"I wondered what was the matter with you, Polly," said her mother, tenderly.

"Dear, dear child!" said the tinker, rising and patting her head. "The chaplet on thy brow an' thee weeping!—fairest flower of all!"

"I have wished that I was dead;" the words came in a little moan between sobs.

"Because: Love hath led thee to the great river o' tears? Nay, child, 'tis a winding river an' crosses all the roads."

He had taken her handkerchief, and with a tender touch was drying her eyes.

"Now I can see thee smiling, an' thy lashes, child—they are like the spray o' the fern tip when the dew is on it."

Polly rose and went away into the house. Darrel wiped his eyes, and the widow sat, her chin upon her hand, looking down sadly and thoughtfully. Darrel was first to speak.

"Did it ever occur to ye, Martha Vaughn, this child o' thine is near a woman but has seen nothing o' the world ?"

"I think of that often," said she, the mother's feeling in her voice.

"Well, if I understand him, it's a point of honour with the boy not to pledge her to marriage until she has seen more o' life an' made sure of her own heart. Now, consider this: let her go to the school at Hillsborough, an' I'll pay the cost."

The widow looked up at him without speaking.

"I'm an old man near the end o' this journey, an' ye've known me many years," Darrel went on. "There's nothing can be said against it. Nay; I'll have no thanks. Would ye thank the money itself, the bits o' paper? No; nor Roderick Darrel, who, in this business, is no more worthy o' gratitude. Hush! who comes?"

It was Polly herself in a short, red skirt, her arms bare to the elbows. She began to busy herself about the house.

"Too bad you took off that pretty dress, Polly," said Trove, when he returned.

She came near and whispered to him.

"This," said she, looking down sadly, "is like the one I wore when you first came."

"Well, first I thought of your arms," said he, "they were so lovely! Then of your eyes and face and gown, but now I think only of the one thing,—Polly."

The girl was happy, now, and went on with the work, singing, while Trove lent a hand.

A score of people came up the hill from Pleasant Valley that night. Tunk went after the old maids and came with them in the chaise at supper time. There were two wagon-loads of young people, and, before dusk, men and their wives came sauntering up the roadway and in at the little gate.

Two or three of the older men wore suits of black broadcloth, the stock and rolling collar—relics of "old decency" back in Vermont or Massachusetts or Connecticut. Most were in rough homespun over white shirts with no cuffs or collar. All gathered about Darrel, who sat smoking outside the door. He rose and greeted each one of the women with a bow and a compliment. The tinker was a man of unfailing courtesy, and one thing in him was extremely odd,—even there in that land of pure democracy,—he treated a scrubwoman with the same politeness he would have accorded the finest lady. But he was in no sense a flatterer; none that saw him often were long in ignorance of that. His rebuke was even quicker than his compliment, as many had reason to know. And there was another curious thing about Darrel,— these people and many more loved him, gathering about his chair as he tinkered, hearing with delight the lore and wisdom of his tongue, but, after all, there were none that knew him now any better than the first day he came. A certain wall of dignity was ever between him and them.

Half an hour before dark, the yard was thronged with people.

Irving Bacheller

They listened with smiles or a faint ripple of merry feeling as he greeted each.

"Good evening, Mrs. Beach," he would say. "Ah! the snow is falling on thy head. An' the sunlight upon thine, dear girl," he added, taking the hand of the woman's daughter.

"An' here's Mr. Tilly back from the far west," he continued. "How fare ye, sor?"

"I'm well, but a little too fat," said Thurston Tilly.

"Well, sor, unless it make thy heart heavy, be content."

"Good evening, Mrs. Hooper,—that is a cunning hand with the pies."

"Ah, Mrs. Rood, may the mouse never leave thy meal bag with a tear in his eye."

"Not a gray hair in thy head, Miss Tower, nor even a gray thought."

"An' here's Mrs. Barbour—'twill make me sweat to carry me pride now. How goes the battle?"

"The Lord has given me sore affliction," said she.

"Nay, dear woman," said the tinker in that tone so kindly and resistless, "do not think the Lord is hitting thee over the ears. It is the law o' life.

"Good evening, Elder, what is the difference between thy work an' mine?"

"I hadn't thought of that."

"Ah, thine is the dial of eternity—mine that o' time." And so he greeted all and sat down, filling his pipe.

"Now, Weston, out with the merry fiddle," said he, "an' see it give us happy thoughts."

A few small boys were gathered about him, and the tinker began to hum an Irish reel, fingers and forearm flying as he played an imaginary fiddle. But, even now, his dignity had not left him. The dance began. All were in the little house or at the two doors, peering in, save Darrel, who sat with his pipe, and Thurston Tilly, who was telling him tales of the far west. In the lull of sound that followed the first figure, Trove came to look out upon them. A big, golden moon had risen above the woods, and the light and music and merry voices had started a sleepy twitter up in the dome of Robin's Inn.

"Do you see that scar?" he heard Tilly saying.

"I do, sor."

"Well, a man shot me there."

"An' what for?" the tinker inquired.

"I was telling him a story. It cured me. Do you carry a gun?"

"I do not, sor."

"Wal, then, I'll tell you about the man I work for."

Tunk, who had been outside the door in his best clothes, but who, since he put them on, had looked as if he doubted the integrity of his suspenders and would not come in the house, began to laugh loudly.

"That man Tunk can see the comedy in all but himself," was Trove's thought, as he returned with a smile of amusement.

Soon Trove and Polly came out and stood a while by the lilac bush, at the gate.

"You worry me, Sidney Trove," said she, looking off at the moonlit fields.

Then came a silence full of secret things, like the silences of their first meeting, there by the same gate, long ago. This one, however, had a vibration that seemed to sting them.

"I am sorry," said he, with a sigh.

Another silence in which the heart of the girl was feeling for the secret in his.

"You are so sad, so different," she whispered.

Polly waited full half a minute for his answer. Then she touched her eyes with her handkerchief, turned impatiently, and went halfway to the door. Darrel caught her hand, drawing her near him.

"Give me thy hand, boy," said he to Trove, now on his way to the door.

He stood with his arms around the two.

"Every shadow hath the wings o' light," he whispered. "Listen."

The house rang with laughter and the music of Money Musk.

"'Tis the golden bell of happiness," said he, presently. "Go an' ring it. Nay—first a kiss."

He drew them close together, and they kissed each other's lips, and with smiling faces went in to join the dance.

XXIX

AGAIN THE UPHILL ROAD

Again the middle of September and the beginning of the fall term. Trove had gone to his old lodgings at Hillsborough, and Polly was boarding in the village, for she, too, was now in the uphill road to higher learning. None, save Darrel, knew the secret of the young man,—that he was paying her board and tuition. The thought of it made him most happy; but now, seeing her every day had given him a keener sense of that which had come between them. He sat much in his room and had little heart for study. It was a cosey room now. His landlady had hung rude pictures on the wall and given him a rag carpet. On the table were pieces of clear quartz and tourmaline and, about each window-frame, odd nests of bird or insect—souvenirs of wood-life and his travel with the drove. There, too, on the table were mementos of that first day of his teaching,—the mirror spectacles with which he had seen at once every corner of the schoolroom, the sling-shot and bar of iron he had taken from the woodsman, Leblanc.

One evening of his first week at Hillsborough that term, Darrel came to sit with him a while.

"An' what are these?" said the tinker, at length, his hand

upon the shot and iron.

"I do not know."

"Dear boy," said Darrel, "they're from the kit of a burglar, an' how came they here?"

"I took them from Louis Leblanc," said the young man, who then told of his adventure that night.

"Louis Leblanc!" exclaimed Darrel. "The scamp an' his family have cleared out."

The tinker turned quickly, his hand upon the wrist of the young man.

"These things are not for thee to have," he whispered. "Had ye no thought o' the danger?"

Trove began to change colour.

"I can prove how I came by them," he stammered.

"What is thy proof?" Darrel whispered again.

"There are Leblanc's wife and daughter."

"Ah, where are they? There be many would like to know."

The young man thought a moment.

"Well, Tunk Hosely, there at Mrs. Vaughn's."

"Tunk Hosely!" exclaimed the tinker, with a look that seemed to say, "God save the mark! An' would they believe him, think?"

Trove began to look troubled as Darrel left him.

"I'll go and drop them in the river," said Trove to himself.

It was eleven o'clock and the street dark and deserted as he left his room.

"It is a cowardly thing to do," the young man thought as he walked slowly, but he could devise no better way to get rid of them.

In the middle of the big, open bridge, he stopped to listen. Hearing only the sound of the falls below, Trove took the odd tools from under his coat and flung them over the rail.

He turned then, walking slowly off the bridge and up the main street, of Hillsborough. At a corner he stopped to listen. His ear had caught the sound of steps far behind him. He could hear it no longer, and went his way, with a troubled feeling that robbed him of rest that night. In a day or two it wore off, and soon he was hold of the bit, as he was wont to say, and racing for the lead in his work. He often walked to school with Polly and went to church with her every Sunday night. There had been not a word of love between them, however, since they came to the village, until one evening she said:—

"I am very unhappy, and I wish I were home."

"Why?"

She was not able to answer for a moment.

"I know I am unworthy of you," she whispered.

His lungs shook him with a deep and tremulous inspiration.

For a little he could not answer.

"That is why you do not love me?" she whispered again.

"I do love you," he said with a strong effort to control himself, "but I am not worthy to touch the hem of your garment."

"Tell me why, Sidney?"

"Some day—I do not know when—I will tell you all. And if you can love me after that, we shall both be happy."

"Tell me now," she urged.

"I cannot," said he, "but if you only trust me, Polly, you shall know. If you will not trust me—"

He paused, looking down at the snow path.

"Good night!" he added presently.

They kissed and parted, each going to the company of bitter tears.

As of old, Trove had many a friend,—school-fellows who came of an evening, now and then, for his help in some knotty problem. All saw a change in him. He had not the enthusiasm and good cheer of former days, and some ceased to visit him. Moreover they were free to say that Trove was getting a big head. For one thing, he had become rather careless about his clothes,—a new trait in him, for he had the gift of pride and the knack of neatness.

A new student sought his acquaintance the very first week of the term,—that rather foppish young man who got off the cars at Hillsborough the day of their first coming. He was from Buffalo, and, although twenty-two years of age, was preparing to enter college. His tales of the big city and his frank good-fellowship made him a welcome guest. Soon he was known to all as "Dick"—his name being Richard Roberts. It was not long before Dick knew everybody and everybody knew Dick, including Polly, and thought him a fine fellow. Soon Trove came to know that when he was detained a little after school Dick went home with Polly. That gave him no concern, however, until Dick ceased to visit him, and he saw a change in the girl.

One day, two letters came for Trove. They were in girlish penmanship and bore no signature, but stung him to the quick.

"For Heaven's sake get a new hat," said one.

"You are too handsome to neglect your clothes," said the other.

As he read them, his cheeks were burning with his shame. He went for his hat and looked it over carefully. It was faded, and there was a little rent in the crown. His boots were tapped and mended, his trousers threadbare at the knee, and there were two patches on his coat.

"I hadn't thought of it," said he, with a sigh. Then he went for a talk with Darrel.

"Did you ever see a more shabby-looking creature?" he inquired, as Darrel came to meet him. "I am so ashamed of myself I'd like to go lie in your wood box while I talk to you."

"'What hempen homespun have we swaggering here?'"

Darrel quoted in a rallying voice.

"I'll tell you." Trove began.

"Nay, first a roundel," said the tinker, as he began to shuffle his feet to the measure of an old fairy song.

"If one were on his way to the gallows, you would make him laugh," said Trove, smiling.

"An I could, so would I," said the old man. "A smile, boy, hath in it 'some relish o' salvation.' Now, tell me, what is thy trouble?"

"I'm going to leave school," said Trove.

"An' wherefore?"

"I'm sick of this pinching poverty. Look at my clothes; I thought I could make them do, but I can't."

He put the two notes in Darrel's hand. The tinker wiped his spectacles and then read them both.

"Tut, tut, boy!" said he, presently, with a very grave look. "Have ye forgotten the tatters that were as a badge of honour an' success? Weeks ago I planned to find thee better garments, but, on me word, I had no heart for it. Nay, these old ones had become dear to me. I was proud o' them—ay, boy, proud o' them. When I saw the first patch on thy coat, said I, 'It is the little ensign o' generosity.' Then came another, an', said I, 'That is for honour an' true love,' an' these bare threads—there is no loom can weave the like o' them. Nay, boy," Darrel added, lifting an arm of the young man and kissing one of the patches, "be not ashamed o' these— they're beautiful, ay, beautiful. They stand for the dollars ye gave Polly."

Trove turned away, wiping his eyes.

He looked down at his coat and trousers and began to wonder if he were, indeed, worthy to wear them.

"I'm not good enough for them," said he, "but you've put new heart in me, and I shall not give up. I'll wear them as long as I can make them do, and girls can say what they please."

"The magpies!" said Darrel. "When they have a thought for every word they utter, Lord! there'll be then a second Sabbath in the week."

Next evening Trove went to see Polly.

As he was leaving, she held his hand in both of hers and looked down, blushing deeply, as if there were something she would say, had she only the courage.

"What is it, Polly?" said he.

"Will you—will you let me buy you a new hat?" said she, soberly, and hesitating much between words.

He thought a moment, biting his lip.

"I'd rather you wouldn't, Polly," said he, looking down at the faded hat. "I know it's shabby, but, after all, I'm fond o' the old thing. I love good clothes, but I can't afford them now."

Then he bade her good night and came away.

XXX

EVIDENCE

It was court week, and the grand jury was in session. There were many people in the streets of the shire town. They moved with a slow foot, some giving their animation to squints of curiosity and shouts of recognition, some to profanity and plug tobacco. Squire Day and Colonel Judson were to argue the famous maple-sugar case, and many causes of local celebrity were on the calendar.

There were men with the watchful eye of the hunter, ever looking for surprises. They moved with caution, for here, indeed, were sights and perils greater than those of the timber land. Here were houses, merchants, lawyers, horse-jockeys, whiskey, women. They knew the thickets and all the wild creatures that lived in them, but these things of the village were new and strange. They came out of the stores and, after expectorating, stood a moment with their hands in their pockets, took a long look to the right and a long look to the left and threw a glance into the sky, and then examined the immediate foreground. If satisfied, they began to move slowly one way or the other and, meeting hunters presently, would ask:—

"Here fer yer bounties?"

"Here fer my bounties," another would say. Then they both took a long look around them.

"Wish't I was back t' the shanty."

"So do I."

"Scares me."

"Too many houses an' too many women folks."

"An' if ye wan' t' git a meal o' vittles, it costs ye three mushrats."

Night and morning the tavern offices were full of smart-looking men,—lawyers from every village in the county, who, having dropped the bitter scorn of the court room, now sat gossiping in a cloud of tobacco smoke, rent with thunder-peals of laughter and lightning flashes of wit. Teams of farmer folk filled the sheds and were tied to hitching-posts, up and down the main thoroughfare of the village. Every day rough-clad, brawny men led their little sons to the courthouse.

"Do ye see that man with the spectacles and the bald head?" they had been wont to whisper, when seated in the court room, "that air man twistin' his hair,—that's Silas Wright; an' that tall man that jes' sot down?—that's John L. Russell. Now I want ye t' listen, careful. Mebbe ye'll be a lawyer, some-time, yerself, as big as any of 'em."

The third day of that week—it was about the middle of the afternoon—a score of men, gossiping in the lower hall of the court building, were hushed suddenly. A young man came hurrying down the back stairs with a look of excitement.

"What's up?" said one.

"Sidney Trove is indicted," was the answer of the young man.

He ran out of doors and down the street. People began crowding out of the court room. Information, surprise, and conjecture—a kind of flood pouring out of a broken dam—rushed up and down the forty streets of the village. Soon, as of old, many were afloat and some few were drowning in it. For a little, busy hands fell limp and feet grew slow and tongues halted. A group of school-girls on their way home were suddenly overtaken by the onrushing tide. They came close together and whispered. Then a little cry of despair, and one of them fell and was borne into a near house. A young man ran up the stairway at the Sign of the Dial and rapped loudly at Darrel's door, Trove and the tinker were inside.

"Old fellow," said the newcomer, his hand upon Trove's arm, "they've voted to indict you, and I've seen all the witnesses."

Trove had a book in his hand. He rose calmly and flung it on the table.

"It's an outrage," said he, with a sigh.

"Nay, an honour," said Darrel, quickly. "Hold up thy head, boy. The laurel shall take the place o' the frown."

He turned to the bearer of these evil tidings.

"Have ye more knowledge o' the matter?"

"Yes, all day I have been getting hold of their evidence," said the newcomer, a law student, who was now facing his friend

Trove. "In the first place, it was a man of blue eyes and about your build who broke into the bank at Milldam. It is the sworn statement of the clerk, who has now recovered. He does not go so far as to say you are the man, but does say it was a man like you that assaulted him. It appears the robber had his face covered with a red bandanna handkerchief in which square holes were cut so he could see through. The clerk remembers it was covered with a little white figure— that of a log cabin. Such a handkerchief was sold years ago in the campaign of Harrison, but has gone out of use. Not a store in the county has had them since '45. The clerk fired upon him with a pistol, and thinks he wounded him in the left forearm. In their fight the robber struck him with a sling- shot, and he fell, and remembers nothing more until he came to in the dark alone. The skin was cut in little squares, where the shot struck him, and that is one of the strong points against you."

"Against me?" said Trove.

"Yes—that and another. It seems the robber left behind him one end of a bar of iron. The other end of the same bar and a sling-shot—the very one that probably felled the clerk—have been found."

The speaker rose and walked half across the room and back, looking down thoughtfully.

"I tell ye what, old fellow," said he, sitting down again, "it is mighty strange. If I didn't know you well, I'd think you guilty. Here comes a detective who says under oath that one night he saw you come out of your lodgings, about eleven o'clock, and walk to the middle of the bridge and throw something into the water. Next morning bar and shot were found. As nearly as he could make out they lay directly under the place where you halted."

Darrel sat looking thoughtfully at the speaker.

"A detective ?" said Trove, rising erect, a stern look upon him.

"Yes—Dick Roberts."

"Roberts, a detective!" said Trove, in a whisper. Then he turned to Darrel, adding, "I shall have to find the Frenchman."

"Louis Leblanc?" the young man asked.

"Louis Leblanc," Trove answered with surprise.

"He has been found," said the other.

"Then I shall be able to prove my point. He came to his home drunk one night and began to bully his family. I was boarding with the Misses Tower and went over and took the shot and iron from his hands and got him into bed. The woman begged me to bring them away."

"He declares that he never saw the shot or the iron."

Darrel rose and drew his chair a bit nearer.

"Very well, but there's the wife," said he, quickly.

"She will swear, too, that she never saw them."

"And how about the daughter?" Trove inquired.

"Run away and nowhere to be found," was the answer of the other young man. "I've told you bad news enough, but there's more, and you ought to know it all. Louis Leblanc is in

Quebec, and he says that a clock tinker lent him money with which to leave the States."

"It was I, an' God bring him to repentance—the poor beggar!" said Darrel. "He agreed to repay me within a fortnight an' was in sore distress, but he ran away, an' I got no word o' him."

"Well, the inference is, that you, being a friend of the accused, were trying to help him."

"I'm caught in a web," said Trove, leaning forward, his head upon his hands, "and Leblanc's wife is the spider. How about the money? Have they been able to identify it?"

"In part, yes; there's one bill that puzzles them. It's that of an old bank in New York City that failed years ago and went out of business."

Then a moment of silence and that sound of the clocks—like footsteps of a passing caravan, some slow and heavy, some quick, as if impatient to be gone.

"Ye speeding seconds!" said Darrel, as he crossed to the bench. "Still thy noisy feet."

Then he walked up and down, thinking.

The friend of Sidney Trove put on his hat and stood by the door.

"Don't forget," said he, "you have many friends, or I should not be able to tell you these things. Keep them to yourself and go to work. Of course you will be able to prove your innocence."

"I thank you with all my heart," said Trove.

"Ay, 'twas friendly," the old man remarked, taking the boy's hand.

"I have to put my trust in Tunk—the poor liar!" said Trove, when they were alone.

"No," Darrel answered quickly. "Were ye drowning, ye might as well lay hold of a straw. Trust in thy honour; it is enough."

"Let's go and see Polly," said the young man.

"Ay, she o' the sweet heart," said the tinker; "we'll go at once."

They left the shop, and on every street they travelled there were groups of men gossiping. Some nodded, others turned away, as the two passed. Dick Roberts met them at the door of the house where Polly boarded.

"I wish to see Miss Vaughn," said Trove, coolly.

"She is ill," said Roberts.

"Could I not see her for a moment?" Trove inquired.

"No."

"Is she very sick?"

"Very."

Darrel came close to Roberts. He looked sternly at the young man.

"Boy," said he, with great dignity, his long forefinger raised, "within a day ye shall be clothed with shame."

"They were strange words," Trove thought, as they walked away in silence; and when they had come to the little shop it was growing dusk.

"What have I done to bring this upon me and my friends?" said Trove, sinking into a chair.

"It is what I have done," said Darrel; "an' now I take the mantle o' thy shame. Rise, boy, an' hold up thy head."

The old man stood erect by the side of the young man.

"See, I am as tall an' broad as thou art."

He went to an old chest and got a cap and drew it down upon his head, pushing his gray hair under it. Then he took from his pocket a red bandanna handkerchief, figured with a cabin, tying it over his face. He turned, looking at Trove through two square holes in the handkerchief.

"Behold the robber!" said he.

"You know who is the robber?" Trove inquired.

Darrel raised the handkerchief and flung it back upon his head.

"'Tis Roderick Darrel," said he, his hand now on the shoulder of the young man.

For a moment both stood looking into each other's eyes.

"What joke is this, my friend?" Trove whispered.

"I speak not lightly, boy. If where ye thought were honour an' good faith, there be only guilt an' shame, can ye believe in goodness?"

For his answer there were silence and the ticking of the clocks.

"Surely ye can an' will," said the old man, "for there is the goodness o' thy own heart. Ah, boy, though I have it not, remember that I loved honour an' have sought to fill thee with it. This night I go where ye cannot follow."

The tinker turned, halting a pendulum.

Trove groaned as he spoke, "O man, tell me, quickly, what do you mean?"

"That God hath laid his hand upon me," said Darrel, sternly. "I cannot see thee suffer, boy, when I am the guilty one. O Redeemer o' the world! haste me, haste me now to punishment."

The young man staggered, like one dazed by the shock of a blow, stepped backward, and partly fell on a lounge against the wall. Darrel came and bent over him. Trove sat leaning, his hand on the lounge, staring up at the tinker, his eyes dreadful and amazed.

"You, you will confess and go to prison!" he whispered.

"Fair soul!" said the old man, stroking the boy's head, "think not o' me. Where I go there be flowers—lovely flowers! an' music, an' the bards an' prophets. Though I go to punishment, still am I in the Blessed Isles."

"You are doing it to save me," Trove whispered, taking the

hand of the old man. "I'll not permit it. I'll go to prison first."

"Am I so great a fool, think ye, as to claim an evil that is not mine? An' would ye keep in me the burning o' remorse when I seek to quench it? I warn thee, meddle not with the business o' me soul. That is between the great God an' me."

Darrel stood to his full height, the red handkerchief covering his head and falling on his back. He began with a tone of contempt that changed quickly into one of sharp command. There was a little silence and then a quick rap.

"Come in," Darrel shouted, as he let the handkerchief fall upon his face again.

The district attorney, a constable, and the bank clerk, who had been injured the night of the robbery, came in.

"He is not guilty," said Trove, rising quickly.

"I command ye, boy, be silent," said Darrel, sternly.

"Have ye ever seen that hand," he added, approaching the clerk, and pointing at a red mark as large as a dime on the back of his left hand.

"Yes," the clerk answered with surprise, looking from hand to handkerchief. Then, turning to the lawyer, he added, "This is the man."

"Now," Darrel continued, rolling up his sleeve, "I'll show where thy bullet struck me in the left arm. See, there it seared the flesh!"

They saw a star, quite an inch long, midway from hand to elbow,

"Do you mean to say that you are guilty of this crime?" the attorney asked.

"I am guilty and ready for punishment," Darrel answered. "Now, discharge the boy."

"To-morrow," said the attorney. "That is for the court to do."

Darrel went to Trove, who now sat weeping, his face upon his hands.

"Oh the great river o' tears!" said Darrel, touching the boy's head. "Beyond it are the green shores of happiness, an' I have crossed, an' soon shalt thou. Stop, boy, it ill becomes thee. There is a dear, dear child whose heart is breaking. Go an' comfort her."

Trove sat as if he had not heard. The tinker went to his table and hurriedly wrote a line or two, folding and directing it.

"Go quickly, boy, an' tell her, an' then take this to Riley Brooke for me."

The young man struggled a moment for self-mastery, rose with a sigh and a stern look, and put on his hat.

"It is about bail?" said he, in a whisper.

"Yes," Darrel answered.

Trove hurried away. A woman met him at the door, within which Polly boarded.

"Is she better?" Trove asked.

"Yes; but has asked me to say that she does not wish to

see you."

Trove stood a moment, his tongue halting between anger and surprise. He turned without a word, walking away, a bitter feeling in his heart.

Brooke greeted him with unexpected heartiness. He was going to bed when the young man rapped upon his door.

Brooke opened the letter and read the words aloud: "Thanks, I shall not need thy help."

"What!" Trove exclaimed.

"He says he shall not need the help I offered him," Brooke answered.

"Good night!" said Trove, who, turning, left the house and hurried away. Lights were out everywhere in the village now. The windows were dark at the Sign of the Dial. He hurried up the old stairs and rapped loudly, but none came to admit him. He called and listened; within there were only silence and that old, familiar sound of the seconds trooping by, some with short and some with long steps. He knew that soon they were to grow faint and weary and pass no more that way. He ran to the foot of the stairs and stood a moment hesitating. Then he walked slowly to the county jail and looked up at the dark and silent building. For a little time he leaned upon a fence, there in the still night, shaken with sobs. Then he began walking up and down by the jail yard. He had not slept an hour in weeks and was weary, but he could not bear to come away and walked slower as the night wore on, hearing only the tread of his own feet. He knew not where to go and was drifting up and down, like a derelict in the sea. By and by people began to pass him,—weary crowds,—and they were pointing at the patches on his coat, and beneath them he could feel a kind of burning, but the crowd was dumb. He tried to say, "I am not to blame," but his heart smote him when it was half said. Then, suddenly, many people were beside him, and far ahead on a steep hill, in dim, gray light, he could see Darrel toiling upward. And sometimes the tinker turned, beckoning him to follow. And Trove ran, but the way was long between them. And the tinker called to him; "Who drains the cup of another's bitterness shall find it sweet." Quickly he was alone, groping for his path in black darkness and presently coming down a stairway into the moonlit chamber of his inheritance. Then the men of the dark and a feeling of faintness and great surprise and a broad, blue field all about him and woods in the distance, and above the growing light of dawn. His bones were aching with illness and overwork, his feet sore. "I have been asleep," he said, rubbing his eyes, "and all night I have been walking."

He was in the middle of a broad field. He went on slowly and soon fell of weakness and lay for a time with his eyes closed. He could hear the dull thunder of approaching hoofs; then he felt a silky muzzle touching his cheek and the tickle of a horse's mane. He looked up at the animal, feeling her face and neck. "You feel like Phyllis, but you are not Phyllis—you are all white," said the young man, as he patted her muzzle. He could hear other horses coming, and quickly she, that was bending over him, reared with an open mouth and drove them away. She returned again, her long mane falling on his face. "Don't step on me," he entreated. "'Remember in the day o' judgment God'll mind the look o' yer master.'" He took hold of those long, soft threads, and the horse lifted him gently to his feet, and they walked, his arm about her neck, his face in the ravelled silk of her mane. "I don't know whose horse you are, even, or where you are taking me," he said. They went down a long lane and came at length to a bar-way, and Trove crawled through.

He saw near him a great white house—one he had never seen before—and a beautiful lady in the doorway. He turned toward her, and it seemed a long journey to the door, although he knew it was only a few paces. He fell heavily on the steps, and the woman gave a little cry of alarm. She came quickly and bent over him. His clothes were torn, his face pale and haggard, his eyes closed.

"I am sick," he whispered faintly.

"Theron! Theron! come here! Sidney is sick," he heard her calling.

"Is it you, mother?" the boy whispered, feeling her face. "I thought it was a great, white mansion here, and that you— that you were an angel."

XXXI

A MAN GREATER THAN HIS TROUBLE

For a month the young man lay burning with fever, his brain boiled in hot blood until things hideous and terrible were swarming out of it, as if it were being baned of dragons. Two months had passed before he was able to leave his bed. He remembered only the glow of an Indian summer morning on wood and field, but when he rose they were all white with snow. For weeks he had listened to the howl of the fir trees and had seen the frost gathering on his window, but knew not how swiftly the days had gone, so that when he looked out of doors and saw the midwinter he was filled with astonishment.

"I must go," said he.

"Not yet, my boy," said Mary Allen. "You, are not strong enough."

"Darrel has taken my trouble on him, and I must go."

"I have heard you say it often since you fell on the doorstep," said she, stroking his hand. "There is a letter from him;" and she brought the letter and put it in his hands. Trove opened it eagerly and read as follows:—

"DEAR SIDNEY: It is Sunday night and all day I have been walking in the Blessed Isles. And one was the Blessed Isle of remembrance where I met thee and we talked of all good things. If I knew it were well with thee I should be quite happy, boy, quite happy. I was a bit weary of travel and all the roads had grown long. I miss the tick of the clocks, but my work is easy and I have excellent good friends. I send thee my key. Please deliver the red, tall clock to Betsy Hale, who lives on the road to Waterbury Hill, and kindly take that cheerful youngster from Connecticut—the one with the walnut case and a brass pendulum—to Mrs. Henry Watson. You remember that ill-tempered Dutch thing, with a loud gong and a white dial, please take that to Harry Warner, I put some work on them all but there's no charge. The other clocks belong to me. Do with them as thou wilt and with all that is mine. The rent is paid to April. Then kindly surrender the key. Now can ye do all this for a man suffering the just punishment of many sins? I ask it for old friendship and to increase the charity I saw growing in thy heart long ago. At last I have word of thy father. He died a peaceful, happy death, having restored the wealth that cursed him to its owner. For his sake an' thine I am glad to know it. Now between thee and the dear Polly there is no shadow. Tell her everything. May the good God bless and keep thee; but the long road of Happiness, that ye must seek and find.

"Yours truly,
"R. DARREL of the Blessed Isles."

Trove read the letter many times, and, as he grew strong, he began to think with clearness and deliberation of his last night in Hillsborough. Darrel was the greatest problem of all. Pondering he saw, or thought he saw, the bottom of it. Events were coming, however, that robbed him utterly of his conceit and all the hope it gave him. The sad lines about his father kept him ever in some doubt. A week more, and he was in the cutter one morning, behind Phyllis, on his way to Robin's Inn. As he drew up at the old, familiar gate the boys ran out to meet him. Somehow they were not the same boys—they were a bit more sober and timid. Tunk came with a "Glad to see ye, mister," and took the mare. The widow stood in the doorway, smiling sadly.

"How is Polly?" said Trove.

For a moment there was no answer. He walked slowly to the steps, knowing well that some new blow was about to fall upon him.

"She is better, but has been very sick," said the widow.

Trove sat down without speaking and threw his coat open.

"You, too, have been very sick," said Mrs. Vaughn.

"Yes, very," said he.

"I heard of it and went to your home one day, but you didn't know me."

"Tell me, where is Polly?"

"In school, and I am much worried."

"Why?"

"Well, she's pretty, and the young men will not let her alone. There's one determined she shall marry him."

"Is she engaged?"'

"No, but—but, sir, I think she is nearly heartbroken."

"I'm sorry," said Trove. "Not that she may choose another, but that she lost faith in me."

"Poor child! Long ago she thought you had ceased to love her," said the widow, her voice trembling,

"I loved her as I can never love again," said he, his elbow resting on a table, his head leaning on his hand. He spoke calmly.

"Don't let it kill you, boy," said she.

"No," he answered. "A man must be greater than his trouble; I have work to do, and I shall not give up. May I go and see Polly?"

"Not now," said the widow, "give her time to find her own way. If you deserve her love it will return to you."

"I fear that you, too, have lost faith in me," said Trove.

"No," she answered, "but surely Darrel is not the guilty one. It's all such a mystery."

"Mrs. Vaughn, do not suffer yourself to think evil of me or of Darrel. If I do lose your daughter, I hope I may not lose your good opinion." The young man spoke earnestly and his eyes were wet.

"I shall not think evil of you," said the woman.

Trove stood a moment, his hand upon the latch.

"If there's anything I can do for you or for Polly," said he, "I should like to know it. Let's hope for the best. Some day you must let me come and—" he hesitated, his voice failing him for a moment, "and play a game of checkers," he added.

Paul stood looking up at him sadly, his face troubled.

"It's an evil day when the heart of a child is heavy," said Trove, bending over the boy. "What is the first law, Paul?"

"Thou shalt learn to obey," said the boy, quickly.

"And who is the great master?"

"Yourself."

"Right, boy! Let's command our hearts to be happy."

The great, bare maple was harping dolefully in the wind. Trove went for the mare, and Tunk rode down the hill with him in the cutter.

"Things here ain't what they used t' be," said Tunk.

"No?"

"Widder, she takes on awful. Great changes!"

There was a moment of silence.

"I ain't the same dum fool I used t' be," Tunk added presently.

"What's happened to you?"

"Well, they tol' me what you said about lyin'. Ye know a man in the hoss business is apt t' git a leetle careless, but I ain't no such dum fool as I used t' be. Have you heard that Teesey Tower was married?"

"The old maid?"

"Yes, sir; the ol' maid, to Deacon Haskins, an' he lives with 'em, an' now they're jes like other folks. Never was so surprised since I was first kicked by a hoss."

Tunk's conscience revived suddenly and seemed to put its hand over his mouth.

"Joe Beach is goin' to be a doctor," Tunk went on presently.

"I advised him to study medicine," Trove answered.

"He's gone off t' school at Milldam an' is workin' like a beaver. He was purty rambunctious 'til you broke him to lead."

They rode then to the foot of the hill in silence.

"Seems so everything was changed," Tunk added as he left the cutter. "Ez Tower has crossed the Fadden bridge. Team run away an' snaked him over. They say he don't speak to his hosses now."

Trove went on thoughtfully. Some of Tunk Hosely's talk had been as bread for his hunger, as a harvest, indeed, giving both seed and sustenance. More clearly than ever he saw before him the great field of life where was work and the joy of doing it. For a time he would be a teacher, but first there were other things to do.

XXXII

THE RETURN OF THURST TILLY

Trove sat in council with Mary and Theron Allen. He was now in debt to the doctor; he needed money, also, for clothing and boots and an enterprise all had been discussing.

"I'll give you three hundred dollars for the mare," said Allen.

Trove sat in thoughtful silence, and, presently, Allen went out of doors. The woman got her savings and brought them to her son.

"There is twenty-three dollars, an' it may help you," she whispered.

"No, mother; I can't take it," said the young man. "I owe you more now than I can ever pay. I shall have to sell the mare. It's a great trial to me, but—but I suppose honour is better than horses."

"Well, I've a surprise for you," said she, bringing a roll of cloth from the bedroom. "Those two old maids spun the wool, and I wove it, and, see, it's all been fulled."

"You're as good as gold, mother, and so are they. It's grand to wear in the country, but I'm going away and ought to have an extra good suit. I'd like to look as fine as any of the village boys, and they don't wear homespun. But I'll have plenty of use for it."

Next day he walked to Jericho Mills and paid the doctor. He went on to Milldam, buying there a handsome new outfit of clothing. Then he called to see the President of the bank—that one which had set the dogs of the law on him.

"You know I put three thousand dollars in the bank of Hillsborough," said Trove, when he sat facing the official. "I took the money there, believing it to be mine. If, however, it is yours, I wish to turn it over to you."

"It is not our money," said the President. "That bundle was sent here, and we investigated every bill—a great task, for there were some three hundred of them. Many are old bills and two the issue of banks gone out of business. It's all a very curious problem. They would not have received this money, but they knew of the robbery and suspected you at once. Now we believe absolutely in your honour."

"I shall put that beyond all question," said Trove, rising.

He took the cars to Hillsborough. There he went to the Sign of the Dial and built a fire in its old stove. The clocks were now hushed. He found those Darrel had written of and delivered them. Returning, he began to wind the cherished clocks of the tinker—old ones he had gathered here and there in his wandering—and to start their pendulums. One of them —a tall clock in the corner with a calendar-dial—had this legend on the inner side of its door:—

"Halted in memory of a good man,

Its hands pointing to the moment of his death,
Its voice hushed in his honour."

Trove shut the door of the old clock and hurried to the public attorney's office, where he got the address of Leblanc. He met many who shook his hand warmly and gave him a pleasant word. He was in great fear of meeting Polly, and thought of what he should do and say if he came face to face with her. Among others he met the school principal.

"Coming back to work?" the latter inquired.

"No, sir; I've got to earn money."

"We need another teacher, and I'll recommend you."

"I'm much obliged, but I couldn't come before the fall term," said Trove.

"I'll try to keep the place for you," said his friend, as they parted.

Trove came slowly down the street, thinking how happy he could be now, if Darrel were free and Polly had only trusted him. Near the Sign of the Dial he met Thurston Tilly.

"Back again?" Trove inquired.

"Back again. Boss gi'n up farmin'."

"Did he make his fortune?"

"No, he had one give to him."

"Come and tell me about it."

Tilly followed Trove up the old stairway into the little shop.

"Beg yer pardon," said Thurst, turning, as they sat down, "are you armed?"

"No," said Trove, smiling.

"A man shot me once when I wan't doin' nothin' but tryin' t' tell a story, an' I don't take no chances. Do you remember my boss tellin' that night in the woods how he lost his money in the fire o' '35?"

"Yes."

"Wal, I guess it had suthin' t' do with that. One day the boss an' me was out in the door-yard, an' a stranger come along. 'You're John Thompson,' says he to the boss; 'An' you're so an' so,' says the boss. I don't eggzac'ly remember the name he give." Tilly stopped to think.

"Can you describe him?" Trove inquired.

"He was a big man with white whiskers an' hair, an' he wore light breeches an' a short, blue coat."

"Again the friend of Darrel," Trove thought.

"Did you tell the tinker about your boss the night we were all at Robin's Inn last summer?"

"I told him the whole story, an' he pumped me dry. I'd answer him, an' he'd holler 'Very well,' an' shoot another question at me."

"Well, Thurst, go on with your story."

"Couldn't tell ye jest what happened. They went off int' the house. Nex' day the boss tol' me he wa'n't no longer a poor man an' was goin' t' sell his farm an' leave for Califurny. In a tavern near where we lived the stranger died sudden that night, an' the funeral was at our house, an' he was buried there in Iowy."

Trove walked to the bench and stood a moment looking out of a window.

"Strange!" said he, returning presently with tearful eyes. "Do you remember the date?"

"'Twas a Friday, 'bout the middle o' September."

Trove turned, looking up at the brazen dial of the tall clock. It indicated four-thirty in the morning of September 19th.

"Were there any with him when he died?"

"Yes, the tavern keeper—it was some kind of a stroke they told me."

"And your boss—did he go to California?" Trove asked.

"He sold the farm an' went to Californy. I worked there a while, but the boss an' me couldn't agree, an' so I pulled up an' trotted fer home."

"To what part of California did Thompson go?"

"Hadn't no idee where he would stick his stakes. He was goin' in t' the gold business."

Trove sat busy with his own thoughts while Thurston Tilly, warming to new confidence, boiled over with enthusiasm for the far west. A school friend of the boy came, by and by, whereupon Tilly whistled on his thumb and hurried away.

"Did you know," said the newcomer, when Trove and he were alone, "that Roberts—the man who tried to send you up—is a young lawyer and is going to settle here? He and Polly are engaged."

"Engaged!"

"So he gave me to understand."

"Well, if she loves him and he's a good fellow, I 've no right to complain," Trove answered.

"I don't believe that he's a good fellow," said the other.

"Why do you say that?"

"Well, a detective is—is—"

"A necessary evil?" Trove suggested.

"Just that," said the other. "He must pretend to be what he isn't and—well, a gentleman is not apt to sell himself for that purpose, Now he's trying to convince people that you knew as much about the crime as Darrel. In my opinion he isn't honest. Good looks and fine raiment are all there is to that fellow—take my word for it."

"You're inclined to judge him harshly," said Trove. "But I'm worried, for I fear he's unworthy of her and—and I must leave town to-morrow."

"Shall you go to see her?"

"No; not until I know more about him. I have friends here and they will give her good counsel. Soon they'll know what kind of a man he is, and, if necessary, they'll warn her. I'm beset with trouble, but, thank God, I know which way to turn."

XXXIII

THE WHITE GUARD

Next morning Trove was on his way to Quebec—a long, hard journey in the wintertime, those days. Leblanc had moved again,—so they told him in Quebec,—this time to Plattsburg of Clinton County, New York. There, however, Trove was unable to find the Frenchman. A week of patient inquiry, then, leaving promises of reward for information, he came away. He had yet another object of his travels—the prison at Dannemora—and came there of a Sunday morning late in February. Its towers were bathed in sunlight; its shadows lay dark and far upon the snow. Peace and light and silence had fallen out of the sky upon that little city of regret, as if to hush and illumine its tumult of dark passions. He shivered in the gloom of its shadow as he went up a driveway and rang a bell. The warden received him kindly.

"I wish to see Roderick Darrel,—he is my friend,' said Trove, as he gave the warden a letter.

"Come with me," said the official, presently. "He is talking to the men."

They passed through gloomy corridors to the chapel door. Trove halted to compose himself, for now he could hear the voice of Darrel.

"Let me stand here a while—I cannot go in now," he whispered.

The words of the old man were vibrant with colour and dramatic force.

"Night!" he was saying, "the guard passes; the lights are out; ye lie thinking. Hark! a bell! 'Tis in the golden city o' remembrance. Ye hear it calling. Haste away, men, haste away. Ah, look!—flowers by the roadside! an' sunlight, an', just ahead, spires o' the city, an' beneath them—oh! what is there beneath them ye go so many times to see?

"Who is this?"

"Here is a man beside ye."

"'Halt!' he says, an cuts ye with a sword."

"Now the bell is tolling—the sky overcast. The spires fall, the flowers wither. Ye turn to look at the man. He is a giant. See the face of him now. It makes ye tremble. He is the White Guard an' he brings ye back. Ah, then, mayhap ye rise in the dark, as I have heard ye, an' shake the iron doors. But ye cannot escape him though ye could fly on the wind. Know ye the White Guard? Dear man! his name is thy name; he is thyself; day an' night he sits in the watch tower o' thy soul; he has all charge o' thee. Make a friend o' him, men, make a friend o' him. Any evening send for me, an' mayhap they'll let me come an' tell thee how."

He paused. Trove could hear the tread of guards in the chapel. They seemed to enter the magnetic field of the speaker and quickly halted.

"Mind the White Guard! Save him ye have none to fear."

"Once, at night, I saw a man smiling in his sleep. 'Twas over there in the hospital. The day long he had been sick with remorse, an' I had given him, betimes, a word o' comfort as well as the medicine. Now when I looked the frown had left his brow. Oh, 'twas a goodly sight to see! He smiled an' murmured o' the days gone. The man o' guilt lay dead—the child of innocence was living. An' he woke, an' again the shadow fell upon him, an' he wept.

"'I have been wandering in the land o' love,' he said."

"'Get thee back, man, get thee back,' said I to him."

"'Alas! how can I?' said he; 'for 'tis only Sleep that opens the door.'"

"'Nay, Sleep doth lift the garment o' thy bitterness, but only for an hour,' said I. 'Love, Love shall lift it from thee forever.' An' now, I thank the good God, the smile o' that brief hour is ever on his face. Ye know him well, men. Were I to bid him stand before ye, there's many here would wish to kiss his hand. Even here in the frowning shadow o' these walls he has come into a land o' love, an' when he returns to his people ye shall weep, men, ye shall weep, an' they shall rejoice. O the land o' love! it hath a strong gate. An' the White Guard, he hath the key."

"Remember, men, ye cannot reap unless ye sow. If any would reap the corn, he must plant the corn."

"Have ye stood of a bright summer day to watch the little people o' the field?—those millions that throng the grass an' fly in the sunlight—bird an' bee an' ant an' bug an' butterfly? 'Tis a land flowing with milk an' honey—but hear me, good men, not one o' them may take as much as would fill the mouth of a cricket unless he pays the price.

"One day I saw an ant trying to rob a thistle-blow. Now the law o' the field is that none shall have honey who cannot sow for the flower. While a bee probes he gathers the seed-dust in his hairy jacket, an' away he flies, sowing it far an' wide. Now, an ant is in no-wise able to serve a thistle-blow, but he is ever trying to rob her house. Knowing her danger, she has put around it a wonderful barricade. Down at the root her stem has a thicket o' fuzz an' hair. I watched the little thief, an' he was a long time passing through it. Then he came on a barrier o' horny-edged leaves. Underneath they were covered with thick, webby hairs an' he sank over his head in them an' toiled long; an' lo! when he had passed them there was yet another row o' leaves curving so as to weary an' bewilder him, an' thick set with thorns. Slowly he climbed, coming ever to some dread obstruction. By an' by he stood looking up at the green, round wall o' the palace. Above him were its treasure an' its purple dome. He started upward an' fell suddenly into a moat, full o' sticky gum, an' there perished. Men, 'tis the law o' God: unless ye sow the seed that bears it, ye shall not have the honey o' forgiveness. An' remember the seed o' forgiveness is forgiveness. If any have been hard upon thee, bearing false witness an' robbing thee o' thy freedom an' thy good name, go not hence until ye forgive.

"Ah, then the White Guard shall no longer sit in the tower."

The voice had stopped. There was a moment of deep silence. Some power, greater, far greater, than his words, had gone out of the man. Those many who sat before him and they standing there by the door had felt it and were deeply moved. There was a quick stir in the audience—a stir of hands and handkerchiefs. Trove entered; the chaplain was now reading a hymn. Darrel sat behind him on a raised platform, the silken spray upon his brows, long and white as snow, his face thoughtful and serious. The reading over, he came and sat among the men, singing as they sang. The benediction, a stir of feet, and the prisoners began to press about him, some kissing his hands. He gave each a kindly greeting. It was like the night of the party on Cedar Hill. A moment more, and the crowd was filing away, some looking back curiously at Trove, who stood, his arms about the old man.

"Courage, boy!" the latter was saying; "I know it cuts thee like a sword, an' would to God I could have spared thee even this. Look! in yon high window I can see the sunlight, an', believe me, there is not a creature it shines upon so happy as I. God love thee, boy, God love thee!"

He put his cheek upon that of the boy and stroked his hair gently. Then a little time of silence, and the storm had passed.

"A fine, fine lad ye are," said Darrel, looking proudly at the young man, who stood now quite composed. "Let me take thy hand. Ay, 'tis a mighty arm ye have, an' some day, some day it will shake the towers."

"You will both dine with me in my quarters at one," said the warden, presently.

Trove turned with a look of surprise.

"Thank ye, sor; an' mind ye make room for Wit an' Happiness," said the tinker.

"Bring them along—they're always welcome at my table," the warden answered with a laugh.

"Know ye not they're in prison, now, for keeping bad

company?" said Darrel, as he turned. "At one, boy," he, added, shaking the boy's hand. "Ah, then, good cheer an' many a merry jest."

Darrel left the room, waving his hand. Trove and the warden made their way to the prison office.

"A wonderful man!" said the latter, as they went. "We love and respect him and give him all the liberty we can. For a long time he has been nursing in the hospital, and when I see that he is overworking I bring him to my office and set him at easy jobs."

Darrel came presently, and they went to dinner. The tinker bowed politely to the warden's wife and led her to the table.

"Good friends," said he, as they were sitting down, "there is an hour that is short o' minutes an' yet holds a week o' pleasure—who pan tell me which hour it is?"

"I never guessed a riddle," said the woman.

"Marry, dear madam, 'tis the hour o' thy hospitality," said the old man.

"When you are in it," she answered with good humour.

"Fellow-travellers on the road to heaven," said Darrel, raising his glass, "St. Peter is fond of a smiling face."

"And when you see him you'll make a jest," were the words of the warden.

"For I believe he is a lover o' good company," said Darrel.

The warden's wife remarked, then, that she had enjoyed his

talk in the chapel.

"I'm a new form o' punishment," said Darrel, soberly.

"But they all enjoy it," she answered.

"I'm not so rough as the ministers. They use fire an' the fume o' sulphur."

"And the men go to sleep."

"Ay, the cruel master makes a thick hide," said Darrel, quickly. "So Nature puts her hand between the whip an' the horse, an' sleep between cruelty an' the congregation."

"Nature is kind," was the remark of the warden.

"An' shows the intent o' the Almighty," said Darrel. "There are two words. In them are all the sermons."

"And what are they?" the woman asked.

"Fear," Darrel answered thoughtfully; "that is one o' them." He paused to sip his tea.

"And the other is?"

"Love."

There was half a moment of silence.

"Here's Life to Love an' Death to Fear," the tinker added, draining his cup. "Ay, madam, fill again—'tis memorable tea."

The woman refilled his cup.

"Many a time I've sat at meat an' thought, O that mine enemy could taste thy tea! But this, dear lady, this beverage is for a friend."

So the dinner went on, others talking only to encourage the tongue of Darrel. Trove, well as he knew the old man, had been surprised by his fortitude. Far from being broken, the spirit in him was happy, masterful, triumphant. He had work to do and was earning that high reward of happiness—to him the best thing under heaven. The dinner over, all rose, and Darrel bowed politely to the warden's wife. Then he quoted:—

"'Like as the waves make toward the pebbled shore,
So do our minutes hasten to their end.'"

"Dear madam, they do hasten but to come as well as to go. Thanks an' au revoir."

Darrel and Trove went away with the warden, who bade them sit a while in his office. Tinker and young man were there talking until the day was gone. The warden sat apart, reading. Now and again they whispered earnestly, as if they were not agreed, Darrel shaking his forefinger and his head, Trove came away as the dark fell, a sad and thoughtful look upon him.

XXXIV

MORE EVIDENCE

Trove went to the inn at Dannemora that evening he left Darrel and there found a letter. It said that Leblanc was living near St. Albans. Posted in Plattsburg and signed "Henry Hope," the letter gave no hint of bad faith, and with all haste he went to the place it named. He was there a fortnight, seeking the Frenchman, but getting no word of him, and then came a new letter from the man Hope. It said now that Leblanc had moved on to Middlebury. Trove went there, spent the last of his money, and sat one day in the tavern office, considering what to do; for now, after weeks of wandering, he was, it seemed, no nearer the man he sought. He had soon reached a thought of some value: this information of the unknown correspondent was, at least, unreliable, and he would give it no further heed. What should he do? On that point he was not long undecided, for while he was thinking of it a boy came and said:

"There's a lady waiting to see you in the parlour, sir."

He went immediately to the parlour above stairs, and there sat Polly in her best gown—"the sweetest-looking creature," he was wont to say, "this side of Paradise." Polly rose, and his amazement checked his feet a moment. Then he advanced quickly and would have kissed her, but she turned her face away and Stood looking down. They were in a silence full of history. Twice she tried to speak, but an odd stillness followed the first word, giving possibly the more adequate expression to her thoughts.

"How came you here?" he whispered presently.

"I—I have been trying to find you." said she, at length.

He turned, looking from end to end of the large room; they were quite alone.

"Polly," he whispered, "I believe you do love me."

For a little time she made no answer.

"No," she whispered, shaking her head; "that is, I—I do not think I love you."

"Then why have you come to find me?"

"Because—because you did not come to find me," she answered, glancing down at the toe of her pretty shoe.

She turned impatiently and stood by an open window. She was looking out upon a white orchard. Odours of spring flower and apple blossom were in the soft wings of the wind. Somehow they mingled with her feeling and were always in her memory of that hour. Her arm moved slowly and a 'kerchief went to her eyes. Then, a little tremor in the plume upon her hat Trove went to her side.

"Dear Polly!" he said, as he took her hand in his. Gently she pulled it away.

"I—I cannot speak to you now," she whispered.

Then a long silence. The low music of a million tiny wings came floating in at the window. It seemed, somehow, like a voice of the past, with minutes, like the bees, hymning indistinguishably. Polly and Trove were thinking of the same things. "I can doubt him no more," she thought, "and I know—I know that he loves me." They could hear the flutter of bird wings beyond the window and in the stillness they got some understanding of each other. She turned suddenly, and went to where he stood.

"Sidney," she said, "I am sorry—I am sorry if I have hurt you."

She lifted one of his hands and pressed her red cheek upon it fondly. In a moment he spoke.

"Long ago I knew that you were doubting me, but I couldn't help it," he said.

"It was that—that horrible secret," she whispered.

"I had no, right to your love," said he, "until—" he hesitated for a little, "until I could tell you the truth."

"You loved somebody else?" she whispered, turning to him. "Didn't you, now? Tell me."

"No," said he, calmly. "The fact is—the fact is I had learned that my father was a thief."

"Your father!" she answered. "Do you think I care what your father did? Your honour and your love were enough for me."

"I did not know," he whispered, "and I should have made my

way to you, but—" he paused again.

"But what?" she demanded, impatiently.

"Well, it was only fair you should have a chance to meet others, and I thought you were in love with Roberts."

"Roberts! He would have been glad of my love, I can tell you that." She looked up at him. "I have endured much for you, Sidney Trove, and I cannot keep my secret any longer. He says that Darrel is now in prison for your crime."

"And you believe him?" Trove whispered.

"Not that," she answered quickly, "but you know I loved the dear old man; I cannot think him guilty any more than I could think it of you. But there's a deep mystery in it all. It has made me wretched. Every one thinks you know more than you have told about it."

"A beautiful mystery!" the young man whispered. "He thought I should be convicted—who wouldn't? I think he loved me, so that he took the shame and the suffering and the prison to save me."

"He would have died for you," she answered; "but, Sidney, it was dreadful to let them take him away. Couldn't you have done something?"

"Something, dear Polly! and I with a foot in the grave?"

"Where did you go that night?"

"I do not know; but in the morning I found myself in our great pasture and was ill. Some instinct led me home, and, as usual, I had gone across lots." Then he told the story of that day and night and the illness that followed.

"I, too, was ill," said Polly, "and I thought you were cruel not to come to me. When I began to go out of doors they told me you were low with fever. Then I got ready to go to you, and that very day I saw you pass the door. I thought surely you would come to see me, but—but you went away."

Polly's lips were trembling, and she covered her eyes a moment with her handkerchief.

"I feared to be unwelcome," said he.

"You and every one, except my mother, was determined that I should marry Roberts," Polly went on. "He has been urgent, but you, Sidney, you wouldn't have me. You have done everything you could to help him. Now I've found you, and I'm going to tell you all, and you've got to listen to me. He has proof, he says, that you are guilty of another crime, and—and he says you are now a fugitive trying to escape arrest."

A little silence followed, in which Trove was thinking of the Hope letters and of Roberts' claim that he was engaged to Polly.

"You have been wrapped in mysteries long enough. I shall not let you go until you explain," she continued.

"There's no mystery about this," said Trove, calmly. "Roberts is a rascal, and that's the reason I'm here."

She turned quickly with a look of surprise.

"I mean it. He knows I am guilty of no crime, but he does know that I am looking for Louis Leblanc, and he has fooled me with lying letters to keep me out of the way and win you with his guile."

A serious look came into the eyes of Polly.

"You are looking for Louis Leblanc," she whispered.

"Yes; it is the first move in a plan to free Darrel, for I am sure that Leblanc committed the crime. I shall know soon after I meet him."

"How?"

"If he should have a certain mark on the back of his left hand and were to satisfy me in two other details, I'd give my life to one purpose,—that of making him confess. God help me! I cannot find the man. But I shall not give up; I shall go and see the Governor."

Turning her face away and looking out of the window, she felt for his hand. Then she pressed it fondly. That was the giving of all sacred things forever, and he knew it. He was the same Sidney Trove, but never until that day had she seen the full height of his noble manhood, ever holding above its own the happiness of them it loved. Suddenly her heart was full with thinking of the power and beauty of it.

"I do love you, Polly," said Trove, at length. "I've answered your queries,—all of them,—and now it's my turn. If we were at Robin's Inn, I should put my arms about you, and I should not let you go until—until you had promised to be my wife."

"And I should not promise for at least an hour," said she, smiling, as she turned, her dark eyes full of their new discovery. "Let us go home."

"I'm going to be imperative," said he, "and you must answer before I will let you go—"

"Dear Sidney," said she, "let's wait until we reach home. It's too bad to spoil it here. But—" she whispered, looking about the room, "you may kiss me once now."

"It's like a tale in *Harper's*," said he, presently. "It's 'to be continued,' always, at the most exciting passage."

"I shall take the cars at one o'clock," said she, smiling. "But I shall not allow you to go with me. You know the weird sisters."

"It would be impossible," said Trove. "I must get work somewhere; my money is gone."

"Money!" said she, opening her purse. "I'm a Lady Bountiful. Think of it—I've two hundred dollars here. Didn't you know Riley Brooke cancelled the mortgage? Mother had saved this money for a payment."

"Cancelled the mortgage!" said Trove.

"Yes, the dear old tinker repaired him, and now he's a new man. I'll give you a job, Sidney."

"What to do?"

"Go and see the Governor, and then—and then you are to report to me at Robin's Inn. Mind you, there's to be no delay, and I'll pay you—let's see, I'll pay you a hundred dollars."

Trove began to laugh, and thought of this odd fulfilling of the ancient promises.

"I shall stay to-night with a cousin at Burlington. Oh, there's one more thing—you're to get a new suit of clothes at Albany, and, remember, it must be very grand."

It was near train time, and they left the inn.

"I'm going to tell you everything," said she, as they were on their way to the depot. "The day after to-morrow I am to see that dreadful Roberts. I'm longing to give him his answer."

Not an hour before then Roberts had passed them on his way to Boston.

XXXV

AT THE SIGN OF THE GOLDEN SPOOL[1]

[1 The author desires to say that this chapter relates to no shop now in existence.]

It was early May and a bright morning in Hillsborough. There were lines of stores and houses on either side of the main thoroughfare from the river to Moosehead Inn, a long, low, white building that faced the public square. Hunters coming off its veranda and gazing down the street, as if sighting over gun-barrels at the bridge, were wont to reckon the distance "nigh on to forty rod." There were "Boston Stores" and "Great Emporiums" and shops, modest as they were small, in that forty rods of Hillsborough. Midway was a little white building, its eaves within reach of one's hand, its gable on the line of the sidewalk overhanging which, from a crane above the door, was a big, golden spool. In its two windows were lace and ribbons and ladies' hats and spools of thread, and blue shades drawn high from seven o'clock in the morning until dark. It was the little shop of Ruth Tole—a house of Fate on the way from happening to history. There secrets, travel-worn, were nourished a while and sent on their way; reputations were made over and often trimmed with excellent taste and discrimination. The wicked might prosper for a time, but by and by the fates were at work on them, there in the little shop, and then every one smiled as the sinner passed, with the decoration of his rank upon him. And the sinner smiled also, seeing not the badge on his own back but only that on the back of his brother, and was highly pleased, for, if he had sin deeper than his brother's he had some discretion. Relentless and not over-just were they of this weird sisterhood. Since the time of the gods they have been without honour but never without work, and often they have had a better purpose than they knew. Those of Hillsborough did their work as if with a sense of its great solemnity. There was a flavour of awe in their nods and whispers, and they seemed to know they were touching immortal souls. But now and then they put on the masque of comedy.

Ruth Tole was behind the counter, sorting threads. She was a maiden of middle life and severe countenance, of few and decisive words. The door of the little shop was ajar, and near it a woman sat knitting. She had a position favourable for eye and ear. She could see all who passed, on either side of the way, and not a word or move in the shop escaped her. In the sisterhood she bore the familiar name of Lize. She had been talking about that old case of Riley Brooke and the Widow Glover.

"Looks to me," said she, thoughtfully, as she tickled her scalp with a knitting-needle, "that she took the kinks out o' him. He's a good deal more respectable."

"Like a panther with his teeth pulled," said a woman who stood by the counter, buying a spool of thread. "Ain't you heard how they made up?"

"Land sakes, no!" said the sister Lize, hurriedly finishing a stitch and then halting her fingers to pull the yarn.

The shopkeeper began rolling ribbons with a look of indifference. She never took part in the gossip and, although she loved to hear it, had, mostly, the air of one without ears.

"Well, that old tinker gave 'em both a good talking to," said the customer. "He brings 'em face to face, and he says to him, says he, 'In the day o' the Judgment God'll mind the look o' your wife,' and then he says the same to her."

"Singular man!" said the comely sister Lize, who now resumed her knitting.

"He never robbed that bank, either, any more 'n I did."

"Men ain't apt to claim a sin that don't belong to 'em—that's my opinion."

"He did it to shield another."

"Sidney Trove?" was the half-whispered query of the sister Lize.

"Trove, no!" said the other, quickly. "It was that old man with a gray beard who never spoke to anybody an' used to visit the tinker."

She was interrupted by a newcomer—a stout woman of middle age who fluttered in, breathing heavily, under a look of pallor and agitation.

"Sh-h-h!" said she, lifting a large hand. She sank upon a chair, fanning herself. She said nothing for a little, as if to give the Recording Angel a chance to dip her pen. The customer, who was now counting a box of beads, turned quickly, and she that was called Lize dropped her knitting.

"What is it, Bet, for mercy's sake?" said the latter.

"Have you heard the news?" said she that was called Bet.

"Land sakes, no!" said both the others.

Then followed a moment of suspense, during which the newcomer sat biting her under lip, a merry smile in her face. She was like a child dallying with a red plum.

"You're too provoking!" said the sister Lize, impatiently. "Why do you keep us hanging by the eyebrows?" She pulled her yarn with some violence, and the ball dropped to the floor, rolling half across it.

"Sh-h-h!" said the dear sister Bet again. Another woman had stopped by the door. Then a scornful whisper from the sister Lize.

"It's that horrible Kate Tredder. Mercy! is she coming in?"

She came in. Long since she had ceased to enjoy credit or confidence at the little shop.

"Nice day," said she.

The sister Lize moved impatiently and picked up her work. This untimely entrance had left her "hanging by the eyebrows" and red with anxiety. She gave the newcomer a sweeping glance, sighed and said, "Yes." The sister Bet grew serious and began tapping the floor with her toe.

"I've been clear 'round the square," said Mrs. Tredder, "an' I guess I'll sit a while. I ain't done a thing to-day, an' I don't b'lieve I'll try 'til after dinner. Miss Tole, you may give me another yard o' that red silk ribbon."

She sat by the counter, and Miss Tole sniffed a little and began to measure the ribbon. She was deeply if secretly offended by this intrusion.

"What's the news?" said the newcomer, turning to the sister Bet.

"Oh, nothing!" said the other, wearily.

"Ain't you heard about that woman up at the Moosehead?"

"Heard all I care to," said the sister Bet, with jealous feeling. Here was another red plum off the same tree.

"What about her?" said the sister Lize, now reaching on tiptoe, as it were. The sister Bet rose impatiently and made for the door.

"Going?" said she that was called Lize, a note of alarm in her voice.

"Yes; do you think I've nothing else to do but sit here and gossip," said sister Bet, disappearing suddenly, her face red.

The newcomer sat in a thoughtful attitude, her elbow on the counter.

"Well?" said the sister Lize.

"You all treat me so funny here I guess I'll go," said Mrs. Tredder, who now got up, her face darkening, and hurried away. They of the plums had both vanished.

"Wretch!" said the sister Lize, hotly; "I could have choked her." She squirmed a little, moving her chair roughly.

"She's forever sticking her nose into other people's business," were the words of the customer who was counting beads. She seemed to be near the point of tears.

"Maybe that's why it's so red," the other answered with unspeakable contempt. "I'm so mad I can hardly sit still."

She wound her yarn close and stuck her needle into the ball.

"Thank goodness!" said she, suddenly; "here comes Serene."

The sister Serene Davis, a frail, fair lady, entered.

"Well," said the latter, "I suppose you've heard—" she paused to get her breath.

"What?" said the sister Lize, in a whisper, approaching the new arrival.

"My heart is all in a flutter—don't hurry me."

The sister Lize went to the door and closed it. Then she turned quickly, facing the other woman.

"Serene Davis," she began solemnly, "you'll never leave this room alive until you tell us."

"Can't you let a body enjoy herself a minute?"

"Tell me," she insisted, threatening with a needle.

Ruth Tole regarded them with a look of firmness which seemed to say, "Stab her if she doesn't tell."

"Well," said the sister Serene, "you know that stylish young widow that came a while ago to the Moosehead—the one that wore the splendid black silk the night o' the ball?"

"Yes."

"She was a detective,"—this in a whisper.

"What!" said the other two, awesomely.

"A detective."

Then a quick movement of chairs and a pulling of yarn. Ruth dropped a spool of thread which rattled, as it fell, and rolled a space and lay neglected.

The sister Serene was now laughing.

"It's ridiculous!" she remarked.

"Go on," said the others, and one of them added, "Land sakes! don't stop now."

"Well, she got sick the other day and sent for a lawyer, an' who do you suppose it was?"

"I dunno," said Ruth Tole. The words had broken away from her, and she covered her mouth, quickly, and began to look out of the window. The speaker had begun to laugh again.

"'Twas Dick Roberts," she went on. "He went over to the tavern; she lay there in bed and had a nurse in the room with her—a woman she got in Ogdensburg. She tells the young lawyer she wants him to make her will. Then she describes her property and he puts it down. There was a palace in Wales and a castle on the Rhine and pearls and diamonds and fifty thousand pounds in a foreign bank, and I don't know what all. Well, ye know, she was pert and handsome, and he began to take notice."

The sisters looked from one to another and gave up to gleeful smiles, but Ruth was, if anything, a bit firmer than before.

"Next day he brought her some flowers, and she began to get better. Then he took her out to ride. One night about ten o'clock the nurse comes into the room sudden like, and finds him on his knees before the widow, kissing her dress an' talking all kinds o' nonsense."

"Here! stop a minute," said the sister Lize, who had now dropped her knitting and begun to fan herself. "You take my breath away." The details were too important for hasty consideration.

"Makin' love?" said she with the beads, thoughtfully.

"I should think likely," said the other, whereupon the three began to laugh again. Their merriment over, through smiles they gave each other looks of dreamy reflection.

"Now go on," said the sister Lize, leaning forward, her chin upon her hands.

"There he knelt, kissing her dress," the narrator continued.

"Why didn't he kiss her face?"

"Because she wouldn't let him, I suppose."

"Oh!" said the others, nodding their heads, thoughtfully.

"When the nurse came," the sister Serene continued, "the widow went to a desk and wrote a letter and brought it to Dick. Then says the widow, says she: 'You take this to my uncle in Boston. If you can make him give his consent, I'd be glad to see you again.'

"Dick, he rushed off that very evening an' took the cars at Madrid. What do you suppose the letter said?"

The sister Serene began to shake with laughter.

"What?" was the eager demand of the two sisters.

"Well, the widow told the nurse and she told Mary Jones and Mary told me. The letter was kind o' short and about like this:—

"'Pardon me for introducing a scamp by the name of Roberts. He's engaged to a very sweet young lady and has the impudence to make love to me. I wish to get him out of this town for a while, and can't think of any better way. Don't use him too roughly. He was a detective once himself.'"

"Well, in a couple of days the widow got a telegraph message from her uncle, an' what do you suppose it said?"

The sister Serene covered her face and began to quiver. The other two were leaning toward her, smiling, their mouths open.

"What was it?" said the sister Lize.

"'Kicked him downstairs,'" the narrator quoted.

"Y!" the two whispered.

"Good enough for him." It was the verdict of the little shopkeeper, sharply spoken, as she went on with her work.

"So I say,"—this from the other three, who were now quite serious.

"He'd better not come back here," said the sister Lize.

"He never will, probably."

"Who employed the widow?"

"Nobody knows," said the sister Serene. "Before she left town she had a check cashed, an' it come from Riley Brooke. Some think Martha Vaughn herself knows all about it. Sh-h-h! there goes Sidney Trove."

"Ain't he splendid looking?" said she with the beads.

Ruth Tole had opened the door, and they were now observing the street and those who were passing in it.

"One of these days there'll be some tall love-making up there at the Widow Vaughn's," said she that was called Lize.

"Like to be behind the door"—this from her with the beads.

"I wouldn't," said the sister Serene.

"No, you wouldn't!"

"I'd rather be up next to the young man." A merry laugh, and then a sigh from the sister Lize, who looked a bit dreamy and began to tickle her head with a knitting-needle.

"What are you sighing for?" said she with the beads,

"Oh, well," said the other, yawning, "it makes me think o' the time when I was a girl."

"Look! there's Jeanne Brulet,"—it was a quick whisper.

They gathered close and began to shake their heads and frown. Now, indeed, they were as the Fates of old.

"Look at her clothes," another whispered.

"They're better than I can wear. I'd like to know where she gets the money."

Then a look from one to the other—a look of fateful import, soon to travel far, and loose a hundred tongues. That moment the bowl was broken, but the weird sisters knew not the truth.

She that was called Lize, put up her knitting and rose from her chair.

"There's work waiting for me at home," said she.

"Quilting?"

"No; I'm working on a shroud."

XXXVI

THE LAW'S APPROVAL

Trove had come to Hillsborough that very hour he passed the Golden Spool. In him a touch of dignity had sobered the careless eye of youth. He was, indeed, a comely young man, his attire fashionable, his form erect. Soon he was on the familiar road to Robin's Inn. There was now a sprinkle of yellow in the green valley; wings of azure and of gray in the sunlight; a scatter of song in the silence. High on distant hills, here and there, was a little bank of snow. These few dusty rags were all that remained of the great robe of winter. Men were sowing and planting. In the air was an odour of the harrowed earth, and up in the hills a shout of greeting came out of field or garden as Trove went by.

It was a walk to remember, and when he had come near the far side of Pleasant Valley he could see Polly waving her hand to him at the edge of the maple grove.

"Supper is waiting," said she, merrily, as she came to meet him. "There's blueberries, and biscuit, and lots of nice things."

"I'm hungry," said be; "but first, dear, let us enjoy love and kisses."

Then by the lonely road he held her close to him, and each could feel the heart-beat of the other; and for quite a moment speech would have been most idle and inadequate.

"Now the promise, Polly," said he soon. "I go not another step until I have your promise to be my wife."

"You do not think I'd let one treat me that way unless I expected to marry him, do you ?" said Polly, as she fussed with a ribbon bow, her face red with blushes. "You've mussed me all up."

"I'm to be a teacher in the big school, and if you were willing, we could be married soon."

"Oh, dear!" said she, sighing, and looking up at him with a smile; "I'm too happy to think." Then followed another moment of silence, in which the little god, if he were near them, must have smiled.

"Won't you name the day now?" he insisted.

"Oh, let's keep that for the next chapter!" said she. "Don't you know supper is waiting?"

"It's all like those tales 'to be continued in our next,'" he answered with a laugh.

Then they walked slowly up the long hill, arm in arm.

"How very grand you look!" said she, proudly. "Did you see the Governor?"

"Yes, but he can do nothing now. It's the only cloud in the sky."

"Dear old man!" said Polly. "We'll find a way to help him."

"But he wouldn't thank us for help—there's the truth of it," said Trove, quickly. "He's happy and content. Here is a letter that came to-day. 'Dear Sidney,' he writes. 'Think of all I have said to thee, an', if ye remember well, boy, it will bear thee up. Were I, indeed, as ye believe, drinking the cup o' bitterness for thy sake, know ye not the law will make it sweet for me? After all I have said to thee, are ye not prepared? Is my work wasted; is the seed fallen upon the rocks? And if ye hold to thy view, consider—would ye rob the dark world o' the light o' sacrifice? "Nay," ye will answer. Then I say: "If ye would give me peace, go to thy work, boy, and cease to waste thyself with worry and foolish wandering."'

"Somehow it puts me to shame," said Trove, as he put the letter in his pocket. "I'm so far beneath him. I shall obey and go to work and pray for the speedy coming of God's justice."

"It's the only thing to do," said she. "Sidney, I hope now I have a right to ask if you know who is your father?"

"I believe him to be dead."

"Dead!" there was a note of surprise in the word.

"I know not even his name."

"It is all very strange," said Polly. In a moment she added, "I hope you will forgive my mother if she seemed to doubt you."

"I forgive all," said the young man. "I know it was hard to believe me innocent."

"And impossible to believe you guilty. She was only waiting for more light."

The widow and her two boys came out to meet them.

"Mother, behold this big man! He is to be my husband." The girl looked up at him proudly.

"And my son?" said Mrs. Vaughn, with a smile, as she kissed him. "You've lost no time."

"Oh! I didn't intend to give up so soon," said Polly, "but—but the supper would have been ruined."

"It's now on the table," said Mrs. Vaughn.

"I've news for you," said Polly, as they were sitting down. "Tunk has reformed."

"He must have been busy," said Trove, "and he's ruined his epitaph."

"His epitaph?"

"Yes; that one Darrel wrote for him: 'Here lies Tunk. O Grave! where is thy victory?'"

"Tunk has one merit: he never deceived any one but himself," said the widow.

"Horses have run away with him," Trove continued. "His character is like a broken buggy; and his imagination—that's the unbroken colt. Every day, for a long time, the colt has run away with the wagon, tipping it over and dragging it in the ditch, until every bolt is loose, and every spoke rattling, and every wheel awry. I do hope he's repaired his 'ex.'"

"He walks better and complains less," the widow answered.

"Often he stands very straight and walks like you," said Polly, laughing.

"He thinks you are the only great man," so spoke the widow.

"Gone from one illusion to another," said Trove. "It's a lesson; every one should go softly. Tom, will you now describe the melancholy feat of Theophilus Thistleton?"

The fable was quickly repeated.

"That Mr. Thistleton was a foolish fellow, and there's many like him," said Trove. "He had better have been thrusting blueberries into his mouth. I declare!" he added, sitting back with a look of surprise, "I'm happy again."

"And we are going to keep you so," Polly answered with decision.

"Darrel would tell me that I am at last in harmony with a great law which, until now, I have been defying. It is true; I have thought too much of my own desires."

"I do not understand you," said Polly. "Now, we heard of the shot and iron—how you came by them and how, one night, you threw them into the river at Hillsborough. That led, perhaps, to most of your trouble. I'd like to know what moral law you were breaking when you flung them into the river?"

"A great law," Trove answered; "but one hard to phrase."

"Suppose you try."

"The innocent shall have no fear," said he. "Until then I had kept the commandment."

There was a little time of silence.

"If you watch a coward, you'll see a most unhappy creature." It was Trove who spoke. "Darrel said once, 'A coward is the prey of all evil and the mark of thunderbolts.'"

"I'll not admit you're a coward," were the words of Polly.

"Well," said he, rising, "I had fear of only one thing,—that I should lose your love."

Reaching home next day, Trove found that Allen had sold Phyllis. The mare had been shipped away.

"She brought a thousand dollars," said his foster father, "and I'll divide the profit with you."

The young man was now able to pay his debt to Polly, but for the first time he had a sense of guilt.

Trove bought another filly—a proud-stepping great-granddaughter of old Justin Morgan.

A rough-furred, awkward creature, of the size of a small dog, fled before him, as he entered the house in Brier Dale, and sought refuge under a table. It was a young painter which Allen had captured back in the deep woods, after killing its dam. Soon it rushed across the floor, chasing a ball of yarn, but quickly got under cover. Before the end of that day Trove and the new pet were done with all distrust of each other. The big cat grew in size and playful confidence. Often it stalked the young man with still foot and lashing tail, leaping stealthily over chairs and, betimes, landing upon Trove's back.

*　*　*　*　*　*

It was a June day, and Trove was at Robin's Inn. A little before noon Polly and he and the two boys started for Brier Dale. They waded the flowering meadows in Pleasant Valley, crossed a great pasture, and came under the forest roof. Their feet were muffled in new ferns. Their trail wavered up the side of a steep ridge, and slanted off in long loops to the farther valley. There it crossed a brook and, for a mile or more, followed the mossy banks. On a ledge, mottled with rock velvet, by a waterfall, they sat down to rest, and Polly opened the dinner basket. Somehow the music and the minted breath of the water and the scent of the moss and the wild violet seemed to flavour their meal. Tom had brought a small gun with him, and, soon after they resumed their walk, saw some partridges and fired upon them. All the birds flew save a hen that stood clucking with spread wings. Coming close, they could see her eyes blinking in drops of blood. Trove put his hand upon her, but she only bent her head a little and spread her wings the wider.

"Tom," said he, "look at this little preacher of the woods. Do you know what she's saying?"

"No," said the boy, soberly.

"Well, she's saying: 'Look at me and see what you've done. Hereafter, O boy! think before you pull the trigger.' It's a pity, but we must finish the job."

As they came out upon Brier Road the boys found a nest of hornets. It hung on a bough above the roadway. Soon Paul had flung a stone that broke the nest open. Hornets began to buzz around them, and all ran for refuge to a thicket of young firs. In a moment they could hear a horse coming at a slow trot. Trove peered through the bushes. He could see

Ezra Tower—that man of scornful piety—on a white horse. Trove shouted a warning, but with no effect. Suddenly Tower broke his long silence, and the horse began to run. The little party made a detour, and came again to the road.

"He did speak to the hornets," said Polly.

"Swore, too," said Paul.

"Nature has her own way with folly; you can't hold your tongue when she speaks to you," Trove answered.

Near sunset, they came into Brier Dale. Tunk was to be there at supper time, and drive home with Polly and her brothers. The widow had told him not to come by the Brier Road; it would take him past Rickard's Inn, where he loved to tarry and display horsemanship.

Mary Allen met them at the door.

"Mother, here is my future wife," said Trove, proudly.

Then ruddy lips of youth touched the faded cheek of the good woman.

"We shall be married in September," said Trove, tossing his hat in the air. "We're going to have a grand time, and mind you, mother, no more hard work for you. Where is Tige?" Tige was the young painter.

"I don't know," said Mary Allen. "He's up in a tree some-where, maybe. Come in, all of you; supper's ready."

While they were eating. Trove heard a sound of wheels, and went to the door. Tunk had arrived. He had a lump, the size of an apple,-on his forehead; another on his chin. As Trove approached him, he spat over a front wheel, and sat looking down sadly.

"Tunk, what's the matter ?"

"Kicked," said he, with growing sadness.

"A horse?" Trove inquired, with sympathy.

Tunk thought a moment.

"Couldn't say what 'twas," he answered presently.

"I fear," said Trove, smiling, "that you came by the Brier Road."

Suddenly there was a quick stir of boughs and a flash of tawny fur above them. Then the young painter landed full on the back of Tunkhannock Hosely. There was a wild yell; the horse leaped and ran, breaking through a fence and wrecking the wagon; the painter spat, and made for the woods, and was seen no more of men. Tunk had picked up an axe, and climbed a ladder that stood leaning to the roof. Trove and Allen caught the frightened horse.

"Now," said the former, "let's try and capture Tunk."

"He's taken to the roof," said Allen.

"Where's that air painter?" Tunk shouted, as they came near.

"Gone to the woods."

"Heavens!" said Tunk, gloomily. "I'm all tore up; there ain't nothin' left o' me—boots full o' blood. I tell ye this country's a leetle too wild fer me."

He came down the ladder slowly, and sat on the step and drew off his boots. There was no blood in them. Trove helped him remove his coat; all, save his imagination, was unharmed.

"Wal," said he, thoughtfully, "that's what ye git fer doin' suthin' ye hadn't ought to. I ain't goin' t' take no more chances."

XXXVII

THE RETURN OF SANTA CLAUS

Did ye hear the cock crow? By the beard of my father, I'd forgotten you and myself and everything but the story. It's near morning, and I've a weary tongue. Another log and one more pipe. Then, sir, then I'll let you go. I'm near the end.

"Let me see—it's a winter day in New York City, after four years. The streets are crowded. Here are men and women, but I see only the horses,—you know, sir, how I love them. They go by with heavy truck and cab, steaming, straining', slipping in the deep snow. You hear the song of lashes, the whack of whips, and, now and then, the shout of some bedevilled voice. Horses fall, and struggle, and lie helpless, and their drivers—well, if I were to watch them long, I should be in danger of madness and hell-fire. Well, here is a big stable. A tall man has halted by its open door, and addresses the manager.

"'I learn that you have a bay mare with starred face and a white stocking.' It is Trove who speaks."

"'Yes; there she is, coming yonder.'"

"The mare is a rack of bones, limping, weary, sore. But see

her foot lift! You can't kill the pride of the Barbary. She falters; her driver lashes her over the head. Trove is running toward her. He climbs a front wheel, and down comes the driver. In a minute Trove has her by the bit. He calls her by name—Phyllis! The slim ears begin to move. She nickers. God, sir! she is trying to see him. One eye is bleeding, the other blind. His arms go round her neck, sir, and he hides his face in her mane. That mare you ride—she is the granddaughter of Phyllis. I'd as soon think of selling my wife. Really, sir, Darrel was right. God'll mind the look of your horses."

So spake an old man sitting in the firelight. Since they sat down the short hand of the clock had nearly circled the dial. There was a little pause. He did love a horse—that old man of the hills.

"Trove went home with the mare," he continued. "She recovered the sight of one eye, and had a box-stall and the brook pasture—you know, that one by the beech grove. He got home the day before Christmas. Polly met him at the depot—a charming lady, sir, and a child of three was with her,—a little girl, dark eyes and flaxen, curly hair. You remember Beryl?—eyes like her mother's.

"I was there at the depot that day. Well, it looked as if they were still in their honeymoon."

"'Dear little wife!' said Trove, as he kissed Polly. Then he took the child in his arms, and I went to dinner with them. They lived half a mile or so out of Hillsborough."

"'Hello!' said Trove, as we entered. 'Here's a merry Christmas!'"

"Polly had trimmed the house. There against the wall was a

tapering fir-tree, hung with tinsel and popcorn. All around the room were green branches of holly and hemlock."

"'I'm glad you found Phyllis,' said she."

"'Poor Phyllis!' he answered. 'They broke her down with hard work, and then sold her. She'll be here to-morrow.'"

"'You saw Darrel on the way?'"

"'Yes, and he is the same miracle of happiness. I think he will soon be free. Leblanc is there in prison—convicted of a crime in Whitehall. As I expected, there is a red mark on the back of his left hand. Day after to-morrow we go again to Dannemora. Sweetheart! I hurried home to see you.' And then—well, I do like to see it—the fondness of young people."

"Night came, dark and stormy, with snow in the west wind. They were sitting there by the Christmas tree, all bright with candles—Polly, Trove, and the little child. They were talking of old times. They heard a rap at the door. Trove flung it open. He spoke a word of surprise. There was the old Santa Claus of Cedar Hill—upon my word, sir—the very one. He entered, shaking his great coat, his beard full of snow. He let down his sack there by the lighted tree. He beckoned to the little one.

"'Go and see him—it is old Santa Claus,' said Polly, her voice trembling as she led the child."

"Then, quickly, she took the hand of her husband."

"'He is your father,' she whispered."

"A moment they stood with hearts full, looking at Santa

Claus and the child. That little one had her arms about a knee, and, dumb with great wonder, gazed up at him. There was a timid appeal in her sweet face.

"The man did not move; he was looking down at the child. In a moment she began to prattle and tug at him. They saw his knees bend a bit. Ah, sir, it seemed as if the baby were pulling him down. He gently pushed the child away. They heard a little cry—a kind of a wailing 'Oh-o-o,'—like that you hear in the chimney. Then, sir, down he went in his tracks—a quivering little heap,—and lay there at the foot of the tree. Polly and Trove were bending over him. Cap and wig had fallen from his head. He was an old man.

"'Father!' Trove whispered, touching the long white hair. 'O my father! speak to me. Let me—let me see your face.'"

"Slowly—slowly, the old man rose, Trove helping him, and put on his cap. Then, sir, he took a step back and stood straight as a king. He waved them away with his hand."

"'Nay, boy, remember,' he whispered. 'Ye were to let him pass.' And then he started for the door."

"Trove went before him and stood against it."

"'Hear me, boy, 'tis better that ye let him sleep until the trumpet calls an' ye both stand with all the quick an' the dead.'"

"'No, I have waited long, and I love—I love him,' Trove answered."

"Those fair young people knelt beside the old man, clinging to his hands."

"The good saint was crying."

"'I came not here to bring shame,' said he presently."

"'We honour and with all our souls we love you,' Trove answered."

"'Who shall stand before it?' said the old man. 'Behold— behold how Love hath raised the dead!' He flung off his cap and beard."

"'If ye will have it so, know ye that I—Roderick Darrel—am thy father.'"

"Now, sir, you may go. I wish ye merry Christmas!" said that old man of the hills.

But the other tarried, thoughtfully puffing his pipe.

"And the father was not dead?"

"'Twas only the living death," said the old man, now lighting a lantern. "You know that grave in a poem of Sidney Trove:

'It has neither sod nor stone;
It has neither dust nor bone.'

He planned to be as one dead to the world."

"And the other man of mystery—who was he?"

"Some child of misfortune. He was befriended by the tinker and did errands for him."

"He took the money to Trove that night the latter slept in the woods?"

"And, for Darrel, returned to Thompson his own with usury. Thompson was the chief creditor."

"With usury?"

"Yes; for years it lay under the bed of Darrel. By and by he put the money in a savings bank—all but a few dollars."

"And why did he wait so long, before returning it?"

"He tried to be rid of the money, but was unable to find Thompson. And Trove, he lived to repay every creditor. Ah, sir, he was a man of a thousand."

"That story of Darrel's in the little shop—I see—it was fact in a setting of fiction."

"That's all it pretended to be," said the old man of the hills.

"One more query," said the other. He was now mounted. "I know Darrel went to prison for the sake of the boy, but did some one set him free?"

"His own character. Leblanc came to love him—like the other prisoners—and, sir, he confessed. I declare!—it's daylight now and here I am with the lantern. Good-by, and Merry Christmas!"

The other rode away, slowly, looking back at the dim glow of the lantern, which now, indeed, was like a symbol of the past.

*   *   *   *   *   *

ABOUT THE AUTHOR

Born in Pierrepont, New York, **Irving Bacheller** graduated from St. Lawrence University in 1882 after which he accepted a job with a New York City newspaper. Two years later, he established a business to provide specialized articles to the major Sunday newspapers. It was through the Bacheller Syndicate that he brought to American readers the writings of British authors such as Joseph Conrad, Arthur Conan Doyle, and Rudyard Kipling. And, to the reading public he introduced New Jersey author Stephen Crane through arranging the serialization of his story, The Red Badge of Courage.

Irving Bacheller began writing himself, publishing "The Master of Silence" in 1892 and "Still House of O'Darrow" in 1894. Although he was appointed Sunday editor of the New York World in 1898, he soon chose to pursue a full-time career as a fiction writer and two years later gave up his journalist position.

Although he continued to turn out a string of books, Bacheller also served as a war correspondent in France during World War I.

Irving Bacheller died in White Plains, New York in 1950. In recent years, several of his works have been reprinted and a previously unpublished manuscript titled Lost in the Fog was published in 1990.

Choose from Thousands of 1stWorldLibrary Classics By

A. M. Barnard	Booth Tarkington	Edward Everett Hale
Ada Leverson	Boyd Cable	Edward J. O'Biren
Adolphus William Ward	Bram Stoker	Edward S. Ellis
Aesop	C. Collodi	Edwin L. Arnold
Agatha Christie	C. E. Orr	Eleanor Atkins
Alexander Aaronsohn	C. M. Ingleby	Eleanor Hallowell Abbott
Alexander Kielland	Carolyn Wells	Eliot Gregory
Alexandre Dumas	Catherine Parr Traill	Elizabeth Gaskell
Alfred Gatty	Charles A. Eastman	Elizabeth McCracken
Alfred Ollivant	Charles Amory Beach	Elizabeth Von Arnim
Alice Duer Miller	Charles Dickens	Ellem Key
Alice Turner Curtis	Charles Dudley Warner	Emerson Hough
Alice Dunbar	Charles Farrar Browne	Emilie F. Carlen
Allen Chapman	Charles Ives	Emily Bronte
Alleyne Ireland	Charles Kingsley	Emily Dickinson
Ambrose Bierce	Charles Klein	Enid Bagnold
Amelia E. Barr	Charles Hanson Towne	Enilor Macartney Lane
Amory H. Bradford	Charles Lathrop Pack	Erasmus W. Jones
Andrew Lang	Charles Romyn Dake	Ernie Howard Pie
Andrew McFarland Davis	Charles Whibley	Ethel May Dell
Andy Adams	Charles Willing Beale	Ethel Turner
Angela Brazil	Charlotte M. Braeme	Ethel Watts Mumford
Anna Alice Chapin	Charlotte M. Yonge	Eugene Sue
Anna Sewell	Charlotte Perkins Stetson	Eugenie Foa
Annie Besant	Clair W. Hayes	Eugene Wood
Annie Hamilton Donnell	Clarence Day Jr.	Eustace Hale Ball
Annie Payson Call	Clarence E. Mulford	Evelyn Everett-green
Annie Roe Carr	Clemence Housman	Everard Cotes
Annonaymous	Confucius	F. H. Cheley
Anton Chekhov	Coningsby Dawson	F. J. Cross
Archibald Lee Fletcher	Cornelis DeWitt Wilcox	F. Marion Crawford
Arnold Bennett	Cyril Burleigh	Fannie E. Newberry
Arthur C. Benson	D. H. Lawrence	Federick Austin Ogg
Arthur Conan Doyle	Daniel Defoe	Ferdinand Ossendowski
Arthur M. Winfield	David Garnett	Fergus Hume
Arthur Ransome	Dinah Craik	Florence A. Kilpatrick
Arthur Schnitzler	Don Carlos Janes	Fremont B. Deering
Arthur Train	Donald Keyhoe	Francis Bacon
Atticus	Dorothy Kilner	Francis Darwin
B.H. Baden-Powell	Dougan Clark	Frances Hodgson Burnett
B. M. Bower	Douglas Fairbanks	Frances Parkinson Keyes
B. C. Chatterjee	E. Nesbit	Frank Gee Patchin
Baroness Emmuska Orczy	E. P. Roe	Frank Harris
Baroness Orczy	E. Phillips Oppenheim	Frank Jewett Mather
Basil King	E. S. Brooks	Frank L. Packard
Bayard Taylor	Earl Barnes	Frank V. Webster
Ben Macomber	Edgar Rice Burroughs	Frederic Stewart Isham
Bertha Muzzy Bower	Edith Van Dyne	Frederick Trevor Hill
Bjornstjerne Bjornson	Edith Wharton	Frederick Winslow Taylor

Friedrich Kerst
Friedrich Nietzsche
Fyodor Dostoyevsky
G.A. Henty
G.K. Chesterton
Gabrielle E. Jackson
Garrett P. Serviss
Gaston Leroux
George A. Warren
George Ade
Geroge Bernard Shaw
George Cary Eggleston
George Durston
George Ebers
George Eliot
George Gissing
George MacDonald
George Meredith
George Orwell
George Sylvester Viereck
George Tucker
George W. Cable
George Wharton James
Gertrude Atherton
Gordon Casserly
Grace E. King
Grace Gallatin
Grace Greenwood
Grant Allen
Guillermo A. Sherwell
Gulielma Zollinger
Gustav Flaubert
H. A. Cody
H. B. Irving
H. C. Bailey
H. G. Wells
H. H. Munro
H. Irving Hancock
H. R. Naylor
H. Rider Haggard
H. W. C. Davis
Haldeman Julius
Hall Caine
Hamilton Wright Mabie
Hans Christian Andersen
Harold Avery
Harold McGrath
Harriet Beecher Stowe
Harry Castlemon
Harry Coghill
Harry Houidini

Hayden Carruth
Helent Hunt Jackson
Helen Nicolay
Hendrik Conscience
Hendy David Thoreau
Henri Barbusse
Henrik Ibsen
Henry Adams
Henry Ford
Henry Frost
Henry James
Henry Jones Ford
Henry Seton Merriman
Henry W Longfellow
Herbert A. Giles
Herbert Carter
Herbert N. Casson
Herman Hesse
Hildegard G. Frey
Homer
Honore De Balzac
Horace B. Day
Horace Walpole
Horatio Alger Jr.
Howard Pyle
Howard R. Garis
Hugh Lofting
Hugh Walpole
Humphry Ward
Ian Maclaren
Inez Haynes Gillmore
Irving Bacheller
Isabel Cecilia Williams
Isabel Hornibrook
Israel Abrahams
Ivan Turgenev
J. G.Austin
J. Henri Fabre
J. M. Barrie
J. M. Walsh
J. Macdonald Oxley
J. R. Miller
J. S. Fletcher
J. S. Knowles
J. Storer Clouston
J. W. Duffield
Jack London
Jacob Abbott
James Allen
James Andrews
James Baldwin

James Branch Cabell
James DeMille
James Joyce
James Lane Allen
James Lane Allen
James Oliver Curwood
James Oppenheim
James Otis
James R. Driscoll
Jane Abbott
Jane Austen
Jane L. Stewart
Janet Aldridge
Jens Peter Jacobsen
Jerome K. Jerome
Jessie Graham Flower
John Buchan
John Burroughs
John Cournos
John F. Kennedy
John Gay
John Glasworthy
John Habberton
John Joy Bell
John Kendrick Bangs
John Milton
John Philip Sousa
John Taintor Foote
Jonas Lauritz Idemil Lie
Jonathan Swift
Joseph A. Altsheler
Joseph Carey
Joseph Conrad
Joseph E. Badger Jr
Joseph Hergesheimer
Joseph Jacobs
Jules Vernes
Julian Hawthrone
Julie A Lippmann
Justin Huntly McCarthy
Kakuzo Okakura
Karle Wilson Baker
Kate Chopin
Kenneth Grahame
Kenneth McGaffey
Kate Langley Bosher
Kate Langley Bosher
Katherine Cecil Thurston
Katherine Stokes
L. A. Abbot
L. T. Meade

L. Frank Baum
Latta Griswold
Laura Dent Crane
Laura Lee Hope
Laurence Housman
Lawrence Beasley
Leo Tolstoy
Leonid Andreyev
Lewis Carroll
Lewis Sperry Chafer
Lilian Bell
Lloyd Osbourne
Louis Hughes
Louis Joseph Vance
Louis Tracy
Louisa May Alcott
Lucy Fitch Perkins
Lucy Maud Montgomery
Luther Benson
Lydia Miller Middleton
Lyndon Orr
M. Corvus
M. H. Adams
Margaret E. Sangster
Margret Howth
Margaret Vandercook
Margaret W. Hungerford
Margret Penrose
Maria Edgeworth
Maria Thompson Daviess
Mariano Azuela
Marion Polk Angellotti
Mark Overton
Mark Twain
Mary Austin
Mary Catherine Crowley
Mary Cole
Mary Hastings Bradley
Mary Roberts Rinehart
Mary Rowlandson
M. Wollstonecraft Shelley
Maud Lindsay
Max Beerbohm
Myra Kelly
Nathaniel Hawthrone
Nicolo Machiavelli
O. F. Walton
Oscar Wilde

Owen Johnson
P.G. Wodehouse
Paul and Mabel Thorne
Paul G. Tomlinson
Paul Severing
Percy Brebner
Percy Keese Fitzhugh
Peter B. Kyne
Plato
Quincy Allen
R. Derby Holmes
R. L. Stevenson
R. S. Ball
Rabindranath Tagore
Rahul Alvares
Ralph Bonehill
Ralph Henry Barbour
Ralph Victor
Ralph Waldo Emmerson
Rene Descartes
Ray Cummings
Rex Beach
Rex E. Beach
Richard Harding Davis
Richard Jefferies
Richard Le Gallienne
Robert Barr
Robert Frost
Robert Gordon Anderson
Robert L. Drake
Robert Lansing
Robert Lynd
Robert Michael Ballantyne
Robert W. Chambers
Rosa Nouchette Carey
Rudyard Kipling
Saint Augustine
Samuel B. Allison
Samuel Hopkins Adams
Sarah Bernhardt
Sarah C. Hallowell
Selma Lagerlof
Sherwood Anderson
Sigmund Freud
Standish O'Grady
Stanley Weyman
Stella Benson
Stella M. Francis

Stephen Crane
Stewart Edward White
Stijn Streuvels
Swami Abhedananda
Swami Parmananda
T. S. Ackland
T. S. Arthur
The Princess Der Ling
Thomas A. Janvier
Thomas A Kempis
Thomas Anderton
Thomas Bailey Aldrich
Thomas Bulfinch
Thomas De Quincey
Thomas Dixon
Thomas H. Huxley
Thomas Hardy
Thomas More
Thornton W. Burgess
U. S. Grant
Upton Sinclair
Valentine Williams
Various Authors
Vaughan Kester
Victor Appleton
Victor G. Durham
Victoria Cross
Virginia Woolf
Wadsworth Camp
Walter Camp
Walter Scott
Washington Irving
Wilbur Lawton
Wilkie Collins
Willa Cather
Willard F. Baker
William Dean Howells
William le Queux
W. Makepeace Thackeray
William W. Walter
William Shakespeare
Winston Churchill
Yei Theodora Ozaki
Yogi Ramacharaka
Young E. Allison
Zane Grey